KITTY TAKES A HOLIDAY

"Standout entertainment . . . truly memorable."
—*RT BOOKreviews Magazine*

"Vaughn's universe is convincing and imaginative."
—*Publishers Weekly*

KITTY GOES TO WASHINGTON

"[A] fun read."   —*Kansas City Star*

"Fans of *Kitty and The Midnight Hour* will be pleased with this fast-paced follow-up."
—MonstersAndCritics.com

KITTY AND THE MIDNIGHT HOUR

"Engaging . . . funny . . . very entertaining."
—*Denver Post*

"I relished this book. Enough excitement, astonishment, pathos, and victory to satisfy any reader."
—Charlaine Harris, *New York Times* bestselling author

"Fresh, hip, fantastic . . . Don't miss this one. You're in for a real treat!"
—L. A. Banks, author of
The Vampire Huntress Legends series

BOOKS BY CARRIE VAUGHN

ATTENTION CORPORATIONS AND ORGANIZATIONS:
Most HACHETTE BOOK GROUP books are available
at quantity discounts with bulk purchase for educational,
business, or sales promotional use. For information,
please call or write:

**Special Markets Department, Hachette Book Group
237 Park Avenue, New York, NY 10017
Telephone: 1-800-222-6747 Fax: 1-800-477-5925**

Kitty's
House of Horrors

CARRIE VAUGHN

GRAND CENTRAL
PUBLISHING

NEW YORK   BOSTON

If you purchase this book without a cover you should be aware that this book may have been stolen property and reported as "unsold and destroyed" to the publisher. In such case neither the author nor the publisher has received any payment for this "stripped book."

This book is a work of fiction. Names, characters, places, and incidents are the product of the author's imagination or are used fictitiously. Any resemblance to actual events, locales, or persons, living or dead, is coincidental.

Copyright © 2010 by Carrie Vaughn, LLC
All rights reserved. Except as permitted under the U.S. Copyright Act of 1976, no part of this publication may be reproduced, distributed, or transmitted in any form or by any means, or stored in a database or retrieval system, without the prior written permission of the publisher.

Grand Central Publishing
Hachette Book Group
237 Park Avenue
New York, NY 10017
Visit our website at www.HachetteBookGroup.com

Grand Central Publishing is a division of Hachette Book Group, Inc. The Grand Central Publishing name and logo is a trademark of Hachette Book Group, Inc.

Printed in the United States of America

First Printing: January 2010

10 9 8 7 6 5 4 3 2 1

To Daniel and Mike
Comrades in Arms

The Playlist

Tom Petty, "You Don't Know How It Feels"

Vampire Weekend, "M79"

Billie Holiday, "What a Little Moonlight Will Do"

The Bangles, "Angels Don't Fall in Love"

Too Much Joy, "Sort of Haunted House"

The Cure, "A Forest"

Gaelic Storm, "Black Is the Colour"

The Tim O'Brien Band, "Another Day"

The Dresden Dolls, "Good Day"

Sarah McLachlan, "Black"

Public Image Ltd., "The Order of Death"

Pink Floyd, "On the Turning Away"

Jeff Oster, "Tibet"

chapter 1

I knew if I stayed in this business long enough, I'd get an offer like this sooner or later. It just didn't quite take the form I'd been expecting.

The group of us sat in a conference room at KNOB, the radio station where I based my syndicated talk show. Someone had tried to spruce up the place, mostly by cleaning old coffee cups and takeout wrappers off the table. Not much could be done with the worn gray carpeting, off-white walls filled with bulletin boards, thumbtack holes where people hadn't bothered with the bulletin boards, and both of those covered with photocopied concert notices and posters for CD releases. The tables were fake wood-grain-colored plastic, refugees from the 1970s. We'd replaced the chalkboard with a dry erase board only a couple of years ago. That was KNOB, on the cutting edge.

I loved the room, but it didn't exactly scream high-powered style. Which made it all the funnier to see a couple of Hollywood guys sitting at the table in their Armani suits and metrosexual savoir faire. They seemed to

be young hotshots on the way up—interchangeable. I had
to remember that Joey Provost was the one with slicked-
back light brown hair and the weak chin, and Ron Valenti
was the one with dark brown hair who hadn't smiled yet.
They worked for a production company called SuperByte
Entertainment, which specialized in reality television. I'd
looked up some of their shows, such sparkling gems as
Jailbird Moms and *Stripper Idol*.

They were here to invite me onto their next show, the
concept of which they were eager to explain.

"The public is *fascinated* with the supernatural. The
popularity of your show is clearly evidence of that. Over
the last couple of years, as more information has come
out, as more people who are part of this world come
forward, that fascination is only going to increase. But
we're not just trying to tap into a market here—we hope
to provide a platform to *educate* people. To erase some
of the myths. Just like you do with your show," Provost
said. Provost was the talker. Valenti held the briefcase and
looked serious.

"We've already secured the participation of Jerome
Macy, the pro wrestler, and we're in talks with a dozen
other celebrities. *Name* celebrities. This is our biggest
production yet, and we'd love for you to be a part of it."

I'd met Jerome Macy, interviewed him on my show,
even. He was a boxer who'd been kicked out of boxing
when his lycanthropy was exposed and then turned to a
career in pro wrestling, where being a werewolf was an
asset. He was the country's second celebrity werewolf.

I was the first.

While working as a late-night DJ here at KNOB, I
started my call-in talk-radio show dispensing advice

about all things supernatural, and came out as a werewolf live on the air about three years ago. Sometimes it seemed like yesterday. Sometimes it seemed like a million years had passed. A lot had happened in that time.

Arms crossed, I leaned against a wall, away from the table where the two producers sat. I studied them with a narrowed gaze and a smirk on my lips. In wolf body language, I was an alpha sizing them up. Deciding whether to beat them up because they were rivals—or eat them because they were prey. They probably had been talking to Jerome Macy, because they seemed to recognize the signals, even if they didn't quite know what they meant. They both looked nervous and couldn't meet my gaze, even though they tried.

This was all posturing.

"That's great. Really," I said. "But what is this show going to be *about?*"

"Well," Provost said, leaning forward, then leaning back again when he caught sight of my stare. "We have access to a vacation lodge in Montana. Out in the middle of nowhere, a really beautiful spot, nice view of the mountains. We'll have about a dozen, give or take, well-known spokespeople for the supernatural, and this will be a chance for them—you—to talk, interact. We'll have interviews, roundtable discussions. It'll be like a retreat."

My interpretation: we're going to put you all in a house and watch you go at it like cats and dogs. Or werewolves and vampires. Whatever.

"So . . . you're not using the same model that you've used on some of your other shows. Like, oh, say, *Cheerleader Sorority House.*"

He had the grace to look a tiny bit chagrined. "Oh, no. This is nothing like that."

I went on. "No voting people off? No teams and stupid games? And definitely no shape-shifting on camera. Right?"

"Oh, no, the idea behind this is education. Illumination."

Ozzie, the station manager and my boss, was also at the meeting, sitting across from the two producers and acting way too obsequious. He leaned forward, eager, smiling back and forth between them and me. So, he thought this was a good idea. Matt, my sound guy, sat in the back corner and pantomimed eating popcorn, wearing a wicked grin.

I had a feeling I was being fed a line, that they were telling me what would most likely get me to agree to their show. And that they'd had a totally different story for everyone else they'd talked to.

I hadn't built my reputation on being coy and polite, so I laid it out for Mr. Provost. "Your shows aren't exactly known for . . . how should I put this . . . having any redeeming qualities whatsoever."

He must have dealt with this criticism all the time, because he had the response all lined up. "Our shows reveal a side of life that most people have no access to."

"Trainwrecks, you mean."

Valenti, who had watched quietly until now, opened his briefcase and consulted a page he drew out. "We have Tina McCannon of *Paradox PI* on board. Also . . . Jeffrey Miles, the TV psychic. I think you're familiar with them?" He met my gaze and matched my stare. One predator sizing up another. Suddenly, I was the one who wanted to look away.

"You got Tina to agree to this? And Jeffrey?"

Both of them were psychics; Tina worked with a team of paranormal investigators on prime-time TV, and Jeffrey did the channeling-dead-relatives thing on daytime talk shows. I'd had adventures with them both, and the prospect of spending two weeks in a cabin in the middle of nowhere taping a TV show was a lot more attractive if I'd be doing it with them.

"What do you think, Kitty? Do we have a deal?"

I needed to make some phone calls. "Can I get back to you on that? I need to check my schedule. Talk it over with my people." Most of my people were already in the room, but the Hollywood talk amused me.

"Of course. But don't take too long. We want to move on this quickly. Before someone else steals the idea." Provost actually winked at that, and his smile never faltered. Valenti had settled back and was regarding me coolly.

"You're not scheduling this over a full moon, are you?" I said.

"Oh, no, certainly not," Provost said, way too seriously.

"Just one more question," I said. "Have you signed on Mercedes Cook?"

Provost hesitated, as if unsure which answer would be the right one. I knew which answer was the right one: if the Broadway star/vampire/double-crossing fink was on the show, I was staying as far away as possible.

"No," he said finally. "She turned us down flat."

Wonders never ceased. But they'd asked her. And she'd said no, so that was a point in the show's favor. "Ah. Good," I said, and Provost relaxed.

We managed polite farewells and handshakes. Ozzie and I walked the two producers outside to their rented

BMW. Provost continued to be gracious and flattering. Valenti stayed in the background. Sizing me up, I couldn't help but think.

After they'd driven away, we returned to the building. The summer sun beat down. It had been a beautiful day, a recent heat spell had broken, and the air felt clean. Smelled like rain.

I turned to Ozzie. "Well?"

He shrugged. "I think it's a great opportunity. But it's up to you. You're the one who's going to have to go through with it."

"I just wish I knew what kooky tricks they have up their sleeves. What are going to be the consequences if I do this?"

"What's the worst that could happen?" he said.

I hated that question. Reality always came up with so much worse than I could imagine. "I could make an idiot of myself, ruin my reputation, lose my audience, my ratings, my show, and never make a living in this business again."

"No, the worst that could happen is you'd die on film in a freak accident, and how likely is that?" Trust Ozzie to be the realist. I glared at him.

"Who knows? At best it'll draw in a whole new audience. To tell you the truth, with people like Tina and Jeffrey involved, it kind of sounds like fun."

"You know what I'm going to say," Ozzie said. "Any publicity is good publicity."

So far in my career, that had been true. I was waiting for the day when it wasn't. "Let me call Tina and Jeffrey and find out why they signed on."

* * *

I had Tina's cell phone number stored on speed dial—she was one of my go-to people on all things weird—and called her as soon as I got back to my office and shut the door. I expected it to roll over to voice mail but was pleasantly surprised when she answered on the second ring.

"Kitty!" she said, before hello even. Caller ID made everyone psychic, at least with phone calls.

"Hi, Tina. How are you?"

"It's so good to hear from you! Is everything okay?"

People always sounded worried when I called them. Maybe because I only ever called a lot of them when I was in trouble and needed help. I needed to set up more lunch dates or have more parties, to cure people of the idea that a call from me automatically equaled danger. Then again, that was probably a lost cause.

"Everything's fine for once, I think."

"I love how you never sound sure when you say that," Tina said cheerfully.

I sighed. "I'm afraid if I relax at all the universe will decide I need a challenge." Which brought me to the business at hand. "I've just had a visit from a couple of guys with SuperByte Entertainment."

"Oh yeah," she said. "*Those* guys. What a couple of freaks, huh?"

I agreed; I'd found them eerily plastic, like they'd been pressed from a mold: Hollywood sleazebag. "This show they're putting together? They said you were on board, and I wanted to ask you why you agreed to it. Do you think it's a good publicity opportunity? Did you . . . I don't know . . . get a good vibe from those guys or what?"

She paused for long enough I thought we'd lost the connection. "Tina?"

When she finally spoke, she sounded confused. "Um . . . I mostly signed on because they said that you'd already signed on."

"What?"

"They told me you'd already agreed to do the show. I figured if you'd decided it was okay, it was a good idea, and I thought it'd be fun hanging out with you again."

"Tina—I heard about this for the first time this afternoon. I hadn't agreed to anything."

"God, they lied to me. I shouldn't be surprised." I imagined her planting her hand on her forehead.

I tried not to sound angry. "You're psychic! Can't you tell when somebody's lying?"

"I'm psychic—that doesn't mean I can read minds," she shot back. "Kitty, you met those guys. They were really convincing!"

"You didn't think to call me to talk about it first?"

"No. I mean, face it—this show totally sounds like something you'd do."

Any more arguing stalled in my throat. Because she was right. I had a few crazy publicity stunts of my own under my belt. And why did I get the feeling Jeffrey Miles would give me a similar story? Those bastards had *used* me. Flung my name around like so much currency. I ought to be flattered.

"That's it," I said, grumbling. "I'm not doing a show run by lying Hollywood scumbags."

"Kitty, please, you *have* to sign on. You can't leave me all alone with this thing. You *owe* me."

Crap. That was a pretty compelling argument. If I left

Tina high and dry with this, I'd feel guilty about it for the rest of my life.

"Did you sign anything? Surely if you did you can get out of it."

"Well," she started, and I waited for the other shoe to drop. "Here's the thing: this really could be great publicity." That was going to be everybody's excuse for anything, wasn't it? She continued, "And the other thing is I figure this is the only way we can counter some of the real wackos they're bound to recruit for this. Right?"

"The fake psychics and emo vampires?" I said. I knew exactly what she was talking about: the kind of crap that gave people like us a bad name, that we had to spend half of our time apologizing for.

"Right," she said.

"You've got a point."

"I'm not going to tell you what to do, Kitty. But please think about backing me up on this thing."

"All right. I'll think about it."

"Thanks, Kitty. Come on, it'll be fun!"

Maybe we could *make* it fun. We'd be like two girls at summer camp.

We clicked off, and I dialed another number. Joey Provost had left KNOB only an hour before; he might not even have arrived at the airport yet.

He answered his phone with, "Hey, Kitty, tell me you've decided to say yes. Don't let me get on the plane without hearing yes."

I suddenly wanted to punch him. Sometimes I really hated caller ID. "Why did you lie to Tina and Jeffrey and tell them I'd already agreed to do the show?"

He hesitated only a beat. "Who told you that? Who said I told them that?"

"I called Tina! *She* told me!"

"Well, yes. Okay," he said, barely stumbling on the words.

"Explain," I said.

"All right. I'll level with you. We need names for a production like this, and I had to start somewhere. You were at the top of our list—you were always at the top of the list. With you on board, half our other names didn't hesitate."

"Why didn't you talk to me first? Why did you have to lie about it?" I said.

"I had to have some way of convincing you, didn't I? Once I got the others signed up, I could do that."

The trouble was, he made sense, in a weird corporate-logic way. I understood why he did it; but he wouldn't admit there was anything wrong with it.

I tamped down on my anger. "Well, now you have to convince me why I should agree to work with a scheming liar."

He took a deep breath, and the edge of desperation in his voice made him sound honest and heartfelt. "Look, Kitty, I know I shouldn't have lied, I should have been upfront. I know that, and I'm sorry. But this is my big chance. This is SuperByte's big chance. We probably look like a bunch of bottom-feeders—and I freely admit that's what we've been until now. But we're trying to rise above all that and get out of the late-night cable gutter. We have our sights set on A-list cable, maybe even network prime time. We want to go upscale, and this is our vehicle. Having you on board will help us do that."

The guy gave a good pitch, I had to give him credit for that. I had to admit, I was a tiny bit flattered—me, A-list? Really? This wasn't to say the whole thing still didn't sound as exploitative as hell.

But I was always saying I wanted the supernatural out in the open. Didn't I want to have a hand—or claw—in this? If it turned out well, yes, I did. If it didn't turn out well . . . maybe I just had to take that gamble.

"All right," I said.

"All right, you're in?" Provost said hopefully.

"All right I'll think about it. Seriously."

"That's all I can ask for," he said, back in Hollywood deal-making mode. "Call me if you have any more questions."

Hanging up, I felt like the decision had already been made. But there was still one person I had to talk to about it.

Home was a condo near the Cherry Creek area. I'd spent the whole drive there arranging the coming conversation in my head. Maybe it would even go a little like how I planned it.

The other person I had to talk to was Ben. My husband. We'd been married for a year. And we hadn't killed each other yet, which I was pretty proud about. Not that we would literally do that, but we were both werewolves, and we *could*—if we didn't depend on each other so much.

Ben was a lawyer with his own practice. He worked from home, which meant he was already in the living room watching evening news on TV when I came in, wincing and looking guilty, sure he'd suspect something was going on.

But he hardly noticed. "Good, you're home," he said. "I have some news."

He seemed positively bubbling. I blinked at him. Wow—my conversation was already derailed and it hadn't even started yet.

"So do I," I jumped in. "I need some advice, actually. I just need to talk this over with someone a little more objective than I am."

"You first," he said. "Let's get yours out of the way so we can get to the exciting part. 'Cause mine's better."

Now I was intrigued. I almost argued, but I wanted to have this talk before I chickened out. I slid next to him on the sofa.

"I've got an invitation to appear on a reality TV show—" I held up my hand to stop him because he'd already opened his mouth to argue. "They're inviting a bunch of supernatural celebrities. Remember Tina McCannon from *Paradox PI*? She's signed up, and so has Jeffrey Miles, and I don't know who else they've got. But it looks like they're trying to do this with a little credibility. It'll tape over two weeks in Montana. They've got this hunting lodge or something, and they *say* they want it to be educational. Consciousness-raising. You know?" I realized I was trying to make it sound good. I wanted him to think it was a good idea.

He sat back, brows raised, looking at me like I was a little bit crazy. I'd thought he was long past being surprised by anything I got mixed up in.

"It sounds like the setup for a horror movie to me," he said.

"God, please don't say that. I'm already anticipating nightmares over this."

"Then why are you even thinking about it?"

"Publicity," I said, and I could feel the wild gleam in my eye.

"You show-business people are weird," Ben said.

I liked to pretend I wasn't exactly part of show business. Sure, I was in the business of entertaining people, but I was on radio. On the fringe. And I was even on the fringe as far as radio was concerned. It wasn't like I was in the thick of the Hollywood madness of *real* show business, right? At least, not yet.

But you know? He was right. Show business was weird.

"It pays pretty well. And. Well. What I'm really worried about is being away from you for two weeks."

Ben and I were a pack. Even if we hadn't been the alpha werewolves leading the Denver pack, the two of us were a pair. A matched set. The idea that wolves mate for life isn't accurate—in the wild, wolves will find a new mate if one of their pair dies, and an alpha male will mate with several females if the pack is prosperous. But Ben and I were pretty solid, and since we'd hooked up we hadn't been apart for more than a couple of days. That was the worst part of this whole deal. I'd gotten used to having him in my life, and I didn't like the prospect of being without. Of not having my guy watching my back.

I saw some of my own thoughts reflected back at me: hesitation, uncertainty. The conflict between human and wolf.

"I don't know," he said, shrugging. "If we were a normal couple and you really needed to do this for your career, it wouldn't even be a question, would it?"

We tried to be normal. We tried not to let our wolf sides overrule us. It was a dominance thing, just like being part of a wolf pack. Every time the wolf side won an argument, we felt a little less human.

"I think I'd still miss you." I leaned my head on his shoulder.

"Thanks." He kissed the top of my head, and I could have stopped talking about anything and just cuddled for the next hour or so. "But you still want to know if I think it's a good idea or a bad idea."

"Yeah."

"It sounds . . . *interesting.*"

"That is *such* a loaded word," I said.

"And you said Tina's agreed to it? She's cool."

"Yeah, and Jeffrey Miles—you remember him, from the hearings in D.C.? He's cool, too."

He pulled back just enough to look at me. "Do you know what I think? I think it'll be good for you to get away for a little while. Since I came along and you took over the pack, you haven't had a chance to do your own thing. You should go. Think of it as a vacation."

I hadn't looked at it that way. "Most men would get suspicious if their wives wanted to go on vacation alone for a couple of weeks. Come to think of it, most women would get suspicious if their husbands suggested they go on vacation alone."

"Honey, I can't hide anything from you. You'd smell it on me."

"Hmm, true." I turned my face to his neck and took

in his scent, distinctively his, soap and sweat, spice and wolf.

He kissed me—a quick peck on my forehead. "I still have my news."

"Is it really better than mine?"

He picked up a letter from the coffee table, marked with some kind of state government seal at the top. Ben was a lawyer; he had dozens of official-looking papers fanned out on the table.

Then he said, "Cormac has a parole hearing."

chapter 2

Moving on to the next call, now. Hello, Audra," I said into the mike.

"Hi, Kitty, yeah, so I'm like a really big fan. I love your show, really."

"Great, thanks very much."

"So, like, I totally need your help. I have this friend who thinks she's a werewolf. But she's totally not. I even went out with her on the last full moon. And I'm like pointing at the sky, pointing at the moon, going, 'Look, you haven't turned into a wolf—you're not a werewolf!' And she's all like, 'But I am on the *inside*. I have the *soul* of a wolf.'"

These potpourri shows were great for when I didn't have anything else planned. Just let people call in with all the problems that have been brewing over the last few weeks. Great—in theory. But it meant I couldn't complain about what calls I *did* get.

I had so much going on in my personal life right now I had a hard time focusing on the call. Cormac's parole hearing was scheduled at the same time I was supposed to be in Montana taping what SuperByte Entertainment was now calling *Supernatural Insider* I wouldn't be here to give him or Ben moral support. That pissed me off. But I was also so darned excited over the prospect of Cormac getting out of prison. Apparently, he'd been a good boy, and that shaved enough time off that now, with almost half of his four-year sentence completed, he was eligible for parole, and Ben said it was all but a done deal. Cormac had friends and family in the area, a place to live, and a plan to look for a job. By all appearances he was completely reformed and repentant. At least, he'd convinced the prison psychologist of it. And what I wouldn't give to be a fly on the wall during those sessions . . .

So in as little as a month from now, he could be out. A free man. I was excited—and more than a little anxious.

I didn't know what to think about Cormac anymore. The first time I met him, he'd tried to kill me, but I talked him out of it. The next time I met him, we traded information, because we were both after the same bad guy. The third time, we'd almost fallen into bed together. We didn't, because he had a thing against werewolves. After that— we were friends. We acted like it, mostly. We'd come to each other's rescue often enough.

I met Cormac before I met Ben. Cormac referred me to Ben—his cousin—when I needed a lawyer. Then Cormac brought Ben to me right after Ben had been bitten and in-fected with lycanthropy. I took care of Ben, and Ben and I—well, we bonded, and Cormac was left out in the cold. Then he came to our rescue, shot and killed a very bad person on our behalf—and was convicted of manslaugh-ter for it. And each of us thought it was our own fault. We had a bumper crop of guilt between us. Not to mention the sparks still lingering between me and Cormac, though I'd gone and gotten married to his cousin and best friend in the meantime. And in the middle of all that I had this sensationalist TV show to deal with.

I needed a radio advice show *I* could call in to.

Audra was still talking. ". . . and I know she listens to your show, too, and I just want you to tell her that she's so full of it."

I leaned in and turned on my snotty voice. "And why should I tell her that?"

"Because she's totally deluding herself. She's not fooling anyone."

"Maybe she isn't trying to fool anyone. Maybe she really honestly feels this way, and if it helps her feel better about herself, and she isn't hurting anything, who are we to argue? As her friend you ought to be a little more supportive, don't you think? She's not actually hurting anyone, is she?"

"Well, no. But it's just so stupid!"

"I think you're being a little judgmental."

"But you're a real werewolf—why are you standing up for her?"

"Because I think, based on what you've told me, that she's right and you're wrong."

Audra made an offended grunt. "That's so not fair!"

Lots of people called in to the show. Lots of people claimed to be fans. Yet they always seemed surprised when I gave them the same smackdown I gave ninety percent of my callers.

"Let me ask you a question, Audra. Why are you so threatened by this? Why does it bother you so much that she calls herself a werewolf when she physically isn't one?"

"Because she's *wrong*. And she's just such a snob about it. Like she's all better than me because she's a werewolf when what she really is is *crazy*."

I straightened. "Why does this girl even hang out with you when you're so mean to her?"

"I'm not mean to her! I'm trying to get her to wake up to reality!"

"To which you've applied a narrow definition."

"And she can't face up to the fact that I'm a vampire."

"Huh?"

"The only reason she keeps going on about being a werewolf is because I'm a vampire, and she's jealous."

I blinked, my brow furrowed in confusion. My lack of a poker face was another reason I was better off on radio than TV. Which was something else that was going to make *Supernatural Insider* interesting.

"Wait a minute," I said. "You're a vampire? Really?" 'Cause right then I would have laid money that she wasn't.

"Well . . ." she said. "I have the *soul* of a vampire."

I didn't know what it was that made people bare their souls and tell me the truth when I had no way of knowing whether they were vampires, lycanthropes, or the Queen of Sheba. Maybe it was that radio was simultaneously so personal and anonymous. They could speak, I could hear them, hear the tears in their voices. But they could stay alone, no one had to see them crying, and as soon as they hung up the phone the confession might never have happened. But I was happy for the confessions, because they made for great entertainment.

"Audra, Audra, Audra," I said. "You know some people believe that vampires don't even have souls?"

"But I *do,* I *understand,* I have the innate sense of style and superiority! I feel the music of the night!"

Oh no. One of *those.* "Audra, do you collect dried red roses in your bedroom? In fact, your whole bedroom is done up in black and red, isn't it? You dress in black and wear a lot of eye makeup? And you listen to a lot of Sarah Brightman?"

"Yes," she said, tentative.

"Okay. Here's what I think. I think you're a bit of a whiner."

"But you're not being *fair!* You're not even *listening* to me!"

Well . . . "I'd like you to try something. I want you to count to ten and exhale slowly. It's a calming exercise. It works for me every time. Can you try it now? Deep breath, and one, two, three—"

"But I *am* calm!"

"Just keep up that counting, Audra, and I bet if you tell your friend that you'll stop making fun of her if she stops making fun of you, you guys'll get along just great." Gratefully, I hit the cutoff. "Next call, what have you got?"

"Hi, Kitty. Thanks for taking my call. I want to talk about bounty hunters. Those guys who go out hunting supernatural monsters."

This night was definitely not going my way. I didn't want to talk about bounty hunters, but who was I to deny my audience? I knew I wasn't going to like where this went. I sighed. "What about them?"

"You've met a lot of these bounty hunters, right? Why don't we hear more about them in the news and stuff? I'd have thought they'd want publicity, that they'd want to get some credit for the work they do."

Looking back on it, I was kind of shocked at how many supernatural bounty hunters I had met. Not by intention, of course. Self-preservation dictated I stay as far away from professional assassins as possible.

"If they started working in public," I said, "then they'd have to be held accountable for what they do. Right now, when they're underground, they don't have to put on a good face for anyone. And when the people they're hunting are also underground, so that no one misses them when they disappear, there's no accountability, no due process, and sometimes no justice."

Except in rare cases, like Cormac's, when he'd been justified in making the kill—and had been convicted for it anyway. The no-win situation. I wasn't going to bring that up if I could help it, which was part of why this topic was making me nervous. It was hitting too close to home. Never mind having to talk to listeners who clearly wanted people like me dead. Weren't they supposed to be fans?

This guy wasn't buying it. "Let's face it, people like that have been around for centuries, right? And the freaks haven't taken over yet, so it must be working. What's wrong with letting them do their jobs?"

Sometimes I thought my listeners were the smartest people around. Sometimes I despaired for the human race.

I said, "I think the question at hand isn't whether or not these hunters should go public, but whether they should be regulated by the government. Licensed, trained, paid regular salaries. Made an extension of existing law enforcement. Hell, train existing law enforcement and let them do the same job for supernatural citizens that they do for everyone else. It's already happening—the police department right here in Denver has a paranatural unit now."

The guy's mocking tone was clear. "Oh yeah, that'll bring a whole lot of protection and justice to the system."

"Come on, people, have a little faith. You have to start somewhere or you end up with anarchy. You end up with guys claiming to be vampire hunters running around staking whoever they please in a self-proclaimed war against evil. Next call, please. Kansas City, you're on the air."

"I'm one of those bounty hunters you're talking about. And let me tell you, you have no *idea* what's out there." The voice was female, with an edge. She sounded like someone who was under a lot of stress. Someone who was used to fighting—all the time. She went on. "Vampires and werewolves aren't even the half of it. Demons, incubi, zombies, warlocks—there's a battle for good and evil out there, and the only thing standing between nice people like your listeners and total chaos are people like me who are willing to sacrifice everything to keep the rest of you safe. And what thanks do we get? Scars and trauma, and not a whole lot else. Naive do-gooders trying to shut us down when you all ought to be on your knees thanking us."

I stared at the mike, because I could think of only one thing to say, and I knew it was the wrong thing. But I couldn't help it; I said it anyway.

"I'm sensing a lot of anger here."

A beat. Then, "Excuse me?"

"Anger. You know: ire, hostility, rage, fury. You have some."

"Oh, you have no idea. I'm angry about *a lot* of things."

I leaned in, getting ready for a nice long chat. I had a wedge with this one, and she seemed willing to talk. We were going to do some digging. Hell, if she didn't like it, she could always hang up. But I didn't think she would, because she was the one who'd called me, and if she hung up now, then I'd just keep talking about her without her input. I loved this gig.

"Why is that?"

"This is a war," she said. "I'm one of the few people out there who are doing something about it. Of *course* I'm angry!"

"A war? Isn't that a little melodramatic? Most people will go through their whole lives and never encounter anything remotely supernatural. Or at least not recognize it. In my experience, most of this stuff prefers to stay out of sight."

"It stays underground because it's afraid of people like me. Not that anybody knows it."

My own problems were temporarily forgotten, because this was interesting. Brain wheels were turning, giving me an idea. My caller wouldn't like it. "Let me try something out on you. You're not really angry about this so-called war you're talking about. You're angry because you don't get any appreciation. Because you're not getting enough love. Am I right?"

"What?" she spat. "That doesn't have anything to do with it. I don't expect anyone to hand me a medal."

Oh, but I was just getting started. "See, I don't think you're as tough as you think you are. Or as tough as you work so hard to make other people think you are. I think you use violence to cover up a lot of insecurities. You have to be the biggest, baddest beast on the block. But that gets kind of lonely, doesn't it? You don't have a lot of friends, do you?"

"You think in this line of work I can trust anyone? You're more naive than I thought."

"Do you have a boyfriend?"

"As a matter of fact, I have several." She sounded smug, bragging.

"Really? How is that working out for you?"

She actually sighed, the barest sign she'd let her guard down. "Not very well."

"I'm sorry to hear that."

She hadn't called to argue with me. She'd called because she needed to vent. She needed to *gush*. And gush she did. "It's so hard when you can't count on the people close to you. They're great guys, they really are, but I feel like they're always judging me. Of course they are— they're way too good for me. They deserve someone better, someone who isn't always getting into trouble, who doesn't have my temper. Someone *prettier*."

"Whoa, hold on there, what has that got to do with anything?" I said.

"I just want people to *like* me. But how can I afford to be nice, doing what I do?"

I turned off the snark. "You're a really strong woman, I can tell. You fight a lot of battles, you stand up to a lot of really bad stuff. I get that. So tell me something: why don't you feel better about yourself? Don't you think there's a certain strength to be had in standing tall, in thinking you're beautiful and acting that way? You don't have anything to prove, right?"

"Easy for you to say—everybody loves you." She

sniffed. Now I wanted to feed her chocolate and give her a big hug.

"Honey, some days I'm not too sure about that. But ever onward, I say. I gotta tell you, I think we're a little out of my league here and I'm really not qualified to offer you guidance. Have you thought about getting counseling?"

She huffed, and whatever moment of honesty and openness had passed. The defenses slammed back into place. "Counseling? I don't need help. I'm not *weak*." She clicked off.

I sighed. "Alrighty, then. Public service announcement here: there's no shame in getting help. Really. Honest. We're all in this together, and life is a little easier when we act like it. Well, it looks like we're out of time. Alas. Now, for next week I'm trying to dig up information on a vampire-only beauty pageant held in New York City last month. Apparently it was all very hush-hush and no one's talking about it. But I'm bound and determined to bring the winner of that pageant on the show for an interview. Join me for the next exciting *Midnight Hour*. This is Kitty Norville, voice of the night."

Two weeks later, I was set to go.

Ben and I stayed awake for a long time the night before I had to fly to Montana. I was still contemplating backing out of the whole thing. If he'd told me right then that he didn't want me to go, I'd have called it off and stayed, just for him.

But we were both trying to pretend that neither of us was that needy.

We'd made love, then made love again, and now lay sweaty and tired, arms around each other. I absently ran my fingers through his hair—scruffy and tangled no matter how much I combed it and smoothed it. It was amazing how long I could focus on his hair. I was comfortable, with his arms around my middle holding me to him like I was a giant pillow. His face nuzzled at my neck, moving along the skin, around my ear, into my hair, as he breathed deeply all the while. Like he was trying to memorize my scent.

"I can't smell that good," I whispered.

"Yes, you can," he whispered back. "I'm not going to wash the sheets 'til you get back."

I pulled away so I could look at him, and so he could see my goofy smile. "That's so romantic."

"It is? I was thinking it was another one of those creepy things that only a lycanthrope would say."

"That, too," I said. "Maybe I can get myself voted off the island early."

"Hmm, cool."

We kissed again, and again, and again.

chapter 3

When Joey Provost said the mountain lodge where the show was being filmed was in the middle of nowhere, he wasn't kidding. I arrived at the Great Falls airport, then had to wait for another, smaller airplane that would take us to the site. The lodge was accessible only via aircraft or a long, hard hike. Was it bad that I kept thinking, limited escape routes?

"Kitty! You're here!" a female voice squealed when I entered the tiny waiting area at the far end of the concourse, and a minute later Tina McCannon had her arms around me.

I resisted an urge to snarl or flee. "Tina, you know better than to sneak up on me like that." But the moment of panic faded—I managed to convince Wolf that just because someone ran at us didn't mean they were attacking— and I hugged Tina back.

Tall, thin, buxom, she was the eye candy for the paranormal-investigator TV show *Paradox PI* and the secret of its success. She had an uncanny sixth sense, and spiritualist tricks like Ouija boards and automatic writing actually worked for her. She always knew which places were really haunted. She was kinda scary—the same way I was kinda scary. We were scary only if someone knew what we were. Otherwise, we must have looked like a couple of really girly girls, hugging and carrying on.

Tina stepped aside, and I glanced past her to see Jeffrey and Ariel, also waiting for the same flight out. TV psychic Jeffrey Miles gave me a big hug. In his thirties, clean-cut, with sandy hair and a photogenic smile, he was handsome and charismatic. Friendly as all get-out. You couldn't help but like him.

"You look great!" he said. And he totally wasn't kidding about that, because he could read auras. At least, he said he could. The first time we met, he'd pegged me as a werewolf before I'd introduced myself. Like Tina, he was too nice and friendly to be *too* scary.

I beamed at him. "Thanks. It's good to see you."

I'd never met twenty-something Ariel in person, but I recognized her because her photo was on her website, and we'd talked on the phone—a lot. Ariel, Priestess of the Night, hosted a talk-radio show like mine, if a bit fluffier. She was way nicer to her callers. Her black hair was pinned up in a bun, and she wore a black dress with a lacy black cardigan, and cool boots. Goth-y, and she wore it well.

"Kitty!" She squealed, just like Tina had. God, this was going to start sounding like a fourth-grade sleepover. She wanted to hug me, too. "I'm so happy you're here and I finally get to meet you."

"God, Kitty. Do you know everyone or what?" Tina said.

"Kinda. Just because I end up interviewing everyone on my show. Come on, sit down, tell me everything."

We traded gossip and recent life stories for about half an hour before the pilot for the local commuter airport came to tell us the plane was ready. We filed out behind him to the tarmac.

My confidence was not boosted. The pilot was brusque, not talkative. He wore what he probably considered to be a uniform, the logo of the tiny commuter airline embroidered on the sleeve of his khaki shirt, tucked into slacks. He wore aviator sunglasses and didn't smile. And the plane—I wasn't convinced it would even get the five of us and our luggage off the ground. We barely fit inside, and the walls seemed paper thin.

I hesitated, staring at the tiny airplane.

"Come on," Jeffrey said, urging me on with a smile. "It'll be an adventure."

"That's what I'm afraid of," I replied, scowling.

But the pilot knew what he was doing, and the little plane did get off the ground. The engine rumbled so loud we couldn't talk—or even think much—which left me staring out the windows at the scenery. We quickly left civilized territory, the city falling away, development growing more sparse, until all I saw were open meadows, forests cut through by hills, then mountains. Forty-five minutes later, we landed on a narrow airstrip nestled in a mountain valley. I closed my eyes during the landing and tried not to think about being trapped in a little metal box, hurtling toward the ground.

The plane pulled to a stop, the pilot opened the doors, and we all piled out. The clean mountain air hit me, and all was forgiven.

Another plane, a bit larger than ours, was parked at the end of the narrow airstrip. The pilot explained that it belonged to the production company and had been used to fly in equipment and supplies. The production crew had a pilot with it—there was our escape route. We wouldn't be completely cut off.

The descriptions I'd been given, variations of "a beautiful mountain retreat," didn't do the place justice. I'd seen mountain lodges that didn't have much thought put into them, squat buildings that looked like they'd been dropped into the landscape by a crane with no consideration of surroundings. This place nestled at the edge of the valley like it had grown there. I had to search for it, where it sat against a hillside—part of the hill, almost. A meadow swept down from it, a clean expanse of rippling green grass dotted with patches of wildflowers. I bet elk and deer grazed here in the mornings. A wide stream ran through the meadow to a lake, and on the other side of the lake—ringing the whole meadow, in fact, up to either side of the lodge—was a forest of tall pines. And beyond the forest, on the horizon, were the mountains. A spur of the Rockies jutted out here, bluish-gray peaks capped with snow even at the end of summer. They were sharp, grouped together like teeth. Clouds were gathering above them. The sun was setting, casting the whole valley in a rich blue twilight. I hoped I got a room with that view.

A few aspens butted up against the lodge itself, which was tasteful log architecture rather than the obnoxious version of it. The whole thing had a warm, rustic atmosphere. My muscles started relaxing.

We spent a few moments just looking around, admiring. I closed my eyes and drew a deep breath of air: trees, stone, a hint of snow, cold water, sun-touched grass, animals in a collage of trails and scents. Untouched wild. So much prey here, my Wolf thought. So many creatures, vegetation, smells all jumbled together, I couldn't make them all out right away. Also, predators: bears, maybe even mountain lions. Their smells were dangerous.

The pilot unloaded our luggage. I turned to thank him, but he had already climbed back into the cockpit and revved the engines. Taxi ride over. We collected our bags and found a path that led to the lodge.

I took out my cell phone just to check, and sure enough: no signal. I couldn't say I was surprised. Middle of nowhere and all that.

We climbed the steps to the lodge's front porch and went inside.

Stopping inside the front door, with the other three crowding around me, I had my first look at the place: the entire first floor was open, with a large, modern kitchen on one side and a living room area on the other. Here, a big stone fireplace dominated the far wall, and a collection of sofas and cushy armchairs gathered in front of it. A couple of cameras and cameramen were set up in opposite corners, staring at us. So, they'd already started collecting footage. One of the cameramen was Ron Valenti, from the meeting with Joey Provost. He'd shed the Armani in favor of jeans and a flannel shirt—very rustic, in a bought-it-out-of-a-high-end-catalog way. He looked at us but didn't acknowledge us. Focused on getting that perfect shot.

People were sitting on the sofas, looking up at us with interest. One of them was Joey Provost.

He stood and came toward me, hand outstretched for shaking. *Another attack,* Wolf growled. We were never going to appreciate aggressive human friendliness, were we? I gritted my teeth, smiled, and shook his hand.

"Hi! Welcome, all of you!" He shook each of our hands in turn. His smile was ferociously pleasant.

"Thanks," I said, glancing around, taking it in. I smelled old soot and the smoke of many fires from the immense fireplace; dinnertime cooking smells from the kitchen, red wine in glasses, and people. Different kinds of people—not entirely human people. My nose was working overtime, trying to take it all in.

"Why don't we come in and make some introductions?" That smile never dimmed, and I sensed an edge of anxiety to it. I didn't envy Provost his job here; he wasn't just going to be producing a TV show, he was going to be playing mediator and camp counselor.

Provost gestured to a large, aggressively muscled black man with a hooded glare sitting on a chair, a little ways from the others.

"Jerome Macy," Provost said.

"Yeah, we've met," I said while the others nodded greetings.

The pro wrestler nodded at me. I nodded back, and we didn't meet gazes—wolf body language that said, *Hey, we're cool, nothing wrong here.* He was another werewolf and understood how weird this all was. I might spend the next couple of weeks being more comfortable around him than anyone else.

"Finally, we get some eye candy," said a guy I didn't know, scoping out Tina, Ariel, and me with a definite leer.

I had to admit, we did sort of look like Charlie's Angels standing together.

He smelled weird. Definitely not human, but a flavor of not-human I hadn't encountered before—and I was racking up quite the scent catalog. Not a vampire, not a werewolf, were-tiger, or were-jaguar. I'd even met a were–African wild dog, but this wasn't any of those. He had a human and something-else smell, like all lycanthropes had. But the something else was kind of . . . fishy. Salty. Wild without the fur. Weird.

"Lee Ponatac," he said in response to my inquiring glare. He had dark hair, and his features were square, young, his eyes brown and shining. He had the scruffy appearance of someone who spent a lot of time outside and didn't care much about polish. It was a nice look, and he pulled it off well. My inquiring glare didn't go away, and he just kept his charismatic smile. "Were-seal. Children of Sedna, we call them back home," he said finally.

My eyes widened. "Really?"

Provost said, "Lee is a state legislator in Alaska. He may be the first publicly acknowledged lycanthrope elected to office in the country. I'm a little surprised we discovered him before you did."

"Yeah. But hey, happy to meet you now. Were-seal? Really? And you don't think this gig will come back to haunt you if you ever decide to run for president?"

He smirked. "I'll cross that bridge when I get to it."

I didn't think there'd ever come a time when I couldn't be surprised, and he seemed pleased at my astonishment. Oh, this was going to be a fun couple of weeks.

The other man, a guy in his thirties, a little overweight and a little balding but not more than average, sat back in an armchair, arms crossed, frowning slightly as he regarded us all. He smelled human. But so did more than half the people in the room.

"And you are?" I asked.

"Conrad Garrett," he said.

"The author?" I said. I'd heard of Garrett, who'd made a profession of writing books debunking the existence of the supernatural, claiming government conspiracy about the NIH's Center for the Study of Paranatural Biology, calling foul on every shred of evidence proving the existence of things like, oh, werewolves. The public recognition of all this was still too new—of course skeptics came forward. "So why don't you return any of my calls?"

"Because acknowledging you only validates your claims," he said, straightforward, like he'd practiced the line.

I huffed. "If you don't believe any of us are real, what are you even doing here?"

"That's putting it a bit existentially," he said. "I just don't believe any of you are what you *claim* you are."

"Wow. Extreme state of denial," Ariel said.

I stared. "Seriously? Really? After everything that's happened? After Congress held hearings and all the stuff on TV?"

"Video footage can be faked," he said. "As for Congress—they're being manipulated by lobbyists. I think it's pharmaceutical companies inventing new 'diseases'"—he actually did the finger quotes—"in order to get research funding that they have no intention of using for research."

I couldn't help it; I giggled. "Shit, you're going to make me shape-shift right here in front of you, aren't you?"

"I look forward to it," he said calmly.

Provost raised a hand to point at the cameras. "Kitty, if you could watch the language? And please—no shape-shifting. Not just yet."

Lee crossed his arms. "*That's* the setup for the show. We're supposed to spend the next two weeks convincing him that all this is real. Then watch him freak out when he can't deny it anymore."

"No, seriously," I said, still stifling giggles. "It'll only take five minutes. I'll shift right now, take a little run— that's some great wolf territory out there. Then we can all go home."

"Kitty," Provost said with forced patience. I had a feeling I was going to be hearing that tone of voice a lot. "We'd like this to be a gradual revelation. If we do it right you won't have to shape-shift at all."

"And we won't break his little mind quite so badly, right?" Tina added.

"Whatever," I said, still giggling. "Is there any of that wine left? I think I could use a drink."

P rovost introduced us to the rest of the crew—Ron Valenti and another co-producer named Eli Cabe would be doing most of the technical work on the show. They'd also brought along a trio of production assistants—Skip, Amy, and Gordon—to help. They were eager twenty-somethings, who seemed giddy to be working on a real show—any show. This was their foot in the door. They looked the part, dressed in casual jeans and funky T-shirts, with headsets permanently attached to their ears and clipboards in their hands. Skip had long, dark hair in a ponytail; Amy was petite and energetic, and she tended to shout across rooms; and Gordon was a bit heavyset and always seemed to be smiling about something. They'd also take care of the catering—the kitchen was fully stocked and we'd have three hot meals a day. This might even turn out to feel like a real vacation.

The lodge had a back room, off the living room, normally set up as a library or reading room. The production crew had taken it over and converted it to a studio, where they parked all their cameras, monitors, and editing equipment. Here, they'd review their footage as it came in and start making the "magic." It was off-limits to participants, of course. I was already thinking of how I could sneak a look in.

The show hadn't officially started taping yet; we were still missing people. The scheduled "activities"—and didn't that sound ominous—would start tomorrow. For now, the cameras were getting footage for some kind of introductory montage, and in the meantime we could all get to know each other. Happily, the lodge had a liberally stocked wine cabinet. It would help to take the edge off whenever I had to talk to Conrad. I had a feeling it was going to be all too easy to bait this guy.

I started in right away, of course. "Conrad, tell me something: you do believe that astronauts have walked on the moon, right?"

"Of course," he said.

"And Lee Harvey Oswald was acting alone when he shot Kennedy?"

"Probably, yes."

"Good, you're not a complete conspiracy nut." Just a partial one. "Hey, I have it on good authority from a vampire in Las Vegas that Oswald used silver bullets. What do you say to that?"

Various skeptical responses followed that announcement. I just grinned. I still hadn't done the research—like did Kennedy use the White House silver when he was in office?—to back that one up. I wasn't sure I believed the vampire who told me this. But I still wondered.

Lee said, "You're even more of a loudmouth in person than you are on your show. I thought it was all an act."

"I became a DJ because I'm a loudmouth, not the other way around," I said.

An artificial noise intruded—the drone of an airplane descending into the valley. Provost stood and looked out the living room's big picture window that gave a view over the porch and into the valley.

"Ah, that's the last shuttle in, I think," he said. He actually rubbed his hands with glee.

Moments later, the front door opened. The man who stepped through it was quite possibly the last person I expected to see here. Oh, the list of people I'd never expect to take part in a show like this was long, and he might not have been quite the last. But he was close.

"Grant!" I said, setting down my wineglass and standing to meet him. My smile grew wide.

Odysseus Grant was a stage magician who fronted an old-fashioned Vaudevillian-style magic show in Las Vegas, complete with rabbits pulled from top hats. The act was more than a stage show: Grant really was a magician, or a sorcerer, or something. A master of arcane knowledge on a crusade against chaos, a real-life Doctor Strange, except even more ominous. He had a box of vanishing that opened into . . . somewhere else. A weird pocket dimension was my theory. He'd said he was going to retire the doorway—I hoped that meant that whatever was inside wasn't going to be getting out anytime soon.

Frankly, I couldn't begin to understand much of what Odysseus Grant really did. But I was still happy to see him.

"Kitty," he said, as warmly as he ever said anything. His smile was thin, but it was there. He was tall, slender, sharp, with pale hair and stony blue eyes. He wore a white button-up shirt and black slacks and held a suit jacket over his arm.

I didn't rush to hug him like I had with my other friends. Grant wasn't a very huggable guy.

"What are you doing here?" I said. "How the hell did they talk you into doing this dog-and-pony show?"

"I've been considering taking my show on the road for some time now. This seemed like a way to start," he said. "I'm not at all surprised to see you here."

I shrugged. I'd reconciled myself to the fact that in some respects, I was very predictable.

"Mr. Grant, welcome." Provost leapt up to shake hands, acting almost deferential toward the magician. Grant had that effect on people.

Provost made introductions again, and Grant greeted everyone neutrally, sizing them up, looking each person in the eye, studying them. Calculating. If I didn't know the guy, and if he hadn't saved my life once, he'd have made me really nervous. In fact, Tina and Jeffrey both seemed wary of him, not greeting him quite as warmly as they could have, keeping a good space between them. I wondered what they saw when they looked at him, what they suspected. If I had to guess what Jeffrey saw in the magician's aura, I'd say "power."

"I suppose you're here because you think you're a real magician," Conrad said.

Grant raised a brow. "I am a real magician." He reached to Conrad's head. Conrad flinched, as if he thought Grant was going to hit him. But Grant only revealed a coin that might have been pulled from behind Conrad's ear.

He handed it to Conrad, who flushed. "Ha, ha," the skeptic said.

"Grant, can I get you a drink?" Macy had moved to the liquor cabinet during the commotion.

"Water is fine," Grant said, which was him all over.

After we'd settled again, and I admired how cozy this all was, gathered on cushy sofas around the rustic fireplace in front of a window with a killer view, Jeffrey said, "Is this everyone?"

"Uh, no," Provost said, and he seemed nervous, shifting his position and clasping his hands. "We have a couple more. They should be getting here any minute."

He glanced outside the huge picture window. Night had fallen; it was full dark. I couldn't hear the sound of an approaching airplane—though a pilot would have to be crazy to try to navigate these mountains at night— so no arrival seemed particularly imminent. But Provost wasn't looking at the clearing in front of the lodge, visible in the porch light. He was looking at the dark sky.

I glanced around the room and noted which prominent

variety of supernatural creature was *not* currently represented here. Then a door in the back of the house opened
and closed.

"Ah," Provost said. "That must be them."

The vampires arrived.

chapter 4

At first glance, the two women seemed pressed straight out of the Eurotrash vampire mold. One had black hair, one had chestnut, both in elaborate buns with apparently no device actually holding them up. They wore blazing red lipstick on pouty lips and had sultry eyes. The chestnut-haired one wore a tight black dress with a low neckline and high hemline. Frighteningly high heels. On anyone else the outfit would have been near-formal cocktail attire, but on her it looked like everyday loungewear, like she'd walk her dog in it. She was beautiful—airbrushed beautiful, with large dark eyes and classic features. You couldn't help but watch her. The other was slightly shorter—though both of them wore high heels that made judging their actual height impossible—with Asian features, dark eyes, and pale ivory skin. She wore flowing black slacks and a cinched-up bustier, embroidered black on black, and a diamond brooch on a choker.

I had no way of judging their actual ages, but for some reason the shorter one struck me as being older. The way she stood just a little in front of her companion gave off a protective, big-sister vibe. They both stood, hands on cocked hips, like they owned the place.

They were so striking, I almost didn't notice the man standing behind them. He smelled human—his heart beat and his warm blood was his own. He was young, muscular under his gray slacks and black T-shirt. Square of jaw and thick of hair. I wanted to look for the label on him that said "Male Model."

He smelled human, but he also smelled a little like the women, who in turn smelled a little like him. They all had an air of coolness, and of fresh blood. Then I figured it out: he was their donor. Their human servant, some vampires called it. I imagined they got a little more than blood out of him. They made quite the trio.

I looked at Provost. "You went out and found the most vampirey vampires you possibly could, didn't you?"

"Vampires," Conrad said flatly. Like he didn't think the show would have the gall to try to convince him that vampires really existed.

Provost hurried to put himself between the vampires and the rest of us. Come on, I wanted to complain. If he thought this was going to cause an epic battle, he should have given us some warning.

I knew better than to go up against vampires. Physically, anyway.

"This is Anastasia and Gemma," Provost introduced the women.

"And this is Dorian," said the shorter, black-haired Anastasia, gesturing to their cabana boy. "So nice to meet you all."

She had a confident voice and an American accent,

which made it hard to place her actual age and point of origin. Her attitude seemed old, experienced.

Nobody said anything. It occurred to me that I might have been the only one here who'd dealt with vampires on anything resembling a regular basis. They tended to be kind of standoffish. But heck, they were people. That was the whole point of my show, that we were all just people, right? So, apparently it was going to be up to me to get this party started.

"So. How did they drag you all into this little shindig?" I couldn't think of a more polite way of asking how they were famous and why hadn't I heard of them.

Anastasia—such a vampire name—gave a gracious tilt to her head, nodding at her companion. "We're here because of Gemma."

I said to Gemma, "And you're here because . . ."

Gemma shifted, cocking a leg and a hip forward, tilting back her shoulders—vamping, for lack of a better word. No pun intended, surely. "I'm the very first Miss Fille de Sang Vampire Pageant winner."

Everyone else goggled at that, except for Provost, who must have been pleased that the cameras were recording all this. But I was kind of pissed off.

"Wait a minute, I heard about this," I said. "In New York, right? Some kind of hoopy vampire nightclub promotional thing. A publicity stunt. I mean, who ever heard of a vampire beauty pageant? The promoters wouldn't talk to me. *Nobody* would talk to me. I wanted to interview the winner and they wouldn't even give me a name." I jabbed a finger at her. "That's no way to get publicity."

"Maybe they thought you weren't the right kind of publicity," Anastasia said. Her smile seemed amused.

"And this is?" I said, pointing at Valenti's camera. Vampires didn't always show up on film. They could play with light, which was why they didn't always have reflections and why cameras didn't always capture them. It was part of how they vanished, how they moved without being seen. They could also control it, when they wanted to. When they wanted the publicity, for example.

"This first pageant was a limited affair," Anastasia said. "Testing the waters, if you will. Like Joey here, I'm interested in what opportunities might be open to us if we go public. However, unlike Joey—and you—I'm not convinced it's safe for us, yet. You live your life in the open, Kitty. You put yourself and what you are out there—and you've faced severe consequences for it. There are still people out there who would be happy to see us all dead. Vampires, werewolves, psychics, everyone." She glanced around at each person in turn.

"We're not so far removed from the days of burning witches. I've heard the argument before."

"Some of us remember."

I wasn't sure how to read Anastasia. I had the impression that dressing to stereotypical vampire standards was an act—it was expected, and if she was going to be public about her vampirism, she would play to those expectations. She probably had a good mind for business—most vampires who survived in wealth and luxury did. But what was the act hiding?

"We wanted to meet other people who are going public and being successful at it. At least, that's why I'm here," Gemma said. She and Anastasia smiled at each other. I was fairly certain Anastasia was her Mistress, the one who made her. I couldn't read all the layers of connection between them.

I said, "So you know all about the proving to Conrad here that we're real and stuff, right?"

"Joey did explain to us the basic premise, yes."

"Wow," I said. "This is going to be so much *fun*."

"Look," Conrad said. "I don't want to be judgmental, especially when it comes to someone's lifestyle choices. But there are such things as artificial fangs. People have ritualistically drunk blood for thousands of years. There's a logical explanation for all of this. And there's really no way of proving any of you are as old as some vampires claim to be."

Jeffrey turned to me. "Kitty, you know a lot of vampires through your show, right? How old is the oldest you've ever met?"

I kept getting pegged as an expert on this stuff. Probably because I kept sticking my neck out. Ah well.

"Most of them aren't very forthcoming about their ages. Information is power, and they don't want to give it away. But the oldest vampire I've ever met is about two thousand years old."

Uncomfortable murmurs and shifting on sofas met the announcement. Even Anastasia looked impressed, narrowing her gaze and studying me as if I had suddenly become interesting.

"But you only have the guy's word for it," Conrad argued. "It's not like you can go back and get a picture or a birth certificate to prove he was alive two thousand years ago."

"Oh, I believed him," I said quietly. The vampire in

question was not someone I ever wanted to meet again. I didn't want to dwell.

"What about you two?" Jeffrey said to the vampires. "How old are you?"

Anastasia smiled. "As Kitty said, we're not forth-coming. Perhaps I'll mention it later. If you're paying attention."

"This is what all these conspiracies and fables have in common," Conrad said. "Lots of mystery and obfuscation, no actual facts. Are you surprised there are skeptics out there?"

I could see it now, we were going to spend the whole two weeks arguing semantics and trying to prove negatives. I said, to no one in particular, "You know what's going to be hard about this? I won't be able to just hang up on someone when they say something stupid."

We settled into conversation, which migrated, as conversations tend to. Whenever the topic veered into controversial territory—or whenever Conrad declared his disbelief in all of us—Ariel was the one who kept things on track, making light observations or drawing anecdotes from us. That was her talent, and the thing that made her radio show different from mine: She made people feel good about themselves, until everyone was comfortable talking. I had to respect her. Jeffrey and Tina told behind-the-scenes stories from their shows, Grant and Macy talked about how they got their starts, and so on. Conrad even asked questions, although he looked like he didn't quite believe the answers.

The remote valley and lodge didn't have cell reception, but Provost provided a satellite phone. Which was good, in case we needed to call the fire department or something—the fire department that would then need two hours and a helicopter to get out here. It was way too soon into this gig to be missing urban living.

The trouble was, there was *one* phone and several people who wanted to use it. Yes, we supernaturals tended to be a lonely lot, drifting hither and yon without friends and family . . . or not. Conrad had a wife and two kids, and he spent half an hour catching up with them. Tina spent ten minutes talking to one of her colleagues from her own TV show. Ariel had a boyfriend whom she was more than happy to talk about. "He has a tattoo parlor, he's a really great artist, everyone in LA goes to him for their tats, he did the ink on my back—that's how we met. Isn't that romantic?" And so on. Lee had a girlfriend in Alaska. I didn't listen in on any of the calls, however much I wanted to. I had some sense of propriety.

Besides, the show people were taping them all, and I'd get to listen when *Supernatural Insider* broadcast.

Finally, it was my turn. I called Ben. He answered on the first ring.

First thing I said was, "This phone call may be recorded to ensure quality exploitative entertainment."

"Right," he answered. "So I guess that means no highly descriptive phone sex."

I blinked. I had to think about that for a second. "You were planning phone sex?" I sounded a little sad.

"And how are you, Kitty?" he said, amused. "Going stir-crazy yet?"

"I haven't even been here a day—how can I be going stir-crazy?"

He chuckled. "Maybe because I am."

Aw, wasn't that sweet? We carried on like a couple

of saps for far too long. Mainly, he kept prompting with questions and I kept talking about the scenery. The show's editors weren't going to get anything juicy out of this conversation.

"How's Cormac's hearing shaping up?" I said. "Is everything on track?"

"Everything's on track," he said. "There's really nothing I can do until the hearing itself. I'd rather not think about it—I'll get even more nervous."

"I'm rooting for you guys."

"I'll let him know," he said.

"I should get going," I said finally, realizing how late it was and how tired I was from traveling. "I'll call again as soon as I can."

"Okay. I'll try to survive."

"You do that. But the next time I go to a remote mountain lodge, you're coming with me," I said.

One by one, the others had all gone to bed, leaving the vampires and their human servant on the sofas in front of the fireplace. It was just them and me now. They looked at me with that sultry, sidewise glance that seemed to come naturally to vampires. The hypnotic gaze that made you want to look at them and made it easier for them to trap you. I frowned back.

"Aren't you guys going to get kind of bored, sitting up all night while everyone else is asleep?"

Anastasia's gaze narrowed. "I'm sure we'll find ways to amuse ourselves."

That made me a little nervous for some reason. "Should I be worried?"

Gemma giggled, and Anastasia's smile grew indulgent. "No more so than usual."

"Though Tina's hung a garlic clove on the inside of her door," Gemma said, still giggling.

Great—the psychic was worried. Did that mean I should be?

I looked at Dorian, the fabulous specimen of manhood sitting on the armchair across from Gemma and Anastasia. He hadn't said a word yet, but we could change that. "What about you, Dorian? Are you enjoying yourself?"

He didn't answer. Smiling, he looked at Anastasia, who said, "I think he's enjoying himself just fine."

Maybe this was going to be a little more of a challenge than I thought. I moved around the room, closer to him, and leaned on the back of the sofa. Not too close. Close enough to look him in the eye. He watched me calmly, a smile playing on his lips. Not bothered, not threatened. Just unworried. I studied him obviously, peering one way or another.

"So. You guys take the master-and-servant thing pretty seriously."

"Dorian's under my protection. It's a duty I take seriously," Anastasia said.

"Here's the thing," I said, moving around to the front of the sofa and taking a seat among them all. "My whole career is based on getting people to talk. Talk radio, that's how it works. So Dorian here may be under orders not to talk, or maybe has decided not to talk, but I see that as a challenge. Because if there was some real reason for him not to talk to anyone, you wouldn't risk him interacting with anyone and leave him in the basement instead. But I'm betting Provost and Valenti and the rest wanted to get this little relationship on camera. So at some point, when you all least expect it, I'm going to get him to talk." I glared the challenge at them all.

"I like her," Dorian said, with a faint precise accent that might have been English.

Pouting, I sat back. Well. So much for that little speech. "Dang. Steal my thunder, why don't you."

His smile was wry, and his eyes gleamed. Damn, he was *hot*. I said, "So now that you're talking can I ask you a question, Dorian? You have a portrait in the attic or what?"

Dorian groaned and shook his head. Anastasia actually threw the pillow from her sofa at me. Throw pillow. Ha.

Gemma stared blankly. "What's so funny?"

"Oh, I forget how young you are," Anastasia said to her. "Never mind, I'll have a book for you to read later."

I took note of that bit of information.

We talked for a while longer, mostly Anastasia asking questions about my show and how I'd gotten my start. She didn't dig too deeply—I didn't tell her anything I hadn't mentioned on the air at one point or another. I expected her to ask how I'd become a werewolf—a traumatic episode on several fronts that I didn't like talking about. But she didn't. Almost like she knew, or suspected that I didn't want to talk about it.

Then I really was too tired to keep my eyes open much longer. As a kid I'd been to sleepovers where if you were the first one to fall asleep you'd wake up with stuff written on your face in lipstick. I didn't want to know what happened when you fell asleep in front of a couple of vampires. So I said good night and trundled upstairs to my room.

My room was on the second floor, in a corner, with a

lovely view. I was looking forward to shutting the door and getting to sleep. Not looking forward to being in bed alone.

Odysseus Grant didn't startle me and make me jump the way he might have. I smelled him first: the clean and quiet smell of a man who didn't like to leave a trace. He stood at the end of the hallway, by the door to my room. "Kitty. Could I speak to you a moment?"

"What is it?"

"I only wanted to ask you to keep your eyes open. Have you heard of something vampires call the Long Game?"

My heart did a double-beat. My smile fell as my whole face went slack.

"Then you have heard of it," Grant said, a wry curl to his lips.

I shook my bemusement away. Tried to clear my head. "Why are you asking? Cleaned up all of Vegas's supernatural problems and need a new challenge?"

"What do you know about it?" he said.

"It's a political thing, I think. It's hard getting a straight answer out of them, but from what I gather there are some vampires trying to consolidate power. Trying to form some kind of monolithic vampire organization. Now, I'm not sure if this means they're trying to take over the world—or if this is just something they play around with because after two thousand years of hanging out a guy gets bored. To tell you the truth, I'm not really sure I want to know. I just want to stay out of it."

He raised a brow. I recognized the expression: wry disbelief. When was I ever able to stay out of anything?

"Will that be possible?" he asked.

"Not if I keep sticking my nose in it. So . . . you're here

because you think this has something to do with the Long Game? You think Anastasia—"

He put a finger over his lips, then said, "Just keep your eyes and ears open for me."

"What have you heard?" I said. But he'd already walked to the other end of the hall and disappeared into his own room.

I looked around for the hidden cameras. Because damned if this wouldn't play well on reality TV.

chapter 5

I was right about the meadow being perfect for elk. The next morning, a herd of them were grazing there. The sun was behind the lodge, behind the hills to the east, but had risen high enough to wash the valley in golden light, which brought out all the colors of the mountains, the grass, and the forest and sparkled off the lake. The elk, about five of them, were perfectly peaceful, moving step by step, noses buried in grass. I sat at the picture window in the living room and watched, breathing in the rich fumes of a cup of gourmet coffee graciously provided by SuperByte Entertainment and Skip the PA. The house was quiet; I could hear birds chirping outside. If I went out on the porch, I'd bet I could smell the beautiful, clean mountain air, the dew on the grass, and even the elk in the meadow. But I didn't want to move and disturb anything. I might even have been relaxed. I was almost startled by the feeling.

It couldn't last. If I'd been here all by myself, settling in for a real vacation, the relaxation might have seeped into my bones. But I was sharing the place with a dozen other people and the production staff. Inevitably, I heard footsteps on the hardwood floor, entering the living room. I took a breath through my nose and sighed at the information.

Jerome Macy wasn't the person I most wanted to see. Like their animal counterparts, werewolves are territorial. Competitive. They have pack structures and hierarchies. I wasn't sure how any of that was going to play out with Jerome and me. We hadn't had a chance to talk about it. I hoped we would talk about it instead of deciding we had to duke it out, however cinematic that would be. However much Provost was *hoping* we'd duke it out. I was just waiting for the request to shape-shift on camera. I might have made a show of teasing Conrad with the possibility, but I wasn't really planning on doing it.

Macy moved up beside me and looked out the window to the meadow and elk. My back muscles stiffened, but I tried not to show it. Tried to keep my shoulders from bunching up, like hackles rising. We were all friends here, right?

"Makes me want to go hunting," Macy said, flexing his hands like he was stretching his claws.

So much for the peaceful morning.

"They're all healthy adults," I said. "Too much work."

"Not if we hunted together." He glanced at me.

Now, that—turning wolf and going on a hunt with a guy I barely knew—was a bad idea. Even if it would give Provost some great footage.

I smiled wryly. "Why would I want to go through all that trouble when there's a lovely staff here that wants nothing more than to feed me, and I don't have to lift a finger?"

His lips curled. "It's not the same."

No, it wasn't. Wolf was salivating at the thought, but I didn't have to tell Macy that. "Sorry. It's just that things around here are going to get weird enough without encouraging that side of it. I like to keep Wolf under wraps when I can."

Being a werewolf isn't an either-or thing. It's not the Jekyll-and-Hyde dichotomy. It's more like a scale, with wolf at one end and human on the other. Some days were a little more wolf than others. Some people were a little more wolf than others. The couple of times I'd met him, I'd had trouble deciding where Macy fell on that line. Did he look kind of burly and mean because he was a boxer turned pro wrestler, or because he was a werewolf who lived right on the edge, who always had a little of his wolf side seeping to the surface? He'd once been the heavyweight world champion. He was huge, solid, like a tree. He'd retain all that mass when he shifted—as a wolf, he'd be monstrous. How much of his fighting instinct came from his wolf side?

After a moment he said, "I know all about keeping it under wraps. Being able to go into a ring and fight it out with somebody without losing my temper, without losing myself? Yeah. But I don't always get to see a stretch of open land like that. Before I leave, I'm going to shift and run out there. I don't always get to have company when I run, either. Thought it'd be nice for a change." His smile turned thoughtful. I considered that maybe there was a real guy hiding in there and not just a thug.

"You don't have a pack at home?"

"Don't need one. You?"

"Yes. A pack, a mate, the works. It's kind of nice having people to watch my back."

He looked back out the window, a cynical curl on his lips. "Too much trouble."

A camera mounted in the corner of the room recorded the entire conversation.

I didn't have anything else I wanted to say. Not much else I could say—I wasn't sure I wanted to know what all went on in Macy's head. I had another two weeks here to get his life story.

The elk were moving off, back to the woods on the far side of the meadow. The grass was so high it brushed their bellies. The idea of running through that meadow on four legs, with wind in my fur and the scent of wild in my nose, did appeal. But I'd rather do it with Ben.

One by one, the lodge's residents woke up and drifted downstairs—except for the vampires and Dorian, who had retired to their sealed basement room before dawn. Breakfast was light—bagels, pastries, yogurt, juice—and so was the conversation. Tina caught me up on the doings of the other investigators on her TV show, Jeffrey talked about the books he'd been writing—self-help inspirational-type stuff about grief and moving on, the kind of thing I'd normally call drivel except this was Jeffrey, whose earnestness made it work. Grant was reticent, not giving any hint about the conspiracy he'd alluded to last night. Ariel sat at the edge of her seat and soaked it all in. I might have been expected to consider her the competition, except she was so darned nice about it. And she was in the business for the same reasons I was: She was insatiably curious about the supernatural, and she wanted to help people cope. She was one of the people *I* called when I got fed up with it all.

But the person here I was probably most curious about was Lee. He was the last one up, and I cornered him in the kitchen on the pretense of refilling my mug of coffee.

"Good morning," I said, watching him pick through the breakfast food set out in the kitchen.

"Hi," he said, wearing a charming smile. He wore a T-shirt and sweats, and his hair was still disheveled from sleeping. "You're looking at me like you want something," he said, glancing at me sideways. He didn't sound put out. Amused, maybe. I must have had a pretty intent look on my face. I was trying to see the seal under his skin. I was still trying to figure out his smell. Not that I'd spent enough time around oceans to know, but I had the feeling he smelled like an ocean.

"Were-seal. I'm trying to imagine how that works."

"Just the way you'd expect it to, I suppose."

"Okay," I said. "But how do you get bitten by a were-seal?"

His smile widened. "You're out hunting seals by kayak, and you run into one that hunts you back."

Well, of course. But what in that statement really got me: "Wait a minute. You hunt seals by kayak?"

He chuckled. "You ask a lot of questions, don't you?"

"Yes. I do."

"Fair enough. I suppose it's as good a way as any to give the cameras what they want, right?"

I shrugged. I was trying not to pay attention to the cameras. I wanted to do this show on my own terms, which meant asking my own questions.

He said, "Alaska still has a lot of little coastal towns

that depend on subsistence hunting. So yeah, I hunt seals. Sometimes I don't use the kayak." He raised a knowing brow.

"Are we going to get to see what that looks like?" I said. "The seal half, I mean."

"I don't know," he said. He looked out the kitchen window to the meadow and mountains. Every window here had a view. "That lake is freshwater. It just wouldn't be the same. I tried to get them to move this to Alaska. Maybe for the second season."

"So will you hate me if I make a 'fish out of water' joke?"

He gave me a long-suffering roll of the eyes.

After a quick breakfast, I explored the rest of the house, which even after a day was beginning to take on the scents and moods of its new residents. It was a wild mix of smells that I wasn't used to, male and female, human, lycanthrope, and vampire, none of them pack or family. If I thought about it too much, if I let it get to me, it wouldn't feel safe.

According to the info I'd been given ahead of time, the lodge was a rental. Usually, it was occupied by groups on various corporate retreats or hunters during hunting season. The lake was supposed to have good fishing. A utility shed at the back of the building held not only the lodge's gas-powered electric generator and solar batteries, but a stash of equipment: fishing poles, kayaks and paddles, snowshoes and cross-country skis. I didn't feel the need to get that adventurous.

The basement, where Anastasia, Gemma, and Dorian stayed, was off-limits, but I wanted to contrive a way to sneak down there at some point. Prurient curiosity was killing me. I knew that actual vampires didn't go in for the coffin thing. So did the three of them share one big bed? Did human Dorian sleep while the two undead women were comatose during the day? Unsurprisingly, I couldn't find any outside basement windows to peer into.

Upstairs, the rest of us had claimed most but not all of the dozen or so bedrooms. Two extra remained. One of them—the least inviting, stuck in the back northwest corner of the house, with no sun and no views—remained clean, crisp, and unused. The other, I couldn't tell, because the door was locked. I rattled the knob. Still locked, and solidly. The door didn't even wiggle against its frame.

"Huh," I said and leaned close, pressing my ear to the wood, taking a deep breath to try and catch a scent. Nothing. Storage, I imagined.

But there was nothing like a locked door to make a place kind of spooky.

The kitchen had a back door, leading outside to a generous pile of chopped wood for the fireplace. *Escape route,* I thought in spite of myself.

After investigating the lodge, I took an hour to study the lay of the land around it. Jerome was right; this countryside practically begged me to shape-shift and go running. The wide, grassy meadow went on for miles, ringed in by even more impressive woods, and it all smelled like it was teeming with good things to eat. Two paths led away from the clearing in front of the house: one led to the airstrip in the middle of the meadow, the other to a hiking trail into the surrounding national forest.

I turned my face to the sun, closed my eyes, and took a deep breath of the world. I couldn't help but relax. I'd have to remember that over the next week. If—when—I got pissed off, count to ten and step outside for a moment.

Joey Provost cornered me on my way back to the lodge. He stepped off the front porch, making a beeline for me. I tried not to let it agitate me; he was just eager, not moving in for the kill. Probably. I stopped and waited for him.

"Kitty! Can I have a word?"

So many snarky ways to respond to that. I refrained; my smile was polite and fake. "What can I do for you?"

"We're going to get started with the meat of the show tonight," he said. "We've come up with this great idea, but I need your help."

Uh-oh. I seemed to remember this clause in the contract I signed regarding playing nice when the producers made requests like this. Then again, it was only the first day—how bad could it possibly be? My smile didn't get any less fake as I waited for him to explain.

"We want people to start opening up, start talking about themselves. Now, I'm not expecting big revelations. But we need to at least break the ice. I figure this is right up your alley. You talk to people all the time—your callers, the people you interview. You're good at asking the incisive questions, and that's all I need you to do here tonight. Just interview everyone, like it's a mini version of your show."

"You want me to do all your work for you," I said.

"I wouldn't put it like that," he said. "I'd rather look at it as showcasing your talents to the benefit of the entire program."

"Ooh, you're good," I said. That was the kind of lingo that sold shows to network executives.

"So that means you're up for it? I'd like to see at least

one question for each of the participants. And I'm sure you'll have no trouble keeping the discussion entertaining."

"That's my job," I said.

"If you could get started as soon as Anastasia and the others join you. That'd be *great*," he said.

"Great," I echoed.

After dinner, I called everyone to the living room and announced, "Okay, kids. Camp counselor Kitty has a game, so gather 'round and play nice for the cameras." Gordon, who was manning the gear this evening, gave me a grin over his camera.

The vampire trio had joined us again, presumably after their dinner. I covertly studied Dorian for puncture wounds but didn't find any. One blood donor for two vampires seemed a bit light. Dorian would be fainting by the end of the first week. Maybe the vampires didn't take much. Maybe that was how they stayed so thin. Their clothing this evening was as stunningly elegant as it had been the night before. Gemma wore a different gorgeous cocktail dress, and Anastasia wore flowing silk trousers and a camisole. Still all in black.

I was starting to really like this room, with its rustic, comfy furniture, warm wood fixtures, and soft lighting. A fire burned in the big stone fireplace, making the room cozy, and I had the feeling of being protected in a cocoon of light and warmth that kept the cool night at bay. Like curling up with my wolf pack.

Sitting cross-legged on one of the big armchairs, I faced the gang spread out around me, seated on sofas, on the hearth in front of the fireplace, and in Lee's case, on the floor. In front of me I held the sheet of paper I'd written my questions on.

I regarded the gathering. "I suppose you're all wondering why I've called you here this evening." I grinned, barely able to keep from giggling, because that line never got old.

Lee smirked. "Did you call us here just so you could say that?"

"No, actually. Mr. Provost put me up to getting the ball rolling tonight. So we're going to play a little game called Kitty's Truth or Dare. Except without the dare part, because I shudder to think what you all would actually be willing to do."

"Maybe we can save that part for next week, when we start getting punchy," Tina said.

"Hm. Wouldn't that be a bad idea? And now that you've said it out loud, Joey is sure to go for it," I said. "Really, this will be painless. I'm just going to ask you a few questions."

"Wait a minute," Tina said. "Show of hands: how many of you has Kitty interviewed on her show?" Jerome, Ariel, Jeffrey, and Tina raised their hands. To me she said, "Is this going to be anything like that?"

Hm, I'd definitely have to come up with a way to get the ones I hadn't interviewed yet on my show. I studied them appraisingly.

"Kitty, you look like you're hunting," Lee said.

"Who, me? So yeah, those guys can vouch for me. It'll be just like that. Nothing to be afraid of." Why did they all look so skeptical? "Look, this is voluntary, and if you have a problem with it you don't have to play along. But

I think it'll be fun. It'll be like those office ice-breaker things."

"Those are never fun," Ariel said darkly.

"Right. Fair enough. So, let's get the rote ones out of the way first. Anastasia, what year were you born?"

"You want that in Gregorian or Julian?"

"Ooh, fancy," I said. "So did you just drop a hint or what?"

"I'm not going to answer that question, Kitty," she said, donning a catty smile.

"Didn't think so. But I wouldn't feel like I'd done my job if I hadn't asked. Gemma, how about you?"

She glanced at Anastasia, like she and Dorian always did, as if asking permission. It irritated me, but I wasn't going to change it by bitching about it. Now, if I could get each of them alone and grill them for a couple of minutes . . .

I didn't detect any sign from Anastasia, no hint that she'd spoken or given Gemma a cue, but the younger vampire turned to me and answered, "Nineteen-eighty."

I blinked. "Holy crap, we're the same age." I looked her up and down, judging her all over again. She looked about twenty, give or take a couple of years. That meant about the same year I'd been attacked and turned into a werewolf, she'd become a vampire. I suddenly felt like I was looking into a "what might have been" mirror. What if it had been a vampire instead of a werewolf that had gotten me?

I wouldn't be winning any beauty pageants, for one thing. Also, to be honest, I was glad I hadn't frozen in time at that age. I'd grown a lot since then. I liked to think

I was a much better person now, and that I wore my age well.

"You know," Conrad said, "*not* claiming to be a thousand years old almost convinces me that you're for real."

"Hey," I said. "Every vampire had to be brand-new at some point, right?" Gemma just smiled, and I recovered, awkwardly. "I guess I won't be asking you any 'wisdom of the ages' questions, then. Next question's for Lee. And this is a serious one, so stop smirking at me." I was getting into a rhythm, just like I did on the show, which was kind of fun. Even more interesting was having everyone sitting here, letting me interact with a live audience. I was glad we were getting this on film.

"Lee: how many were-seals are there, and is there any kind of community? Do you hang out, have packs like werewolves do, anything like that?"

"No," he said. "We're loners. I don't even know how many there are. I know a few others in Alaska; we run into each other occasionally. Usually we give each other a wide berth."

Conrad said, because obviously he couldn't let anything go, "You're asking me to believe in not just werewolves, but were-seals? What about were-bears? Were-poodles? Were-rabbits? Where do you draw the line?"

He was just trying to get my goat. Best thing I could do was play it straight. "Were-rabbit? Not likely. In my experience, only carnivores manifest lycanthropic varieties. But were-bears, yeah, totally, there's some of those."

He gaped, but as I'd hoped, he had no other response to that.

"Moving on!" I said. "Odysseus Grant. Where the hell does your box of vanishing open to *really?*"

"You're fishing. Ask another one." Grant didn't change his expression, didn't miss a beat.

"Box of vanishing?" Conrad said. "Are you implying he does the vanishing-person trick and people actually *vanish?*"

I glared at him. "Are you going to give commentary on everything?"

"That's my job here, isn't it?"

"Alrighty, let's skip forward. Here's my question for Conrad: What's the strangest unexplained thing that's ever happened to you?"

"Well, I don't know that anything like that has really happened to me. Not like you're talking about."

"Forget the werewolves and vampires for a minute. I'm talking just . . . odd. Coincidence, déjà vu, fate, any of that. The wind blew a winning lottery ticket into your hand. You got a call from someone right when you were going to call them. Anything that made you stop and wonder for a minute."

"Let me think." He leaned back, hand on chin. We all watched, quiet and eager. I felt sure he was going to deny that anything strange or odd had ever happened to him, not so much as a shadow in the closet when he was a kid.

So imagine my surprise when he said, "I thought I saw a ghost, once. That is, I was a kid, and I thought it could be a ghost, until I thought about it and realized there was probably a reasonable explanation. A draft from a window or something."

Tina looked like she was about to jump up and say something, but I shot her a look and she settled back. We had something here—I didn't want to scare him off.

"What made you think it was a ghost? What about it made it so strange?"

He shook his head, his expression turning inward, unfocused with the memory. "It was the cold," he said. "It was a warm summer day, but there was this spot in the hallway that turned freezing. It's like that expression, someone walking over your grave. That's what it felt like. I could have sworn that someone was watching me. And that if I'd reached my hand out, someone standing there would have taken it." Unconsciously, he closed his hands into fists.

If Conrad had said something about smoky figures or moving furniture, I might have written off the account to suggestibility. He was a scared kid whose imagination had reinterpreted his fear based on campfire tales. But he didn't. My skin had goose bumps at his story.

"Whoa," I said, in validation. This was my gift, my superpower: making people feel like they could talk about anything. Making them open up and reveal their secrets.

"It could have all been in my head," he said quickly. "It could have all been my imagination."

Tina said, "Radical drops in temperature in localized areas have been reported with some hauntings. That whole incident, it doesn't sound unlikely at all." This didn't seem to comfort Conrad any.

"You weren't afraid of it?" Jeffrey said.

"No," Conrad said. "It mostly made me feel sad."

"Had there been any deaths in your family at the time? Had you lost any friends?" Jeffrey asked. "Might someone have been trying to contact you?"

Conrad thought for a moment, and his face was a blank. "No. No, that couldn't have been it." His voice was stark, and I wondered if he was lying, but suggesting that would have made him turn surly and shut up. Best move on.

My victims . . . er, interview subjects were mostly too clever and too used to the spotlight to slip up and answer my really probing questions. I didn't get stunning confessions from any of them, except the one from Conrad. He was quiet for the rest of the evening, and I wondered what nerve I'd touched.

Around midnight, the group started jumping ship, led by Conrad. I grumbled at the mutiny, but not really, because by the end of it I was left with Anastasia, Gemma, and Dorian. Maybe they'd be more forthcoming without everyone else around.

What was I thinking? We still had cameras focused on us. Probably a lost cause, but I had to try.

I waited until Anastasia and Dorian were involved in a conversation in the kitchen, where he was pouring a glass of wine. I was sure they were trading notes and commentary on their fellow housemates and everything they'd learned. Gemma wasn't interested and went to the window to look out at the nighttime meadow, trimmed with white from a waning moon. I sidled up to join her, not too obviously, I hoped.

"Hey, Gemma, can I ask you a question?"

"I suppose." She had a stunning smile—of course. "Doesn't mean I'll answer it."

"Why? Why become a vampire?"

She rolled her eyes. "That's such a boring question."

"Still. Humor me."

She hesitated, then gave a lopsided shrug, her first unstudied gesture. "I was afraid of getting old." She looked away, refusing to meet my gaze. Like a kid almost—

twenty years old and bored by old people, meaning any-one over twenty-five. How long did it take a vampire to develop that haughty poise that was so common with them? Long enough to realize the world was growing old around them? A generation—when you stop understanding the kids who look like you?

Was that arrogance a shield?

"That's not a very good reason," I said.

She frowned. It damaged her poise, just a bit. "I've been on the pageant circuit since I was eight. It's all I've ever known how to do. When I was fifteen, I went on anti-depressants. I was two inches too short for the model-ing agencies, and my mom acted like it was the end of the world, like I was this huge failure. My looks—it's all I have. I don't know how Anastasia found me. It's like she had this crystal ball and saw me screaming, 'Get me out of here.' She said she could keep me young forever. Like I said, that's all I have. She's taken such good care of me, I never looked back. She has uses for a very beautiful woman. What she does—she can use someone like me. I'm happy to help her."

I was almost afraid to ask what she was talking about. I thought I knew—the vampire entourage. The collection of beautiful people at a Master's—or Mistress's—beck and call. An alpha werewolf could gain status by showing off how many lesser wolves he—or she—could take care of. Vampires did the same thing by showing how many beautiful and powerful vampires owed them loyalty. It was almost feudal. Anastasia could bring Gemma into a room and distract everyone in it. Her adversaries wouldn't even know they were being distracted.

Was Gemma so afraid of growing old she'd make herself into a pawn? I didn't understand it. But then, I hadn't chosen to become what I was. It happened, and I just dealt with it. Making lemonade out of lemons and all that. Bottoms up.

"That seems kind of sad to me," I said. "There's so much more that makes up a person. There's a quote from Coco Chanel: 'Nature gives you the face you have at twenty; it is up to you to merit the face you have at fifty.' I'm kind of curious to see what kind of face I'm going to merit." My smile was wry.

"Oh, you're different," she said. "You couldn't possibly depend on your looks. Oh—I didn't mean it like that." I hadn't even had a chance to react to what she'd said. My smile only got more wry. "You're nice-looking, really cute. But you have so much else along with your looks. That's what I meant," she said. "Never mind. You know what I mean."

"You thought you didn't have anything else to aspire to. Yeah, I think I get it."

Anastasia joined us. Dorian had gone to the basement, I assumed. She put her hands on Gemma's shoulders and leaned in to whisper, "Go on downstairs. I'd like to speak with Kitty."

Ah, here it came, the smackdown for trying to weasel a confession out of Gemma, like Gemma couldn't speak for herself. The younger vampire smiled at me, squeezed her Mistress's hand, and retreated to the basement, leaving Anastasia and me alone.

I waited, but she didn't say anything. She gazed out the window, as Gemma had, a faint smile on her lips, seemingly admiring the beauty. And she *still* didn't say anything.

I couldn't stand it. "Did you really just need a pretty face hanging around you? Because that doesn't seem like the best reason to make someone a vampire," I said.

She didn't react; didn't look angry, or amused. What, then? "There's more to Gemma than her looks," Anastasia said finally. "Even she'll see that someday. I wouldn't have turned her otherwise. But consider this: without the time to grow out of her old life, she might never have discovered that about herself."

"But she's still entering beauty pageants," I said. "I'd have thought a stint with the Peace Corps might have done more to improve her sense of self-worth."

"May I ask you a question now?" she said.

I couldn't say no, even though I felt a bit cornered. I didn't really want to be the focus of this woman's attention. With just the two of us here, looking anywhere but her eyes was difficult. I worked to keep from fidgeting.

"This two-thousand-year-old vampire you said you met," she said. "Who was it?"

I didn't want to talk about this. "He was a little intimidating."

"Let me tell you about him. He's not so tall; average height and build, but he looks like stone. Close-cropped hair. An intense man. He was probably intense even before he turned to vampirism. And he's concerned with power. Political, territorial. He chooses minions, binds them to him. He's preparing allies for a coming conflict."

Weakly, I nodded. "That's right. That's him."

Anastasia leaned forward a little, her full lips in a pouting smile, her gaze searching. "What did he tell you, Kitty? What did he offer you? What did he demand?"

My thin pretense of a smile fell. "What do you know about him? Why are you asking me these things?"

"Evasion," she said, straightening slowly, catlike. "That tells me something, as well."

"Are you trying to figure out whose side I'm on? If Roman succeeded in buying me off?"

"Did he?"

What the hell, just lay it out there. "No."

Her gaze still studied me, assessed me. I got the feeling she didn't believe me, but talking about Roman made all my muscles go tense. Surely she could see that.

"So what's your interest in him?" I said. "Are you one of his?"

She was too good, too experienced to let her expression slip. Too magnificent a poker player. But I thought I knew: if she was one of his, she wouldn't have to ask me about him. The thought actually made me like her better. But I didn't like being in a verbal fencing match with an obviously experienced vampire. I was so outclassed.

"Is he a rival, then?" I asked, when she didn't answer. "How old does that make you?"

Her smile widened and for a moment seemed genuine. Like in another moment she'd laugh and we'd be like old friends. But I also felt like she'd be laughing at me.

She said, "For all our vaunted immortality, old vampires are actually quite rare. They consider each other to be rivals, and they eliminate each other. It's best to keep a low profile."

That so didn't answer my question. "This isn't a low profile."

"Sometimes you have to step into the light to learn what you need to know."

That was a page out of my book. She was still being evasive. "Are you working against Roman? Or are you just another player working for the same goal?"

She tilted her head. "You seem to know more about this than I'd expect from someone of your . . . type."

"You going to give me the old 'werewolves are uncivilized heathens' line now?"

"No, of course not, I wouldn't insult you. I'm far too aware of how some werewolves promote that reputation so people like me will underestimate them."

Over the last couple of years, I'd learned about the so-called Long Game in bits and pieces, like drops of water falling into a bucket. I had gathered enough of those drops to make a mess. And none of those drops suggested that werewolves ever played a part in the Long Game except as tools. As minions. Most of the werewolves I knew just wanted to be left alone, and that didn't give us a whole lot of power in the game Anastasia was playing.

Before I could call her on it, she straightened and smoothed out her trousers, an obvious shift in tone and in topic. "And what do you know of Odysseus Grant?"

Well, shoot. Were these two plotting some sort of underworld scheme against each other? Did the show serve as a backdrop by accident, or had they ended up here by design? Anastasia might have rigged all this as a publicity stunt. Grant? Never. He didn't do stunts. He was always in earnest.

What could I possibly tell the vampire that wouldn't get him in trouble? I wasn't a good liar. I couldn't pretend like I didn't care about him.

"He saved my life once," I said. "As far as I'm concerned, he's one of the good guys."

"Good guys. I wonder what that means to you."

"I just want to be left alone," I said, my voice soft. I didn't know yet if Anastasia was a good guy. I didn't know what that meant to her.

Her gaze narrowed. "I don't believe you. The evidence suggests otherwise."

I looked up, because these were the big issues, and when you started trying to untangle the big issues—of philosophy, of ideology—there often were no right answers. I tended to take things day by day, by gut instinct, and hope for the best.

"Then maybe I want justice," I said.

"Oh," she said, with something like mocking awe. "You're an idealist."

"Yeah. So I'm told."

"Well. Good luck. You'll need it." She gazed outside, like she had just commented on the weather, or the lovely shadows on the grass.

Hand on hip, I turned to her. "Okay, now you're just baiting me."

"We don't move through time," she said. "We exist outside of it. We build our own worlds and carry them with us, cultures within cultures, orbits within orbits. And we look on you as we would on rats in a cage. Studying you."

"If you feel that way, why are you even here? Why bother interacting with us? Is someone like Dorian just your milk cow?"

"Some of us feel differently," she said quickly, almost an apology. "Some of us resist the urge to see the rest of you as livestock. I know you understand—you resist the same urges."

"But I'm mortal. Changes the outlook a bit."

She said, "I'm trying to explain what you're facing. The players in the Game—why consolidate power except to use it? What does anyone use power for but to impose their worldview over everyone?"

"That's a little epic for me to wrap my head around."

"Live long enough and you see where the patterns lead."

"How long?" I took the flyer.

She smiled, thin and wary. "I should retire now. Thank you for speaking with me."

When she offered her hand, I took it—it was smooth, cool, firm. I still wouldn't meet her gaze, and this seemed to amuse her, as well. Then she left, disappearing around the corner to the basement door.

I flopped onto the sofa and buried my face in a cushion.

chapter 6

I managed to get a couple hours of sleep. I should have slept more—it's not like I had to be anywhere—but I kept turning that conversation with Anastasia over in my mind, and I kept worrying.

When I got up, it was still before anyone else. I went for the phone and called Ben. My hand cupped over the mouthpiece, I spoke as softly as I could.

"What's wrong?" he said instantly. I was being so obviously conspiratorial.

"I need you to check on something for me."

"You're still managing to find trouble, aren't you?"

I should have argued this on principle. But really, I didn't have a leg to stand on. "This probably isn't important, but I don't want to be blindsided. You may need to talk to Rick about it."

"Do I have to?"

Rick, Master vampire of Denver. Ben didn't like vampires; I couldn't much blame him. "Come on, Rick's a good guy."

"For certain values of good."

"There's a vampire here. Her name's Anastasia. I'd just like to find out more about her, where she came from, if she has any kind of reputation."

"Is there a reason for the cloak-and-dagger routine?"

"She's been asking me about Roman."

He paused a moment, then said, "Oh. Shit. Is she working for him or something? How are they connected?"

"That's what I need to find out. She didn't seem to be all that thrilled with him, which is a little encouraging."

"The enemy of your enemy is not necessarily your friend."

"I know that. She seems to be trying to find out which side I'm on. Why can't people just leave me alone?"

"You're a popular public figure who volunteered to be on a reality TV show. And you want to be left alone?"

"Okay, point taken." I pouted.

"You know I've got my own situation going on here. I have Cormac's parole hearing in two days."

Crap. I was frustrated all over again that I wasn't going to be there. "How is that going? Are you okay? Is he okay? Is everything going to be okay?"

"If he can keep his nose clean for a couple more days, we should be golden."

My first thought: he'd kept his nose clean for almost two years—surely the next couple of days wouldn't be a problem. But then I thought, this was Cormac we were talking about. "You sound nervous."

He sighed. "I am nervous. This is the perfect time for the universe to drop a bomb on us."

"Don't think like that. It's going to be fine. Everything's going to be fine."

"Just keep saying that. We could use the good vibes."

"You got it," I said, wishing hard that this would work out all right. "Don't worry about my problems—springing Cormac is more important."

"I think I can spare five minutes for a call to Rick. I'll let you know what I find out."

"Thanks. I love you, Ben."

"I love you, too. If Roman shows up, run. Don't try to talk to him, don't get into an argument with him. Just run."

"Yeah. I'll run." Roman wasn't going to show up. Hell, no. That would be too much.

We signed off, and I cursed the universe's bad timing that all this was happening at once.

After the talk with Ben, I emerged from the back of the lodge to the living room just in time to hear Tina yell.

"Oh, *gross!* What the hell?"

A half-dozen of the others were awake by then and ran to the picture window, where Tina was standing, mouth open, looking out with a horrified expression. The usual cameras were there to capture the fun.

A mauled carcass lay at the edge of the meadow. It wasn't very clear, but blood was visible, along with a mound of meat—pink flesh that gleamed wetly in the morning sun. There might have been legs sticking out, maybe a scrap of tawny hide.

"Is that a deer?" Jeffrey said. "It looks like something shredded it."

Conrad said, "Maybe a bear. Or a wolf. A real wolf, I mean." He eyed me.

"They wouldn't leave a kill like that this close to people," Lee said.

I looked around. Tina, Jeffrey, Conrad, Lee, Ariel, me. I had an idea of what had happened.

"Has anyone seen Jerome?" I said wryly. So maybe I hadn't been the first person up this morning.

"What?"

Lee raised a brow. "Seriously?"

Yeah, *he* knew what I was talking about. I stepped outside, went down the porch steps, and took a breath of air. The smell hit me: blood and guts, decay setting in. Crows would be here soon to start picking at it. Circle of life and so on. I also caught the scent of lycanthrope all over the place. I wondered if Macy was trying to be cute, dragging his kill back here.

At that moment, he emerged from around the side of the lodge. He'd probably retreated to the forest on this side of the valley to sleep his wolf off. And he hadn't bothered to bring clothes with him: he was naked. I could see every inch of his sleek, muscular body. He was huge, solid as a brick wall. Well built, all the way around. A-hem.

He'd even managed to clean most of the blood off his face and hands, but I could still smell traces.

When he saw me, he stopped. I met his gaze and smiled. "I see you managed alone just fine."

"You missed out," he said. "The hunting here's great."

"Yeah, that's why they call it a hunting lodge. You're putting on quite a show." I tilted my head toward the window and the audience standing there.

Macy grinned. "I thought I'd shake things up a little."

"Uh, yeah."

I went back inside, leaving the man to his lack of modesty. He followed me in, not caring a bit that the others suddenly looked everywhere else but at him. Except for Lee, who was smirking right along with me. Something about being a lycanthrope made being naked not all that big a deal.

"Convinced yet, Conrad?" I said.

He shook his head. "It's a trick. Provost probably dumped that carcass out there."

The bummer thing was, he wasn't wrong. A scene like this would have been easy to stage.

Macy didn't pause for conversation but went straight to the stairs, where Grant was descending. The two passed each other awkwardly.

Hands in his trouser pockets, Grant faced us. "I seem to have missed some excitement."

Maybe Conrad was half right. Maybe this had been rigged—just not the way he thought. I glanced sidelong at one of the cameras. "I think Provost may have put Jerome up to a little fun," I said. "But hey, we had to get started with the freaky shit sometime."

"Er—language, Kitty," Ariel said.

I shrugged. "That's what editors are for."

Conrad crossed his arms. "Odysseus—despite your name, I think you may be the most rational person here besides me. You really believe all this? You believe Jerome is a werewolf? That Kitty is? I mean, a werewolf named Kitty—how do you expect anyone to buy that?"

"Because I've seen her shape-shift," he said.

Conrad opened his mouth to reply, then closed it again.

"My offer still stands," I said, hitching my thumb toward the door. "I'll go shape-shift right now and we can finish up this whole thing."

Tina raised a hand. "I'd go for that—I haven't seen you shift. And how did he see you shift? What's the story with that?"

"Long," I said. "Complicated."

"I guess that means you're not going to tell us."

"What happens in Vegas, as they say," Grant said, brow lifted.

Did he just crack a joke?

That, then, was going to be the tone for the entire two weeks: something freaky happening, maybe prompted by Provost, maybe not; then Conrad grumbling about how it was all a setup; Valenti, Cabe, and the PAs running around to capture it on film. I assumed the events would escalate—the incidents would get weirder, and Conrad's denials would get lamer, until he had a moment of epiphany. And probably a spectacular nervous breakdown, to boot. Then we'd all reconcile and grow together as human beings. Reality shows liked to convince the TV-viewing public that they were all spontaneous and, you know, real. But a good editor would be able to turn the footage from this week into a retelling of *War and Peace*.

Midmorning, Provost dropped in to see how we were doing. The daily check-in. His producer face was as plastic and smiley as ever. I was sitting on the porch, feet propped on the railing, reading a book when he bounded up the steps, arms spread in greeting.

"Kitty! How's it going? Enjoying yourself?"

"Yes. Quite," I said noncommittally.

"You couldn't find anything more, ah, photogenic to do than read a book?"

"You don't think this is photogenic? Look at it this way, you include footage of me reading, you'll appeal to your intellectual demographic."

He stared blankly, and he was probably right: he didn't have an intellectual demographic. I knew I was in trouble when he pulled over another of the chairs and settled in for a chat. He leaned forward, elbows on knees, acting chummy, but the gesture made me cringe and want to growl. Some people had no respect for personal space. He might have been a high school guidance counselor in a past life.

"I wondered if you could do me a favor," he said.

"Another one?" I said. I was pretty sure I wouldn't like whatever he was about to say.

"There's obviously some kind of history between you and Grant." He gave a certain weight to the word "history" that made me raise my brow. "Now, I don't need any details, but I have to say, there's *a lot* of potential there. And something's definitely going on between Grant and Anastasia. The whole thing screams triangle. Really meaty stuff. I was hoping I could convince you to, you know, maybe play it up a little."

I was under no illusions that reality TV actually depicted reality, so this shouldn't have surprised me. Still, I stared at Provost, disbelieving, but he continued looking hopeful. If I got angry, it would only reinforce any notions he'd developed. Ignoring him probably wouldn't work—he'd just keep bugging me until the two weeks were up. Maybe if I played nice it would throw him off guard.

I said, "You know, the 'history' between Grant and me involves a death-defying escape from a cult of crazies practicing human sacrifice in worship to an ancient Babylonian goddess. You sure you want me to play that up?"

That got him to at least hesitate. The permanent smile remained frozen. "You may be right. The network executives might have a problem with human sacrifice. If we didn't handle it, you know, *tastefully*."

The words "tasteful" and "human sacrifice" should never appear together in the same sentence. Why did I even bother arguing?

"Can I ask you something? Did you put Jerome up to dropping that mauled deer on the driveway?"

"No. That was all him. Great stuff, too. That guy has a good eye for entertainment."

"Must be all the pro wrestling."

"So when are you going to head out for a run yourself? The four-legged kind."

"I try to be a little more civilized," I said. "All joking aside, I wasn't really planning on it at all."

"Too bad you wouldn't let us schedule this over the full moon."

I leaned forward. Bared my teeth in an expression of aggression he wouldn't understand. "If you want it that bad, I hear there's a video you can download off the Internet."

He blinked, gave a nervous smile, and walked away. Maybe he did understand the body language.

He went inside. Through the picture window, I watched him have similar, hushed conversations in corners with Lee and Tina. He tried to have one with Grant, but the magician made a curt apology and walked away.

I was making a map in my mind of who was talking to whom, who had sneaked off, and who could possibly be colluding with Provost. Or Grant. Or Anastasia. Inventing more conspiracies, and probably playing the game exactly the way Provost would want me to.

chapter 7

That night, when the vampires and Dorian arrived and we gathered in the dining room for the official structured-activities portion of the evening, Tina was the last to arrive, and she had a shopping bag with her. The item in it was long, flat, maybe a couple of inches thick.

"Ooh, I know what this is," I said, my eyes getting big, because this was going to be *good*. Tina gave me a smile as she peeled back the bag and revealed the Ouija board box.

"Oh, now, this is interesting," Anastasia said, leaning in.

"Give me a break!" Conrad said, looking away in disgust.

"No, seriously, she's really good with this," I said.

"You're not going to get me to buy that a Ouija board really works. Especially not one that comes in a box from Parker Brothers," Conrad argued.

"These are actually the best kind," Tina said, ripping off the shrink-wrap. "These are clean. You don't want to mess with a board when you don't know where it came from or what it's bccn uscd for."

"I've never had much luck with any boards," Jeffrey said.

"That's because you're all auras and empathy. I'm a little more hands-on," Tina said, and the two grinned at each other like they were sharing a secret.

Did I sense sparks? Were Tina and Jeffrey developing a thing? I'd have to keep an eye on them. The thought made me giddy—they'd be so cute together. I wondered if their kids would be superpsychic. But I was getting ahead of myself.

The eleven of us gathered around the long dining room table. Tina sat in the middle and set up the board. "We're not all going to be able to play, I'm afraid. There's not enough room. But, Jeffrey, if you could sit across from me, I'm betting the two of us should be able to get something."

"I'm game." He always was.

Ariel dimmed the lights and brought out a couple of candles. "It's all about atmosphere."

"And she knows, because she has flapping bat icons on her website," I said.

"Hey!" But she was smiling, so she'd taken the ribbing well. And there was much chuckling. "You're not very formal about this. Some people build up whole rituals, stock phrases, the right colored candles, incense, the works. They say it won't work without it. That it's a way to show the spirits respect."

"Different strokes," Tina said. "I'm self-taught; I never learned any rituals. But it seems like all the ceremonial crap is distracting. Puts up more barriers between us and the other side rather than reducing them. Conrad's right on that score—too much mysticism only confuses people. Makes it easier to dupe them. I'd rather cut through all that. Most of this is instinct anyway. I can't explain what it is I do."

"What are you going to do for us today? Channel Houdini or what?" I said.

"You can't channel Houdini," Conrad said, predictably. Tina rolled her eyes.

"I'm going to try to read something off you," she said to Conrad. "This is supposed to be about shocking you, right?"

"Do your worst," he said.

Across from each other, Tina and Jeffrey placed two fingers from each hand on the plastic planchette in the middle of the board. Then nothing happened.

I'd seen Tina do this before, but it was still spooky. It didn't help that the last time we'd done this, it had initiated some really scary fallout. Buildings spontaneously combusting, demon possession. Yeah. What was going to happen this time? So much of the tension of this came from expectation. The atmosphere of it, as Ariel said. Everyone must have been holding their breaths, the room was so still.

The plastic scritched across the printed cardboard, a tiny scraping noise. Someone might have scuffed a foot. Except that Jeffrey and Tina both held their hands above the Ouija board, tense—and not touching the planchette. It had gotten away from them.

"What was that?" Ariel whispered.

"Shh," Tina hissed. She craned over the board to

see where the arrow pointed. "The letter N. Well, it's a start."

"How are you going to prove to me that you didn't move that yourself?" Conrad said, once again taking a page out of the skeptic's handbook.

"Here's the thing, Conrad," Tina said, sounding frustrated. "I can't. Shall we try again?"

Again, Jeffrey and Tina placed fingers on the plastic. Candles flickered. Their shadows wavered across the board, ghostly. Like something from beyond really was reaching out, nudging.

"We have an N," Tina said. "What is Conrad thinking about that has to do with N?"

They must have sat like that for a couple of minutes. Jeffrey had his eyes closed. Tina's were half-lidded, her gaze on the planchette. Somebody fidgeted; the noise of fabric on fabric seemed loud.

The plastic shifted, again scooting out of Jeffrey and Tina's grasps. This time, we all leaned in. It pointed at A.

"Sleight of hand. It's a stage trick." Conrad looked at Grant. "Right?"

Grant shrugged noncommittally.

"This doesn't prove anything," Conrad said, shaking his head.

"Natalie," Jeffrey said. "Someone named Natalie. Young. A terrible loss."

His eyes were still closed. He pursed his lips, like he was trying to solve a puzzle. He didn't see Conrad staring at him, his mouth open.

"What is it?" Tina asked.

We were all looking at Conrad now. He stammered,

"My-my sister. Natalie. She was a couple years older than me. She died."

"Drowned, right?" Jeffrey said.

"That was twenty-five years ago," Conrad said. "How did you know that?"

"It's a common feeling. You lose someone you love in an accident like that, you spend the rest of your life wondering if you could have prevented it. You may think you've moved on, but the thought of it is always there. It wasn't your fault, Conrad. You couldn't have done anything," Jeffrey said gently.

I knew how Conrad was feeling, because Jeffrey did the same thing to me when I first met him and asked him to prove he could do what he claimed. He pulled a name out of my past and knocked me over with it.

Nothing in the room moved until Conrad shook himself, shuddered almost, like he was waking up from a spell. He glared at Jeffrey.

"You could have learned about that a dozen different ways. It was in the newspapers. Provost dug it up and fed you the line. That's all it is. And it's a cheap stunt, throwing something like that at me. Nice try—for a second there I almost believed you."

Jeffrey shrugged, like it didn't bother him one way or another whether Conrad believed him.

"And just to prove I'm not upset, I'm not going to get up and storm out of the room. That's what you're expecting, isn't it?" Conrad pointed when he said this.

"Right," Tina said. "Let's try something a little lighter. No more invasive information about people who aren't receptive to it, okay?" Tina donned a quirky smile. "Let's find out who's going to hook up by the end of the two weeks."

There was much grumbling, chuckling, and eye rolling at this announcement. Grant and Anastasia were sitting detached, observant but not involved.

"I think it's a good idea," Ariel said. "Let all that subconscious stuff come bubbling to the surface."

"Come on." Tina grinned at Jeffrey. "It'll be fun."

Sighing, he reached over the board, and they returned to their positions on the planchette.

Again, nothing happened. This would try the patience of saints.

I imagined the sound of a ticking clock, which would have been a perfect backdrop. That, and a hard wind beating against the house. Maybe a cat knocking something over. This whole scene was begging for the haunted-house treatment. Gemma giggled, and someone shushed her.

"Maybe nobody hooks up," Jeffrey said. "If there's nothing there, there's nothing there."

"Provost won't be happy about that," I said. "I hear they always rig a hot romance on these things. You have to have at least one cavorting-in-the-hot-tub scene."

"Shh," Tina said, and I ducked, because I should have known better. "I don't like this." She suddenly pulled her hands away, shaking them as if she'd touched something hot.

"Are you getting something?" Jeffrey said.

"No. I'm just not feeling good."

Conrad said, "All this psychic stuff is showmanship. It's all an act."

I was really going to get sick of that tone of voice by the end of the two weeks. Half of us shushed him.

"Try again. Focus on what's causing that feeling," Jeffrey said.

Once again, they placed fingers on the planchette. Again, we waited. Tina had her eyes closed. Jeffrey watched Tina. He seemed worried. My own gaze went back and forth between them.

The candles flickered.

Tina's lips started moving, like she was speaking silently. Her brow furrowed.

"Tina," Jeffrey said and reached for her.

She gasped. The planchette and board jumped, skittering from her touch. She sat back, holding her head, gasping for breath. I rose half out of my chair, along with a few of the others. Jeffrey shoved past us, making his way around the table to her side. He knelt by her, and she clung to his shoulder.

"What happened?" he asked.

"I don't know," she said, her voice strained. "I don't think I like it here."

This wasn't calming my own paranoia at all.

"Could it be something that happened in the past?" Jeffrey said. "A past accident or death?"

"No. That sort of thing isn't this . . . insistent. That's it, I'm done." She pushed her chair away from the table. "Sorry, guys. Obviously the stars are not aligned tonight."

"Can I get you something? A glass of water?" Jeffrey said, and Tina smiled a thanks.

I didn't like it. Tina wouldn't act like that unless something had really gotten to her. She had guts. I'd seen her scared, but she never backed down.

Someone turned the lights back on, and the group

broke into different conversations. Grant and Anastasia were watching Tina closely, studious, like they expected her eyes to roll back in her head while she chanted in tongues. Which I'd seen her do before, but still.

Then they caught each other watching. Exchanged the briefest glance. Grant left the table and made his way to the living room window, to look out at the night. At nothing.

Tina had her hands around the glass of water Jeffrey had brought her, but she hadn't taken a drink yet. Jeffrey was hovering. Something was definitely sparking between those two. If I had my way I'd have shuffled everyone out of the room and let them have their moment. But the cameras were probably eating this up.

I sat at the table and folded the Ouija board out of the way; I had the feeling it was staring at me.

"Jeffrey, are you sensing anything?" I asked.

He hesitated, glancing around like whatever it was had physical form and he could really see it. "It's hard to tell if there's really something here, or if it's the strain of a dozen strangers pushed together in an artificial situation. I wouldn't expect the energy here to be rosy."

"Maybe that's it," Tina said. "Just normal weirdness."

"You know how odd that sounds?" I said, and she smiled.

"Tina," Grant said, turning from the window and marching over. "I'd like to try something, if you're game."

She looked wary. "Depends. I may just have a beer and call it a night."

"Do you trust me?"

"Hell, no," she said, glaring.

"You saw something," he said. "You didn't like it, and I think your mind decided to block it. Now, I suspect you're the kind of person who doesn't scare easily. If something has scared you, I'd really like to know what."

"What do you suggest?"

"I'd like to hypnotize you."

"Can you do that?" Tina said.

"I can try. It may not work. I may be wrong and you may not have any idea what's bothering you, subconsciously or otherwise."

She didn't look convinced. "I've seen a lot of freaky stuff, but I'm not sure how I feel about that."

"We can do it here, in the open," Grant said. "The moment you're uncomfortable, we'll stop."

"Is it dangerous?" I said.

"It can be," he said. And that was why I liked Grant. He could be evasive, but he didn't sugarcoat.

She looked at Jeffrey, gave him some expression I couldn't see. He shrugged and said, "I'm curious to see what would happen."

She took a deep breath. "Okay. We can try it."

Sounding amused, Conrad said, "So, you have a watch on a chain? A crystal ball or something?"

"No," Grant said. "Lie down on the sofa, here. Everyone else, you can watch, but keep your distance."

Under the gathering's watchful, curious stares, Tina moved to the sofa and lay down. Jeffrey didn't leave her side. He sat on the edge, near her knees. She shifted to give him room, and they both looked at Grant, daring him to argue. The magician didn't. He moved a pillow under her head and asked if she was comfortable. She shifted and fidgeted for a moment, then settled. Even I could tell she was tense. The room smelled tangy. It wasn't just the smell of a house filled with people and growing ripe; it was nerves, tension. Lee and Jerome, the other lycanthropes, glanced at me. All our noses were flaring. This was getting thick.

Grant knelt by the sofa near Tina's head.

"Relax," he said, his voice soft, steady. "Take a deep breath. In, and out."

He managed to project even more intensity than usual. Like he had collected all his focus, which had been spread equally around the room, observing, and pointed it toward her. If he had pointed all that attention toward me, I'd probably have jumped out of my skin. Never mind relaxing.

I had to say something: "I'm sorry, weird question, and if I don't ask now I'll forget."

I expected the glare Grant gave me. But it was an indulgent glare—he knew me pretty well by this time. "Yes?"

"Are psychics like Tina more or less susceptible to hypnotism? You know, are their minds more receptive to being open like that, or do they actually have stronger defenses against that kind of prying?"

Grant said, "I wouldn't call it prying. When it's done well, it's more like drawing back a curtain. It all depends on how cooperative the subject is. We'll find out soon how cooperative Ms. McCannon is."

"Just get on with it," Tina said.

Grant raised a brow, asking my permission. I ducked out of the way.

"All right," he said, returning his attention to Tina. "Again. Relax. Breathe in, and out." He spoke slowly, calmly, and in moments her breathing matched the rhythm of his speech. He didn't use any of the movie "you're getting very sleepy" clichés. He just spoke softly, rhythmically, creating a mood, like the peace of a gently rocking boat. I was getting a little woozy listening to it.

The room was dead quiet.

"You're in a dark room, safe and warm. Protected. You feel calm and powerful. Nothing can touch you here. Warm, protected, very safe. In a moment, a light will come on, slowly. A soft, warm light is growing brighter. You start to see what else is in the room. Tina, do you remember the séance you performed a short while ago?"

"Yes," she whispered, her lips barely moving.

"Go back to the start of the séance. Remember what you felt. What you saw. Replay those events, those feelings. Remember what contacted you. What happened first?"

Her lips moved; the words came slowly. "It's moving. I can't feel my hands. I know when it starts because I can't feel my hands." Her brow furrowed. Grant murmured words of comfort.

"Jeffrey is helping," she said. "They trust Jeffrey."

"Who trusts Jeffrey?"

"*Them.*" She wet her lips. "Natalie. Conrad's sister. She's with him, looking after him. She's worried—"

"Now, wait just a minute—" Conrad said, lurching forward. Anastasia caught his arm, held him back. He looked hard at her, as if surprised by the strength of her grip. He met her gaze. And I bet *that* gave him a shock.

Conrad stayed back and stayed quiet.

"That was the first contact you made during the séance," Grant said, his tone never wavering. "Move forward now. You tried again."

"Asked a question. Who hooks up." She smiled a little.

"You felt something."

Tina's smile vanished. "No."

"You're safe here. The room is protected. The scene playing now is only an image, a memory. You can see the memory very clearly. It can't hurt you."

She shook her head, just a little. "It's here, closing around the house."

"What is?"

"It's ugly. No."

Jeffrey reached for her hand, but Grant shook his head sharply, warning him away.

"Whatever you saw, it can't hurt you here," Grant said. "You have control over this memory. What do you see? What is it, closing around the house?"

"Hate," she said.

Grant pursed his lips. "Where does the hate come from?"

"It's a plan—it's all part of the plan. I can't see the plan, I can only see what it means, and it's full of hate. Nobody makes it, nobody—" She grimaced, her head started shaking, and a whine began in her throat, at the edge of a scream. Her whole body tensed. The hair on my neck bristled.

Grant leaned in. "The light is fading, Tina. It's growing dim, fading to a warm, comforting darkness. You're resting, relaxed in every part of your body. Your mind is relaxed, your breathing is relaxed. When I count to three, you'll awake rested, aware, in full control of your memory and yourself. One . . . two . . . three . . ."

She opened her eyes. Looked at Grant, then at Jeffrey. She let out a long sigh.

"So what's out there?" Jerome said, moving closer, from the outskirts of the gathering. "What's closing in?"

She rubbed her face; her frown was despairing. "I couldn't see it. It was almost . . ." She shook the thought away. Jeffrey took her other hand and squeezed tightly.

Urgent, Jerome continued. "Is it a person? An animal? A thing? Another one like us? What?"

"I said I don't know!" She sat up, glaring. Her hands were shaking.

"Whole lot of good that does us," the wrestler said, turning away.

Lee said, "I'm not trying to criticize, or question you, but could this maybe be paranoia? We're in the middle of nowhere, in a weird situation—"

"I'm a paranormal investigator," she said. "I've been in situations way more whacked-out than this."

"I believe her," Anastasia said. "I believe there's more going on here than we think. I would certainly like to know what."

I bet you would, I managed not to mutter. She and Grant were back to studying each other, without looking like they were studying each other. The cynic in me was starting to think they were both plants, in cahoots with Provost to jack up the tension until somebody snapped. All to make the show more exciting. Except I knew Grant wouldn't do that kind of thing. I *thought* Grant wouldn't do that kind of thing. The last thing I needed here was to decide I couldn't trust anyone.

"Clearly, you have an unusual talent," Anastasia said to Tina.

Tina looked away. "I wish I didn't, most of the time."

"That's another way to tell the fakes from the real thing," Grant said, turning to Conrad. "The real psychics tend to treat it as a burden. They tend not to show off."

Tina gave him a thin-lipped smile.

The skeptic crossed his arms, set his expression into a frown. "I'll give you this much, you all are putting on a great show."

"Will you lay off with that?" Tina said.

For my part, I'd about had it with him, and it had only been two days. "That's it," I said, marching to the front door. "I'm doing it right there on the front porch for everyone to see so he'll just shut the hell up."

"Kitty—" Ariel, who was closest, grabbed for my arm. I brushed her away, and a growl cut from my throat.

She backed away, arms up defensively. Something inside me wanted to howl. I closed my eyes, held my head for a moment while taking several deep breaths, and thought of broccoli. Thought of anything that wouldn't make me bare my teeth and snarl.

The room had fallen silent, like the hush at a party after somebody breaks a wineglass. Without the laughing after.

Making the effort to settle, I rolled my shoulders, straightened my back, and opened my eyes to regard my colleagues and housemates with a friendly, nongrowling smile. I suddenly felt exhausted. But some of the tension went out of the room. Everyone could breathe now.

"What just happened?" Conrad said.

"I'm taking a walk. If something's out there, maybe I'll catch a sign of it," I said and went outside.

This whole situation was designed to make me go

crazy. I just had to keep that in mind and not let it get to me. Thank God the nearest full moon was behind me instead of in front of me, or keeping it together would be that much harder.

I stomped down the front steps to the clearing and already felt better. Closer to the earth, more in my element. I shook my arms and let some of the tension fall out of me. Maybe I could shift. Run as Wolf, just for a little while. Take the edge off.

Gordon and his camera followed me out, but I ignored him. Ignoring him was getting easier.

I heard another set of footsteps on the porch and turned back just as I caught Jerome's scent. My shoulders stiffened, like rising hackles. He hesitated, turned sideways. Came down the steps obliquely instead of right at me. It made me only marginally less twitchy.

"Well?" I said. Rather ambiguous, but that was about as articulate as I was feeling at the moment.

"Maybe you have the right idea. If Tina thinks something here's out to get us, maybe we should go looking for it."

"If something here's out to get us, it's because Provost and his people planted it for the sake of the show and it's all a setup."

"Fair enough. But have they planned it because they expect us to go after it and figure it out, or not? Why not play along?"

The bottom line: we'd feel better by actually doing something rather than standing around bitching.

"For somebody who lets himself get beaten up professionally, you seem to have hung on to a few brain cells," I said.

"I think I got out of boxing just in time to save them. Pro wrestling's a little tamer."

I started to say something snide, then stopped. Who was I to judge? "Shall we take a walk around the house? I take clockwise, you take counter, and we'll see if we find anything."

He continued down the steps to join me in looking out over the meadow, the lake with its surface shining metallic in darkness, the shadows of the forest. The light from the lodge's windows extended only to the edge of the clearing. A faint wind was blowing; we both turned our noses into it and breathed deeply. In a way, with just the two of us here, I felt more comfortable. I wasn't so aware of the ways I wasn't human. Jerome wouldn't think I was strange, sniffing the wind, pacing silently, peering into the darkness. Acting like a wolf on the hunt.

Both of us took on that body language, prowling step by step around the house, glancing back to check on the other's progress. Anyone watching from inside would notice it; Conrad would probably say we were only acting. I reached the corner of the lodge and turned my senses outward, letting Wolf bleed into them, letting her instincts tell me if anything was wrong. Moving slowly, I zigzagged to cover more ground, listening for the smallest sounds. What I heard were normal nocturnal noises, the creatures who came out at night, mice or voles in the underbrush, an owl flapping in trees overhead. Nature's white noise.

Around the lodge I smelled people. Humans. Part of the crew, I assumed, or residents of the house who had walked here earlier. Nothing out of the ordinary, nothing that raised my hackles. The night was calm, dark, like it was supposed to be. The lodge had golden light shining in most of the windows, making it an island of welcome warmth. Maybe Wolf wanted to go hunting, but I would be just as happy to go back inside and settle for the evening. As soon as I walked off some of my nerves.

I was looking for anything out of place, and I found it: a circle of glass and metal perched in a tree, pointed at the back door: another one of the remote cameras. I looked up into it, waved a little, wondering if we were following Provost's script.

In the back of the house, I waited to hear footsteps as Jerome and I approached each other. I smelled him first, catching the trace of a fellow werewolf. I marveled at how such a massive man could move so quietly.

We spotted each other across the scrubby clearing behind the house, froze a moment, caught in each other's gazes, then relaxed and moved again. I decided I really did want to see him as a wolf at some point before the show ended. I imagined he was impressive.

"Anything?" I said, and he shook his head.

"You think it's all in Tina's head?"

"I've worked with her before," I said. "She's not one to cry wolf. No pun intended."

"Then what *is* going on?" He huffed.

Did I tell him that I thought the vampires were bringing their own brand of hijinks into the proceedings? That Grant had his own plotline going on in addition to whatever one Provost had worked out for us? I decided I didn't really want to bring all this up with Jerome. We might have both been werewolves, but he was still a stranger. Not part of my pack.

"I don't know," I said softly. "Let's get back in before the others start a rumor about us."

He leered. "Isn't that what this show's all about?"

"I have my guy back home, and I'd really hate for you two to decide you had to duke it out over me." Not to mention Jerome could pound Ben into mush. I loved my husband, but he wasn't built like a tank.

"I think that may give Provost his next show."

I shook my head and marched inside.

None of us found anything weird; nobody could point to anything specifically wrong, except for the feeling that Tina had, which had now spread to the rest of us by the power of suggestion. Predictably, Conrad said, "You're all just trying to scare me," at which point Jerome snarled at him, and half the room jumped. I didn't. I glared at the wrestler, with a silent admonishment: *Cut it out.*

Yeah, I was pretty sure Provost's ulterior motive was to drive us all crazy, to see who snapped first. I hoped there wouldn't be any blood when it happened; Provost was probably hoping otherwise.

In keeping with the seminocturnal schedule, I went to bed a few hours before dawn. My bedroom light had been off only twenty minutes when someone knocked on my door, very softly. If I hadn't been awake and twitchy already, I wouldn't have heard it. I could have called for whoever it was to come in, but I wasn't feeling that trusting and open. I padded to the door and opened it a crack.

Tina stood outside, pressed close, almost pushing her way in. "Can I talk to you?"

"Yeah, of course." I let her in and glanced behind her, expecting to see one of the PAs and a camera, but she'd managed to ditch them. I quickly closed the door.

Tina paced. She was wringing her hands, looking around like she expected something to jump from the walls at her. I turned on the bedside lamp, which gave just enough light to chase away shadows.

"Sit down," I said, settling on the edge of the bed with enough room for her. "Still shaken up?"

She sat, sighed, but remained tense, bracing her arms on the edge of the mattress. "What do you know about Grant? I mean really know about him?"

Whatever was going on here, Grant must have been at the center of it, the way people kept asking about him. Was I going to have to sit him down and ask what he was cooking up?

"He's a magician," I said. "Really a magician. Not just stage tricks. He makes things vanish, he opens doorways to . . . to other places. He knows things. Does things that I've never seen before. I can't explain it, but I always thought he was one of the good guys."

Tina's expression turned confused. "That sounds so . . . epic."

"Yeah. You'd see why I'd rather think of him as one of the good guys."

"I've heard of people like that," she said. "But so much of it is stories. Dr. Dee, Aleister Crowley. They're so shrouded in mystery no one knows what to believe about them. Everything gets written off as tall tales, larger-than-life lies. But you're saying Odysseus Grant is for real?"

"Yeah."

She leaned forward. "He's making Jeffrey and me nervous. Jeffrey says the guy doesn't even *have* an aura."

"Then you know more about what he is than I do."

"Kitty, he's your friend and you went through something together, I understand that. But that hypnotism, or whatever it was, freaked me out. It's not that he was inside my head, it's like he's still there. Poking around my senses, looking through my eyes." The expression in her gaze was wild.

I didn't know what to say. I couldn't begin to understand what she was experiencing. What was strange: I didn't question what she had told me. Odysseus Grant was capable of anything. "Why would he do that?" I said.

"That's what I wanted to ask you. Maybe he doesn't trust me to tell the truth."

"Maybe I could talk to him. Hell, maybe you should talk to him—he's not a mean guy."

"I can't do that!" She leaned forward, setting her head in her hands. "He scares me."

Enough. This was getting out of control. "Tina, I believe you when you say something's going on. But I also think this whole situation is designed to manipulate us, make us paranoid until someone loses it and one of us shape-shifts or starts sucking blood or speaking in tongues. So we just need to keep it together."

Straightening, she took a deep breath. "Okay. Right. You're right. I'm not going to freak out. But you will talk to Grant?"

"Yes. Tomorrow."

She leaned over for a hug, and I complied. Poor Tina. She must have been even more sensitive to living in a house full of weirdos than I was. All that strange psychic energy, with her in the middle of it. At least Jeffrey understood what she was going through. Jeffrey—I smelled him on her hair. Just a little. As if she'd been leaning on his shoulder. Aw . . . I didn't say anything, but I wanted to. Later.

I loved the idea that at least one good thing might come out of this show.

chapter 8

I couldn't sleep, tossing and turning for a couple of hours. Maybe if I got up, took a walk, and drank another glass of wine, I could relax.

Outside, the air had a predawn chill, making my breath fog. I loved mornings like this, especially waking up outside after a full moon, naked, curled up with Ben, my skin tingling at the combination of warm bodies and cool air. I could enjoy the world as it seemed to pause and take a breath before my crazy life started up again. Watch the sky get light, try to notice the moment it turned from night to gray dawn to palest blue, then watch the sun rise.

I went down the path to the edge of the meadow. A mist lay across the valley, drifting over the surface of the lake, clinging to the grass in the meadow, lacework fog waiting for the sun to burn it off. Atmospheric rather than obscuring. I felt better, even if I wouldn't be getting any more sleep.

Back at the lodge, Dorian was standing at the end of the porch, leaning forward against the railing and gazing out over the clearing. I scuffed my feet up the path to make noise, so I wouldn't startle him. He glanced at me slowly, like I'd woken him from a spell.

"Hi," I said. "I wasn't sure I was ever going to see you in daylight, without the escort."

He chuckled but didn't offer any additional commentary. He might have been the quietest guy I'd ever met.

I should have left him alone to enjoy the moment, but I might not have another chance to talk to him without the vampires. I kept my distance, watching him watch the world. The morning sun was still low in the sky, but it turned the valley golden, the light seeming to paint every tree, every blade of grass. The sky was bright blue, and a hawk was soaring over the meadow.

"It's a nice morning," I said, wincing at the awkward conversational gambit.

"Yeah," he said. "I like to do this sometimes. Stay up to watch the sunrise."

"When Anastasia lets you off the leash?"

His smile turned wry. "It isn't like that. I don't have to ask her permission."

"And you can leave her whenever you want?"

"I wouldn't want to."

I'd already gotten more from him than I expected. I should have quit while I was ahead. "Can I ask a personal question?"

He didn't say yes, but he didn't say no. He had a great smile, which suddenly made me want to ask what was so funny.

"Are you in training?" I said. "It's my understanding that some people in your position are serving some kind of apprenticeship, and that they hope to become vampires someday."

"No, I'm not. I'd miss this too much to ever give it up." He nodded at the sunlit world. "Anastasia's offered. To turn me, I mean. But I think I like being alive too much. I stay with her because we're friends. It's not so mysterious."

"I've talked to people who'd give a lot to be in your position. Who'd jump at the offer to become a vampire."

"I listen to your show," he said. "And no offense, but a lot of your callers are either crazy or looking for attention."

I decided I really liked Dorian. He'd never call in to my show, because he knew how to fix his own damn problems.

"Yeah," I said, grinning. "Can't argue. So what about the immortality? The power? You're not attracted to that?"

"There's the price for all that," he said. "I've seen it up close. It's not worth it." He glanced away, shaking his head.

"You are wise beyond your years," I said.

"If you say so," he said. "Now. Can I ask you a personal question?"

"Fire away."

"Are you one of those people who went looking for this? Did you want to be a werewolf?"

I said, "If the first question people ask about vampires is 'How old are you?' that's usually the first question people ask lycanthropes."

"If you don't want to answer, I understand—"

"I was attacked. I wasn't looking for it."

"You seem to have done pretty well with it despite that," he said.

"It was either that or go completely crazy. I got pretty close to that, by the way."

He glanced away for a moment. "That's true of most of this, isn't it? Cope or go crazy."

"Any bets on which way Conrad will go when all this finally hits him?"

"He's a basket case waiting to tip over."

I giggled. Wouldn't that be worth the price of admission? I turned back to the door. "I'll let you enjoy your sunrise. It's been very nice talking to you, Dorian."

"Likewise," he said, with that gorgeous smile.

I left him to his sunny morning. It was hard enough to find a quiet moment of solitude around here without me wrecking it.

Next I called Ben, needing to rant to a friendly ear and hoping to get some outside perspective on whether we were all turning freaky paranoid or if something weird really was going on. Not only was he already awake, he didn't even let me say hello. "Hey," he said. "I've got something for you. A message from Rick."

I perked up. "It's about"—I didn't even want to say her name—"what I asked you about?"

"Yeah. First he wanted to know if this is the Anastasia who's medium height, Chinese, with a sense of humor."

"Yeah, that's her," I said.

"Then he knows her. Met her a hundred or so years ago in San Francisco—and can I just mention how surreal it is talking to Rick about this sort of thing?"

"What does he know about her?" This was the jackpot. I hadn't expected Rick to know Anastasia; I'd been grasping, throwing the name out there hoping he'd have some inkling of her reputation. It turned out vampires moved in a very small world indeed.

"She was the lieutenant of the Master of San Francisco. Sometime in the 1920s, a new Master took over and Anastasia vanished. Rick said he was never sure if she left to save her own skin—or if she'd colluded with the new Master by betraying the old. Since then, he's caught a rumor of her every decade or so. She tends to keep her head down. He was surprised to hear about her being part of this show. He's not sure what her game is or where her loyalties are. He says he likes her but doesn't trust her."

So much for my paranoia being all in my head. The slice of vampire soap opera didn't help me much—I'd have preferred a definite "friend" or "enemy" stamp to put on her. Even Rick telling me to get the hell away from her would have been some help.

"Great. Now what?"

"I don't know. Just keep on sticking it out. Though Rick did say he'd be interested in any good gossip you could pass along."

"I'm sure he would be. It'll have to wait until I've figured out what's going on here."

Ben let out a long-suffering breath in preparation for a speech. It was kind of cute—we'd been married a year, and I could already tell his mood by the sound of his breathing.

"Kitty, have you considered that maybe *nothing's* going on? That maybe the whole reality show setup has you paranoid because you're expecting there to be a plot? Maybe they're having you on."

I rubbed my face. All this conspiracy was making me tired. "I hope you're right."

He hesitated, then said, "Okay. Now I'm worried. You're supposed to argue with me."

I chuckled. I didn't want to argue. "The thing is, Tina's really anxious, and she usually knows what she's talking about."

"All you can do is keep your eyes open. Kitty, I have to get going. I have to be in Cañon City this afternoon."

Cormac's hearing was in the morning. I said, "That's way more important than my little issues. Break a leg."

"I'm not sure that's appropriate here, but thanks. And you be careful."

"Ha—so you do think something weird's going on."

"I'll talk to you later, Kitty," he said, still in the long-suffering voice.

Another day in the funhouse began. My project before lunch was to corner Grant and talk to him about Tina. Jeffrey cornered me first, when I was in the middle of a cup of coffee.

"Kitty, can we talk?"

Oh, why me? I'm a werewolf. I was supposed to be a scary monster, not everyone's favorite confidante.

"Yeah, sure," I said with a sigh. We settled on one of the sofas and leaned in close.

"I'm worried about Tina," he said.

"Me, too," I said. "She came and talked to me last night."

"Whatever's going on here, it's affecting her deeply. I think hypnotizing her may have made it worse. I think Grant may have opened her up to something dangerous."

"Jeffrey. *What* exactly do you think is going on?"

"I don't know," he said, looking forlorn, as sad as I'd ever seen him. "Everyone's nervous, even the crew. But I can't tell if they're nervous because they know something, or because they're sharing a house with werewolves and vampires."

"Here's the problem," I said. "Everyone's convinced something freaky is going on, but nobody knows what. Maybe it's psychosomatic, maybe it's all in our heads. We're letting the atmosphere get to us. But if there is something, we need to brainstorm. Is the place haunted? Is the whole show a conspiracy? If so, why? For what purpose? And who here is in on it?"

He shook his head. For all his talent, empathy, and insight, this was outside his experience. "I couldn't even begin to guess what it means. That's why I wanted to talk to you."

You'd think if we all pooled our experience, we could come up with something. I couldn't imagine a more qualified bunch of people to deal with any problem involving the supernatural. Excepting Conrad, of course.

I said, "Can I just say that I think it's really cute that you're so worried about Tina?"

That got him to blush. Ducking his gaze, he donned a wide, goofy smile. "She's pretty special."

I patted his arm. "We'll figure this out. Don't worry."

Tina came downstairs then, and Jeffrey was at her side in a moment, walking with her to the kitchen and asking if she wanted coffee. They looked like a couple of teenagers.

Maybe we should just chuck the whole freaking-out-

Conrad storyline and call the show *Real World: Supernatural Edition*.

Today was picnic-by-the-lake day. We had more beautiful weather, blue sky and blazing sun. We had a lovely spot, a narrow beach of smooth gravel near a well-kept wooden dock suitable for parking canoes and jumping off of to swim. With the meadow and mountains as a backdrop, the scene was postcard picturesque and would play very well on television. The half dozen of us who took part had spread blankets on the ground and happily munched on another great catered meal.

Tina and Jeffrey sat on the dock, the cuffs of their jeans rolled up, dangling their feet in the water. Ariel stood at the end of the dock in a cute bikini, black with white polka dots, an ensemble that was no doubt making Provost back in the production room very happy. Lee was already swimming—fully human—and trying to get her to join him.

"But it's *really* cold!" she complained after dipping in just a toe.

"It's *great*. This is *perfect!*" he countered.

"Keep in mind, he's used to swimming in the Arctic," Jeffrey said.

"How about I just stay out here and *watch* you?" Ariel said.

Lee slapped the surface and sent a shower of water splashing at her. Predictably, she squealed. Unpredictably, she jumped in after him and they started a full-on splashing water fight. Much laughter and shrieking ensued.

I reminded myself that I was supposed to be enjoying this. That I *would* be enjoying this if I hadn't nearly convinced myself that all this was a front. I should have been sprawling out on my blanket enjoying the scenery, but I was distracted, turned inward, gnawing on the issue like a dog with a bone.

Also present: Conrad and Jerome, who were talking sports together over chicken sandwiches. The vampires and Dorian were inside, tucked safely away in darkness until nightfall. Odysseus Grant also joined us, which surprised me. I didn't associate him with bright sunlight. More like shadowy theaters and stage lights. He sat with his back against the trunk of a tall conifer, up a little ways from the edge of the beach. His sleeves were rolled up past his elbows, but that was the only concession to the great outdoors he'd made in his clothing. I was in shorts and a T-shirt.

I picked myself up and wandered to where Grant was sitting. He watched me. I tried not to be nervous.

"Mind if I join you?" I said.

"Of course not."

I sat cross-legged, nearby. "Your show yesterday made Tina a little edgy."

He gave a thin smile. "That wasn't a show. Stage hypnotism looks completely different."

"I get the feeling that wouldn't make her feel any better."

"She opened a door. Accessed a dark place. She should be nervous."

"This is all so vague. Conrad's not half wrong about some of this stuff. It's hard to believe when it's all just shadows."

"If it was more than shadows, we'd be able to see it clearly. We wouldn't be as terrified."

I wanted to deny that I was terrified. I hadn't reached that level yet. But it wasn't too far a leap from lurking anxiety to terror. "You? Terrified?" I said, smiling to take the edge off my prodding.

"Watchful," he said.

"Don't get me wrong. I trust you implicitly. But I also suspect you don't do much of anything without an ulterior motive. You agreed to do this show because it would bring you in contact with certain people. It would get you access to information. What brought you here? What are you looking for?"

He pursed his lips, looking thoughtfully over the lake, its surface sparkling with sunlight on ripples of water.

"Shadows," he said finally. "The trouble in Las Vegas last year was just a thread in a larger . . . web. I almost called it a tangle, but it's too organized for that. You know it—you've seen it. You've faced it. You tell me whether we ought to be terrified by it."

This was far too serious a conversation to be having in such a beautiful setting. I ought to rip off my clothes and join the others for a swim in the lake. I said, "I've decided to ignore it for as long as I can."

"Implying that you're aware that you won't be able to ignore it forever."

My kingdom was a small one. I had my family, my mate, my pack, my city. I didn't want anything else. I didn't want an empire. But I would fight to protect what I had. I'd fought before, and I'd be an idiot to ignore the forces out there building empires, who would take my world away from me if I let them. Grant was right.

"So this is just another battle in your war against the forces of chaos," I said.

"'Just' another battle. You make it sound mundane."

"And you suspect Anastasia of being part of it?" I said.

He just smiled.

And while we were all discussing various conspiracy theories and secret suspicions, Provost and his crew were recording everything on video. Maybe one of the producers wanted information. What better way to gather intelligence than to bring a bunch of people on the inside together, then record their conversations? What happened when the secret shadow world of vampires and the forces of darkness got discussed on national TV? Wait a minute, who was I kidding? To the average TV-watching audience, these conversations would seem boring. They'd never end up in the final cut.

The gathering by the dock had turned quiet, drawing our attention.

"Lee?" Ariel called. She treaded water, turning slowly and looking out over the surface. "Where'd he go?"

"How long has he been under?" Jeffrey said.

"I don't know," Ariel said. "A while, I think."

"Lee knows how to take care of himself," Tina said. "He's a were-seal, for crying out loud."

"But where is he?" Ariel said.

Except for the ripples Ariel was making, the surface of the lake was still, dark, not a bubble in sight. I stood and wandered to the edge of the water. Grant came with me. A moment later, Jerome was standing with us, all of us looking out, and the nervous rock in my gut was growing heavier.

"Should we call someone?" Jeffrey said.

A body erupted from the water and lunged onto the edge of the dock. Torpedo-shaped, it was big, rubbery, with slick gray skin mottled brown, dripping wet. It had a face like a mashed-up dog's, with huge, shining dark eyes. Opening its mouth wide, it showed off way too many sharp teeth and brayed, a throaty, belchy bark.

Everyone screamed. Except maybe Grant, who raised a curious brow and took a step back. Even Jerome shouted and stumbled away from the water. Tina and Jeffrey scrambled away from the barking seal. Ariel didn't even bother climbing onto the dock. She swam for the shore, splashing in a panic.

The seal—Lee, I assumed—gave another growl. I swore it sounded like laughter. Then he rolled back into the water. Breaking the surface, he splashed his flippers, then swam, fast and hard, away from shore. He broke the surface now and then, his skin gleaming in the sun.

When I'd calmed down, I had to admit I was impressed that Lee had enough control to play a practical joke while in his lycanthropic form. I wouldn't have.

"Ballsy," Jerome said, chuckling nervously. He must have agreed with me.

"You jerk!" Ariel screamed after the now-distant seal. She stomped her feet, splashing in the water. Fuming, she turned to the rest of us. "That was awful! Ooh, I'm going to get him back. I'm so going to get him back for that!"

Tina started laughing. A tad hysterical, but still. All of our hearts were racing. If we didn't laugh, we'd have heart attacks. But I agreed with Ariel—we'd certainly have to find a way to get back at him, wouldn't we?

We were missing someone. I looked around, didn't see him.

"Where's Conrad?" I said. "Where'd he go? He had to have seen this."

"He went back to the house for a minute. Said he had to use the bathroom," Jerome said.

"Are you *kidding* me?" I screeched. Honest-to-God lycanthropic shape-shifting right in front of him—sort of— and he was off using the bathroom? I could have cried.

"Murphy's Law," Grant said. "The most powerful force in the universe."

"Goddammit," I muttered.

Just to make the scene even more cinematic, Conrad came wandering down the path from the lodge then. He stopped when he found us all staring at him with posttraumatized, half-amused, half-murderous looks on our faces.

"What are you all looking at?"

"Were-seal," I said, pointing over my shoulder to the lake. "Lee gave us a show, but he's gone now. Probably off hunting trout or whatever the hell swims in lakes in Montana."

Conrad looked uncertain a moment, then chuckled. "Nice try. But Lee's just hiding in the woods. Right?"

I turned to Skip and the camera. "You can show him the playback, right?"

"Um, we're not really allowed to do that," he said.

I cursed Lee for his bad timing. We just needed Conrad to see the seal—so totally not native to freshwater lakes in landlocked Montana—to chip away at his smug skepticism. Was that too much to ask?

So that was the end of the picnic.

*   *   *

Every reality show had to have a bit where they got you alone and filmed you talking trash about everyone else on the show. It was too much to hope that we'd get through *Supernatural Insider* without it. So there I was, sitting in front of a camera, held by Gordon this time, with the great outdoors as a backdrop. Provost watched from behind the camera, egging me on. I fiddled with the personal mike clipped to my collar.

"Do I have to?" I said for the third time.

"It's in the contract," Provost said, also for the third time.

I sighed and pointed at the camera. "Is that thing on?"

"It's been rolling for a minute now."

There was no getting out of this. I wasn't supposed to want to avoid this—face it, I was one of the biggest attention whores on the show. This bit was designed to give the stage to the attention whores, to give them ample opportunity to make idiots of themselves. And that was the problem, wasn't it? No matter what I said, Provost and his crew would edit it to make me look like an idiot.

Being an attention whore was only fun when I was in charge.

"What exactly are you looking for with this?" I said. "If you give me some idea what you want me to say, I can just say it and save you some time trying to edit it all together." I smiled with teeth.

He grimaced right back. "What do you think about some of your housemates? Anastasia, let's say. Or Jerome."

Predictable.

"Here's the thing," I said, leaning forward, making

like I was going to dispense some gem of juicy gossip. "You want me to sit here and be catty about everyone else. See if I have any juicy bits of gossip to share. But I'm not going to do that, because the only chance I have of looking good when this thing airs is to be as nice as I possibly can. So you know what? I love everybody. I love them all. We all get along great. This is like summer camp."

Provost gave me a level glare. I didn't expect him to like what I said; but he couldn't argue, because at least I'd said *something*. He finally said, "Is that how you *really* feel?"

I thought a minute, then said, "I think Conrad is stubborn."

Gordon giggled but quickly shut up when Provost glared. But I'd decided that Provost didn't have much of a sense of humor.

"Okay," the producer said. "If we can't go for dirt, how about blatant sentimentality? You miss your family? Anything you'd like to tell them? Your family'll love it when they watch the show and know you were thinking of them."

I wasn't sure I wanted to get that sappy any more than I wanted to be a gossipy jerk. My family knew I loved them—I didn't have to say it on national TV. In the end, though, I did miss my family. I missed Ben especially. Things kept happening that I wanted to tell him about, ask him about. On this subject, at least, I couldn't find sarcasm to throw at Provost. Maybe the guy deserved a straight line for once.

Again, I looked at the camera. "Being away from my

family is the hardest thing about being here." I pursed my lips and didn't have to pretend to look sad.

I hoped that would play well enough on TV for Provost. He seemed happy enough and let me loose from the camera's eye.

chapter 9

Toward dinnertime, a sleepy-looking, naked Lee, swim-suit in hand, came sauntering into the house. He waved a hello, then made his way upstairs.

The cameras tracked him, and the editors would prob-ably have a great time fuzzing out the interesting bits.

Conrad said, "If I knew this was going to be *that* kind of show, I might have thought twice about participating."

"The whole thing seems one-sided to me," Jerome said. "When's your turn, Kitty?"

"I keep offering, and you all keep saying no," I said. "You can't change your mind now. With you guys letting it all hang out, I can be a little discreet."

In what had become routine, right around the time we finished eating dinner at the long dining room table, the basement door opened and the trio of the night emerged.

"Have we missed anything interesting?" Anastasia said, striding up to take one of the extra chairs. Gemma settled in beside her. Dorian remained standing, close to the wall, looking over them in a bodyguard stance that probably wasn't just for show.

"You missed a great sunny day by the lake," Jeffrey said.

"You can't miss what you don't want," Anastasia said.

"Lee shape-shifted and scared the bejeezus out of everyone," Tina said.

"I am sorry I missed that."

"It seemed like the thing to do," Lee said. He'd rejoined the group after putting on clothes and seemed to be beaming, like he was proud of the escapade.

"And is our resident skeptic convinced yet?" Anastasia said.

"He walked away for five minutes and missed it."

She chuckled. "How perfect. We'll be able to draw this out for days."

From the kitchen, where he was opening another bottle of wine and pouring drinks, Conrad said, "I haven't seen anything yet that can't be explained by perfectly normal means."

"Hey Conrad," I called. "You know the principle that in a given situation, the simplest explanation is usually the correct one?"

"Occam's razor. Yes."

"What's simpler: that we imported a live seal, brought it a thousand miles inland, and set it loose in an environment that might kill it, for the purpose of playing a joke on you; or that Lee's a lycanthrope?"

He said, "If one of your options is impossible, it doesn't matter how outlandish the only probable one sounds. It has to be the correct one."

"I won't argue with your logic," I said. "Only your assumptions."

"I don't think you imported a seal. I think you're making it all up," he said.

Almost angrily, Tina said, "Is someone *paying* you to be this stubborn?"

Now, there was an idea. I hadn't considered that Conrad might also be part of some conspiracy. Hell, maybe we had more than one conspiracy afoot. Wouldn't that be exciting?

But Conrad denied it. "I'm getting paid the same stipend the rest of you are. At least, I assume I am. I'm just a lowly author and not a TV celebrity, so I may be getting peanuts compared to you."

The door to the study/production room opened, and I jumped. Just a little. Not freaked-out jumped. Just startled. Ghost fur prickled along my back. Looking around, I saw at least a couple of the others had also flinched, startled: Tina, Gemma. All of us stared at Joey Provost, who came into the living room wearing his showbiz smile. He was carrying a shoe box–sized wooden case.

"How's everyone doing?" he said. I clamped shut my jaw so I wouldn't be able to say, *Fine, until you got here.*

"We're all just fine, I think," Anastasia said, eyes half-lidded, purring in perfect vampire allure. It must have been one of the powers they got, along with immortality.

"That's great. You all up for some more fun and games?"

"Another activity rigged for maximum entertainment value," I said. "Excellent."

I couldn't pull off allure like Anastasia could. All I had was snark. Glaring at me, Provost set the box on the coffee table. We gathered around.

"Your instructions are in here. Wait 'til I leave, then

take a look and have at it." He smiled like a guy who was having a lot of fun keeping a secret. Very smarmy. I didn't like it.

The door closed behind him. He was gone, but nobody moved.

"Well?" Tina said. None of us looked all that enthusiastic—none of us were really the types who appreciated being Provost's dancing monkeys. I wondered how they were going to edit the footage to make us look excited.

"Let's get this over with," I said and knelt by the table to open the box.

Inside, on bare wood, lay a folded note, five velvet jewelry boxes, and a stopwatch. I unfolded the page and read aloud.

" 'Treasure Hunt,' " the top of the page said. " 'You all have special talents, ways of searching out the hidden, of doing the impossible. You'll break into the following five teams, and one at a time each team will have a chance to find the other half of the lockets in these boxes, which have been hidden outside the lodge. Conrad will monitor the stopwatch and see who finds the treasure the fastest.' Dude, cliché," I said. Sure enough, each box had a gold locket on a chain with the lid broken off. Each locket was a different shape: oval, circle, square, rectangle, and—of course—a heart. I read off the teams: Jerome and I were on one team, the vampires and Dorian on another. He'd teamed Tina with Ariel and Jeffrey with Lee. Odysseus was all by himself. This ought to be interesting.

"Isn't there supposed to be a prize?" Lee said. "What do we get for winning?"

"The satisfaction of winning?" I said, shrugging. I

didn't really care, because I shuddered to think of what cheesy prize Provost would come up with.

"This isn't very scientific," Tina said. "And I thought we weren't supposed to have competitions."

"Bitching isn't going to get it over with any faster. Think of it as a party game. Like Pin the Tail on the Donkey," I said. "Who's first?" We all glanced guiltily away—no one wanted to be first. We weren't even bothering to look enthusiastic.

"Conrad, you pick, since you seem to be the one in charge," Anastasia said.

"Let's see," Conrad said in a mock-serious tone. "Tina and Jeffrey are supposed to figure out where it is using their psychic powers, right? The werewolves . . . what are you supposed to do, sniff it out?"

"You'd be surprised," Jerome said.

"The vampires do what, fly through the air and use super vision?"

"You watch too many bad movies," Gemma said.

Conrad huffed and said, "And maybe Odysseus can pull it out of his top hat."

Tina looked at Grant. "Can you really do that?"

Grant's lips turned in a thin smile. "Not without preparation and a trapdoor."

Conrad shook his head. "I still can't tell if you think you're for real or not."

"A lot of what we're doing here deals with perception rather than truth," Grant said. "Many would argue that reality depends more on the former than the latter."

There was a pause as we all absorbed that. Gemma's forehead wrinkled, like she was still parsing the sentence.

"Right, yeah," Conrad said finally. "So, I still perceive that you're all deluded or faking. I think Tina and Ariel should go first."

Ariel shrugged. "I don't even have any weird talents. I'm like Kitty, I just talk too much."

"Come on, why us?" Tina said.

"Because I'm betting you'll put on the best show," Conrad said.

And they did. At least Tina did. She started by choosing one of the lockets, closing her eyes, feeling it. Picking up vibes, whatever. I might have believed in the things she could do, but I still didn't understand how it worked.

"What do you want me to do?" Ariel whispered, clearly in awe of the psychic.

"Hold the flashlight," Tina said, retrieving the light from the kitchen counter.

They went outside. Gordon followed them with one of the cameras.

"What if they don't find it?" Jerome said.

Lee sat back and stretched his arms over his head. "It's going to be a long night."

Tina and Ariel returned, prize in hand, about forty minutes later. Which, as long as it seemed, was still more quickly than I would have expected. It didn't bode well, because I was pretty sure we wouldn't be able to find our half so quickly, and I kind of wanted to win. And I hated that I kind of wanted to win, because that meant I was playing Provost's game. I'd just have to be obnoxious about it.

Ariel was bubbling, holding up both halves of the locket for all to see. Tina looked annoyed. She held a crooked, forked stick a couple of feet long that she might have picked up off the ground.

"Is that a dowsing rod?" Jeffrey said. Tina nodded.

"A dowsing rod?" Conrad said. "Are you serious?"

"Took us straight to it," Ariel said.

Jeffrey grinned at Tina. "You are so cool." She blushed.

Conrad shook his head, as skeptical as ever, but he wrote the time down on the sheet of paper anyway.

"It's spooky out there," Tina said. "I'd just as soon not have to go out at night again."

"Spooky?" I said. Meaning: spookier than a nighttime forest usually is?

"Maybe I'm still creeped out by that hypnotism trick last night." She threw Grant a glare.

"You should trust your instincts," Grant said. "If you think something's out there, you should listen to that feeling."

"That's just it, I can listen to my instincts all I want, but unless I get something specific, I'm just panicking." She slumped into an armchair, shrugging off further inquiry. "Who's next?"

Jeffrey and Lee went next. Jeffrey touched the locket like Tina had. Lee held the piece of jewelry to his nose and took a deep breath. Taking in the scent. It took them about forty-five minutes, and when they returned, Tina and Ariel did a little high-five because they were still in the lead.

"These things must not be very well hidden," Conrad observed. "I guess Provost wouldn't want to make it too hard."

"Sometimes when you're looking for something, it just calls out to you," Jeffrey said.

Then came Jerome and me. We both took big draws of air off our locket, the oval one. Not that it would help, because it smelled generic—cheap metal, a little bit tangy, and a little bit like Provost's aftershave. Maybe that would be enough to give me a trail. Really, I didn't know how we were going to manage this. Picking a weak scent out of the wilderness was like looking for a needle in a haystack. No—a specific piece of hay in a haystack.

Jerome and I ended up outside, along with Gordon the PA and his camera, looking into the great outdoors, letting our eyesight adjust to the darkness. I turned my nose up, breathed deep, and caught the trail of Provost's aftershave. Leading right back to the lodge, of course.

"I'm not sure this is going to work," I said.

"Well, let's get started doing something. Crisscross the ground, cover all the area around the house, see what we can pick up." It was as good a plan as any.

We split up, him taking the front of the lodge and me taking the back. I caught the trails of the teams that had gone before us and ignored them. I was looking for Provost.

"Kitty!" Jerome called, and I trotted over to join him.

He was kneeling, resting one hand on the ground, head bent over. His powerful body was taut, like he was ready to run, his gaze up and watchful. He looked animal, a little bit of his wolf bleeding into his gaze. Not wanting to set him off, I approached cautiously, obliquely.

"There," he said, nodding in the direction where the woods joined the meadow, a little ways from the lodge.

Nose flaring, taking in the air, I caught it—Provost. I nod-ded, and we set off, stalking our prey.

We went carefully for about ten minutes. The trail was faint, but we were able to follow it. Especially after we told Gordon he had to stand downwind. A strange, twi-light feeling came over me; I was feeling more wolf than human, even though I wasn't shifting; I was still solid within my human skin, but this felt like hunting. Jerome and I hadn't spoken since we left the lodge—we communi-cated by glances, by tilts of our heads and shoulders. The night blazed with information. I saw everything clearly, heard a hundred little noises in the woods and meadow, from an owl's swoop of wings to insects and mice burrow-ing through grass. Being part of this world felt so natural. I'd be perfectly happy spending the whole night out here and not going back to the lodge. And wouldn't that shake things up?

I followed the trail, but at one point I branched right and Jerome branched left. Brow furrowed, confused, I backtracked, zigzagged over the ground, reading the scents of the world like it was a book. Sure enough, the trail split. Joey Provost had been over this ground twice, in two different directions.

Noticing I had stopped, Jerome looked back at me.

"There are two trails here," I said, wincing because my speech sounded so loud and intrusive. "Which is right?"

Jerome went over the same ground and found what I did. He took a moment to gather words, like he, too, had to remember human speech. "You sure it isn't a false trail? When he was planting the other teams' lockets?"

"It probably is. Just in case, you stick to the main trail

and I'll check this one out. If it goes to the wrong locket, I'll turn back and catch up with you."

"Come on, guys, please don't split up," Gordon said. "Who am I supposed to follow?"

"Easy—whichever one of us takes the right trail, right?" I said. "Did Joey tell you where he hid the thing?"

Gordon almost looked surly. "Jerome, you wait here. I'll follow Kitty first, then come back and follow you."

That was actually a fairly elegant solution. Jerome didn't look happy about it, but he crossed his arms and waited.

We split up.

The trail continued faintly, mostly because there were so many smells, so much to take in. This area may have been isolated, but other people had been through here. Hikers, hunters, whatever.

I lost the scent in a clearing. No—the trail stopped. I walked around the perimeter, and it didn't continue further. Provost had stopped here, but I didn't find a locket piece. His scent didn't linger in any one place; rather, he seemed to have come here, paced around, then left again by the same path.

I did find other signs, though: the remains of a meal, bone and gristle from someone's chicken dinner, haphazardly buried with a thin layer of dirt thrown over it. A mashed-down square space—a tent footprint. A tree that had done latrine duty. Someone had camped here recently.

"Hey, Gordon? Do you know if anyone else has been in the area? Was anyone from the crew camping or something?" I glanced over my shoulder to ask. I showed him what I was talking about, the evidence of occupation.

He had to lower the camera to see what I was looking at. After a cursory glance, he shook his head. "I don't know. I don't think it was any of us."

That moment, Jerome found us hunched at the edge of the camp, staring. My face scrunched up with concentration.

"I got it," he said, holding up a piece of locket on a chain.

"Hey, you were supposed to wait!" Gordon said, then hurried to lift his camera in place and start recording.

Jerome ignored him. "What's wrong?"

"What do you make of this?" I gestured around the clearing and gave Jerome a few minutes to find the same things I had. A normal person without a whole lot of tracking skills would have overlooked the signs. To a werewolf with a hyperactive sense of smell, the evidence jumped out.

Jerome looked at me. "Who do you think was here?"

"Besides Provost? I don't know. There were two others, I think. Valenti maybe?"

"You think maybe someone's spying on us? On the lodge, the production, whatever?" he said.

"Where are they now? Where'd they go?"

The trails went out, then disappeared. Whoever had been here had scattered. I shook my head.

"Should we be worried?" Gordon said.

I sighed. "I'm always worried. We should get back."

We returned to the lodge, and if Jerome and I looked unhappy, the others assumed it was because we had the slowest time yet. Next up, the vampires took about as long as the psychics had, and I couldn't have said how they did it. Maybe they just looked.

Odysseus Grant, all by himself, ended up winning. When his turn came, Conrad started the stopwatch. Grant held the original piece of the locket for a moment, running his thumb along the chain. He set it down on the table, walked out the front door, closed it behind him. Less than half a minute later—not even enough time for the rest of us to sit back and start a conversation—he returned. Holding up the other half of the locket.

I assumed that all four prizes were hidden about an equal distance away from the lodge. Jerome and I had managed to find ours, after some trial and error and a lot of hunting, in an hour. The box with the locket piece itself was at least a quarter mile away—it took fifteen minutes just to walk there and back, so how had Grant returned with it in mere seconds? I wasn't sure I wanted to know. This may have been all about putting the whammy on Conrad, but I had limits.

"Wait. How did you find it so fast?" Conrad said.

"I pulled it out of my top hat," Grant said.

Conrad sputtered, "I thought you said—"

Tina glared. "Odysseus? You don't *have* a top hat."

Grant just smiled.

"I call shenanigans," Conrad said.

"You've been calling shenanigans all week," I said. "Why stop now?"

"But I want to know how he did it." He turned to Grant. "You're in on it, right? You had the other half in your pocket the whole time."

"If you've already decided what to believe, I can't possibly convince you otherwise," Grant said.

"Mr. Grant is full of mystery, isn't he?" Anastasia said, her tone stinging. "Really, Mr. Grant, tell us—are you a ringer? Are you here as one of us—or for another reason entirely?"

I rolled my eyes at the conspiracy. "Oh, please."

But everyone else was looking at Odysseus. Tina, who'd been suspicious of him since the hypnotism; Jeffrey, who couldn't see his aura; the others, who simply didn't know what to think of him. Once again, it would make great TV.

"This is going to go all *Lord of the Flies* on us, isn't it?" I wondered if that was the idea. I shook my head. "We're better than that, people."

That broke the tension, or rather broke it enough for us to stop glaring at each other.

Ariel stood. "It's late. I think I'll head to bed. So, good night, everyone. We'll all feel better in the morning."

Jerome and Lee followed. Then Conrad. Then Tina and Jeffrey, glancing at those of us remaining as they went to the stairs, frowning.

Anastasia and Grant didn't look away from each other. Epic staring match.

"Anastasia?" Dorian said.

"It's all right. You and Gemma go on." Dorian touched the younger vampire, and the two of them walked arm in arm to the basement. "Gordon, you're probably tired. Why don't you call it a night?" And amazingly, the PA listened to her, wandering to the back room and leaving the front of the house without a camera operator.

"Kitty, would you give us some privacy, as well?" Anastasia said. Hint hint.

"Oh no," I said. "Somebody's got to stick around and keep you guys from killing each other."

Her lips flickered a smile. "You really think you could stop us?"

She was right. Both of them could knock me aside, werewolf or no. "I'm not leaving," I said, no matter how unable I was to back up my bravado.

Didn't matter; she proceeded to ignore me.

"Odysseus Grant," the vampire said, in the way of a judge preparing a verdict.

The magician met her gaze, didn't flinch. Shocking, astonishing—vampires had power in their gazes. Grant didn't seem to care. Her gaze didn't affect him.

I didn't necessarily want to be here for this. They faced each other in some kind of silent, telepathic battle.

"You're going to ask me about Roman," Grant said finally. He started pacing, a few steps one way, then back. Calculated, intimidating. "Has he contacted me. Am I working for him. Will I report to him about you. Will I finish you for him."

"You can't finish me."

"The difficulty is, I have some of the same questions about you. What are you working for?"

"Not *who* am I working for?" she said, her voice smooth as silk. He nodded, the barest inclination of his head. "So, are you working for Roman? Has he sent you to kill me?"

"Why should I answer your questions when you haven't answered mine?"

"You guys are idiots," I said. They both looked at me like they'd forgotten I was there. Or like they'd expected me to stay polite and quiet. To merely witness.

Didn't they know me better by now?

"You're the two most powerful people in this house,

but that doesn't automatically make you rivals, does it? So can you please just lay out what you're really worried about and quit with this clandestine bullshit?" Like my bitching would really get them to be reasonable.

And yet, after a moment, Grant said, "All right. I learned about Roman last year—with Kitty's help, I might add. I learned that he controlled Las Vegas—my city— through two different vampires, different fronts that hid his identity. An obfuscating sleight of hand that I can almost appreciate. But I don't, because this is a being who is consolidating power, who doesn't want people to know he's consolidating power. I'm trying to learn more about him. Now, perhaps I should apologize for my suspicion, but you're a vampire, an old one, and it's more likely that you're another front acting on his behalf than an independent force acting against him, as I am. There it is. I've laid it all out."

She considered him. "Telling me exactly what I'd like to hear. What would show you in the best light in my eyes."

"Assuming we're both telling the truth, we're both working for the same thing," Grant said.

"Assuming," she said, painstakingly polite.

"Wait a minute," I said, raising my hand. Thinking hard—I had to get the thought out before I lost it. This was important. "Why is this about Roman? How would he know about this crazy little reality show, and why would he even care? If he wanted to go after you all, or recruit you, or whatever, why would he do it here? Unless— unless the whole show is a front."

Grant had said it himself: fronts behind fronts behind fronts again. This was exactly how Roman operated. Now they were both looking at me, and not as an annoyance. Rather, I was suddenly interesting to them.

The magician followed the thought through. "If someone like Roman wanted to remove some of his rivals, getting them in one place like this is the perfect opportunity."

"Jerome and I found a campsite out in the woods. Like someone's been out here watching the place."

"Roman wouldn't go through all the trouble," Anastasia said. "Would he? That would mean Provost is the one working for him."

I looked away. "I don't know. It's crazy. I'm too full up with conspiracy theories right now. But if you're both working against Roman, you play into his plans by fighting with each other."

"Roman's plans stretch across centuries," Anastasia said. "Nothing's too far-fetched."

"If we're right, what do we do about it?" Grant said.

"We watch," she said. "We wait."

"Ah, the vampire way," I said. "I don't have that much time. I'm going to poke the wasp nest."

I stood and went to the back of the lodge, to Provost's production room.

chapter 10

Grant and Anastasia didn't stop me when I went to the back of the lodge, but I imagined them exchanging one of those "there she goes again" looks.

It was late. Really late. But I had a feeling Joey Provost was still awake and watching the footage we'd produced, cooking up new angles and sensationalist storylines. No time like the present to bug him. Besides, if he had been watching the current conversation via one of the remote cameras and microphones, and he was part of some kind of conspiracy, I wanted to get him before he came up with a cover story to deny it all. I wanted to catch him flat-footed.

I knocked on the library door. Behind it, I could hear an audio track and hushed voices under it. I knocked again and waited.

Amy, who must have been the one on duty with the monitors tonight, finally opened the door.

"Yes?"

"I'd like to speak to Joey," I said.

"Er, ah—" She glanced over her shoulder. Looked like

she was thinking about whether she'd screw up by letting me talk to Provost—or by not letting me talk to him. "Is there a problem?"

"Oh, not really. I just have a couple of suggestions for him. You know. To really make the show pop." Heh. I knew just enough of the lingo to make me dangerous.

"What is it?" Provost called from inside.

I preempted Amy by calling back, "It's me! I wanted to talk to you for a sec. If that's okay."

Provost appeared at the door then, and Amy scampered away and out of the cross fire.

"Kitty! What can I do for you?" He pretended to sound happy to see me. However, the tension in his face showed annoyance.

"Hi. I'm just here breaking the fourth wall. Or fifth wall. I'm not really sure how the metaphor applies here."

"Is there something wrong? What do you need?"

"I have a little theory I want to run by you."

He stepped out of the library and closed the door behind him. We were standing in an isolated corner now, watching each other, waiting.

I said, "Are you really working for SuperByte Entertainment? Or do you report back to someone else, and there's an ulterior motive to all this?"

He chuckled. "That's kind of crazy-sounding," he said.

"Yeah, I know. But look at it from a certain point of view. You've gathered together almost all the public movers and shakers who have anything to do with the supernatural, who personally know lots of others. And now you're tracking their every move, recording their scheming. And it's like you're gathering information. Or waiting for something to happen."

"Like what?"

"That's just it, I don't know. But do you by any chance know a vampire named Roman?"

His expression turned thoughtful. I couldn't tell whether I had touched a nerve or not; he was unreadable. "No. But I'd sure love to meet him. Maybe bring him on if we do a second season."

That would be so very bad . . . "It's not that I'm accusing you personally of anything. But I wonder if we're all dupes, and there's someone who's manipulating all of this. A puppet master pulling the strings."

He stared at me, and I couldn't tell if he thought I was crazy, or if *he* was the crazy one, I'd gotten everything right, and he was about to go gonzo on me.

Finally, he chuckled nervously. The look in his eyes was spooked. So, he thought I was crazy. I could live with that.

"I suppose you'd have to develop a pretty good imagination, and a pretty healthy paranoia, given what you are," he said. "You'd have to believe in the unbelievable."

It wasn't a denial. He didn't give me the smarmy Hollywood reassurances I expected. We continued sizing each other up.

"I guess if you really were in on some kind of conspiracy, I couldn't expect you to come out and admit it. Maybe I just wanted to see the look in your eyes. Just in case."

The smile still looked nervous. Which was probably understandable, given a werewolf was standing here accusing him of plotting.

"There's no conspiracy," he said. Then his expression brightened. "But if you want to play that up, that could be a great thread for the show. I'll mention it to the editors. We could get this whole suspense-thriller thing going."

That was the response I should have expected. "Okay. You do that."

"Now, if you don't mind, I need to get back to it." He pointed a thumb over his shoulder to the library. I waved a quick farewell and trundled back to the living room.

"Well?" Grant said when I'd returned.

"I think he thought I was crazy," I said. "Oh well. I had to try it."

Anastasia tilted her head. "Should we consider that maybe he's a really good actor?"

"I don't know," I said. "I guess we're back to watch and wait." They still held themselves in wary stances. But at least they weren't poking at each other anymore. "You guys are done with all the veiled accusations?"

Anastasia's lip curled. "For now."

I threw up my hands and marched upstairs.

Again, I awoke far too early, and far too grouchy. I was having nightmares about Roman and thinking too much about vampire conspiracies.

I went downstairs to get the coffeemaker started. It wouldn't turn on. In fact, the whole kitchen was quiet, still—no hum from the refrigerator, no rattle from the furnace. I tried the light switch—nothing. The lodge ran on a combination of solar power and gasoline generator. Something must have gone out.

I went to the library door and knocked. Not that Provost and company would be at work this early; I wasn't surprised when no one answered. I went in. A trio of chairs sat in front of wide tables, filled with TV monitors and equipment. All the monitors were dead—nothing was on, not even the red lights on the power strips. Upstairs, Provost and his production crew were using the three rooms at the end of the hallway. I went to Provost's door next. I knocked—and got no answer.

"Kitty, what's wrong?" Grant stood halfway down the hall, near his own room. He was neatly dressed as always. I wondered if he ever changed clothes and went to bed.

"I don't know," I said. "The power's gone out. I was going to tell Provost, but I can't find him."

Brow creased thoughtfully, he went to the light switch at the top of the stairs, flipped it a couple of times. Not because he didn't believe me, I was sure. He just had to try it himself. Nothing happened. "Odd," he said.

I leaned close to the door and called, "Joey?" I took a chance and cracked the door.

The room was empty, the beds undisturbed. The other two crew rooms were also empty, though suitcases sat in the corners and clothes lay on one of the beds. Grant joined me, looking into the rooms over my shoulder.

"Thoughts?" I said. He shook his head, pensive. I squeezed around him and went back downstairs, to retrieve the satellite phone from the library. It ran on batteries, and it was time to make a call.

I looked, searching all the shelves, the tables, behind equipment, under cameras, in drawers. Then I searched the living room, under cushions, behind chairs and sofas.

I opened every drawer and cupboard in the kitchen. Grant joined me in the middle of the search.

"I can't find the phone," I said.

"That's not good," he said, his expression unchanging.

"Should we check on the generator? Maybe we can get the power back, then figure out where Provost and company went." Maybe they were off on a nature hike.

"I think it's in the shed," he said.

Grant and I went out the front door, on our way to the shed at the side of the lodge. I stopped on the porch, hardly noticing the magician crowding behind me. I'd frozen, because I was staring at Dorian's body, lying on the ground by the porch.

chapter 11

Part of the railing around the porch had broken. It looked like the nails or the joints had come loose from the posts and the whole thing toppled to the ground. And it looked like Dorian had been leaning on it when it happened. Stepping out on the porch, I looked over the edge and saw him, lying still and crumpled on the ground. Dark blood pooled by his head. I could smell his body cooling, and his heart was silent.

Of all the stupid, ugly accidents. "He came out here sometimes," I said weakly. "To watch the sunrise."

I went down the steps, approached Dorian, looked back at the porch, trying to figure out what had happened. He'd been leaning on the railing. Maybe it had just given way. He fell wrong, hit his head, maybe even hurt his neck. A stupid accident.

"Kitty?" Grant said. He came down the steps to join me, making the same quick examination I did.

"It doesn't make sense," I said. "*I* leaned on that railing. We all did. That thing was stable. What the hell happened?"

"He's heavier. Maybe he just hit a bad spot."

"A fall like that shouldn't have killed him. It was only a few feet." I started crying. I turned away to hide the silent tears running down my cheeks. I'd just gotten to know him. Just gotten to like him. It wasn't fair.

Grant said, "Provost might have footage from the remote cameras that might explain this."

But were the cameras still running without power? "Except Provost is gone, along with the phones. We can't call for help."

Grant looked around as if he expected some kind of attack, as if searching the treetops for a hidden enemy. "There's a radio in the airplane." He marched out, heading toward the path that led from the lodge to the airstrip.

I hurried after him, taking a last look at Dorian. I hated leaving him alone—but I hated leaving Grant alone, too.

Within sight of the airplane parked at the edge of the meadow, I stopped. A breath of air touched my face, and with it came the smell of carrion.

"What is it?" Grant asked. He studied me; I turned my nose to the air to track the scent. It was making me queasy, making me want to howl.

"Bodies," I whispered. This didn't smell like meat, like the deer Jerome had dropped in front of the house the other day. This smelled like bodies. "It's coming from the plane."

I ran forward, Grant on my heels. The smell grew stronger. I reached the cabin door and rattled the handle, struggling with it a moment before finally wrenching it open.

The three production assistants lay on the floor of the cabin, dead. Side by side, curled up and crammed in, Gordon first, then Skip, then Amy. Purple bruises ringed their necks, as if they'd been garroted. I gripped the door, my heart racing, my breaths stumbling. I wanted to run, and my wolfish instincts howled.

Provost, Valenti, and Cabe were still missing.

"What's it mean?" I said, catching my breath, struggling to stay calm.

Grant moved to the cockpit and opened the door. "Look at this. It's the radio," he said, gesturing to a box that had been gutted, wires hanging out. So much for making contact with the outside world that way.

"What's going on? Who did this?" And where were they now? I turned, looking out over the meadow and surrounding woods. I walked around the airplane, searching, smelling, trying to find a trail. I smelled people, moving back and forth. The whole path smelled like people, and the airstrip smelled like fuel and tire skids overlaying the natural smell of the valley. Nothing stood out, nothing gave me a clue about who had done this or where they'd gone.

Grant was sitting in the pilot seat, flipping switches—that he'd know anything about flying a plane didn't surprise me. The engine coughed, sputtered, and died. "Out of fuel," he said. "Someone's drained the fuel tank."

Leaving us good and stuck. I tried to be shocked but felt resigned.

Grant hopped out of the cockpit and closed the door. I returned to staring at the bodies in the cabin. They didn't deserve this. This had been just another job, and now—

Grant closed the cabin door, blocking my view. I shook myself clear of the image.

"What should we do with them?" I said.

"Leave them for now. We need to wake the others."

As it turned out, we didn't have to wake up the others. We heard a loud, shocked scream as we approached the lodge. This one was different than when Tina discovered Jerome's deer carcass. This one was all about volume and fear. *Not another murder* came my first thought, and I ran. I'd find the murderer, catch him and tear him apart—

Ariel had discovered Dorian's body. She was standing on the front porch, hands over her mouth, looking down. Tina, Jerome, and Jeffrey were with her.

How were we going to tell them that this wasn't the worst of it? Slowly, I climbed the steps. The group on the porch followed me with shocked, questioning gazes, expecting me to say something. I didn't know where to start.

"The power's out," I said. "The phone's gone, and the radio in the airplane is busted. We can't find Provost anywhere."

"What are you saying?" Jerome demanded, angry. Like being fierce could solve this, could make everything right again. "What the hell's going on?"

Grant stepped up beside me, his lip curled into a thin smile. "I think we've been had."

The others went inside to wake up Lee and Conrad and gather everyone in the living room. Grant and I examined the area where Dorian had been standing and where he'd fallen. Looking for footprints, odd smells, hints of foul play. Like some kind of detective novel. Didn't Agatha Christie do this one already?

I smelled Provost. Didn't mean anything, because he'd been in and out of here all week, on the porch, sitting, standing, walking. I found footprints, but again, Provost and his crew had been going back and forth the whole time we'd been here. I didn't know enough about forensics to know if the wound on Dorian's head was caused by the fall or by someone sneaking up on him and hitting him.

Grant found something, a scorch mark at the joint that had held the railing to the post. "A small explosive might have weakened the joint at an opportune time. It wouldn't even have to be loud enough to hear."

"So it's sabotage. Not an accident," I said.

"Seems reasonable."

None of us had touched Dorian up to that point. For a second I entertained the thought that maybe he was just unconscious, and if I put my hand to his neck there'd be a pulse and he'd survive. But the Wolf senses knew otherwise, couldn't be fooled. He smelled dead.

Grant, Jeffrey, and I took a spare blanket, wrapped Dorian in it, and brought him inside to one of the empty bedrooms upstairs. We closed the door softly, out of respect. It seemed almost laughable; we weren't going to wake anyone up. But the whole situation seemed to call for moving softly, carefully.

Then we gathered in the living room to discuss—to confront—the situation.

"So we're stranded," Jeffrey said. "We don't have any power, and there's no way to contact anyone."

"Has anyone checked the generator?" Lee said.

"We were on our way to do that when we found Dorian," I said. "But do you really think this is just a matter of turning the power back on? We're on our own here."

I wanted to pace, but I stayed in my chair, my feet tapping nervously. Jerome did pace, back and forth along the picture window, looking out.

"I don't get this. What does this mean? What are you all saying?" Conrad said, shaking his head. "Because if this is some kind of haunted-house gag for the show, it's in really poor taste."

"There are *bodies,* Conrad," I muttered. "This isn't TV anymore."

Grant said, "Until we contact the authorities, I suggest no one go anywhere alone. We should stay in this central area until we come up with a plan to contact the authorities and find out where Provost is."

"We're what, sixty miles from the nearest town? If I shifted I could run that in a day," Jerome said. "Kitty and I both could."

"There's another resort lodge even closer than that," Lee said. "Thirty miles, maybe. I can check the map."

"That may be our best option," Grant said.

I couldn't explain what had happened—what was happening—but we were coming up with plans, and that was good. That made me feel better. This was a good, sensible, talented group of people to be stuck with.

But there was still something making me nervous. I looked at Grant. "We should go around and look for those remote cameras and shut them down. Put electrical tape or duct tape over the lenses if we can't turn them off. I don't want anyone salvaging footage for any shows out of this."

"Or spying on us?" Grant said.

"I didn't want to say it," I said.

Conrad was pale, breathing too quickly, on the edge of panic. "But if the power's out—"

"Batteries," Jerome said. "They could still be filming."

"We'll do that," Tina said, taking Ariel's hand and urging her to her feet. "I'll bet there's duct tape in the kitchen or toolshed."

Jerome and Grant paired off to check the generator, Tina and Ariel searched the kitchen for tape, and I kept wracking my brains, wondering what we were missing.

Jeffrey said, softly, "Someone should tell Anastasia and Gemma what happened to Dorian. They should know."

Well. That was one of the things I'd forgotten. Or didn't want to think about. I didn't understand the bond the three of them shared, but I knew it was strong. I knew they'd be hurt. Devastated. I couldn't guess how they'd react.

"Isn't it a bad idea, disturbing vampires while they're sleeping?" Ariel said.

"And how disturbed do you think they'll be when they realize we've gone all day without telling them what happened?" I said.

"I don't want to do it," Tina said softly. A couple of the others—Lee, Conrad—looked away, in silent agreement.

"I'll do it," I said and went toward the stairs.

I didn't want to. I didn't like the idea of walking into the vampires' secret lair with this news more than anyone else did. But if it had been me, I'd want someone to tell me right away. Not that I knew how I was going to do it.

I opened the door. The stairwell was pitch-dark. My eyes adjusted quickly; enough light bled from the upstairs to let me see, a little. I should have brought a flashlight. Keeping my hand on the wall, I inched my way down, until I felt the stairwell give way to open room.

The room looked like all the other bedrooms, a typical hotel setup with a king-sized bed, a bureau, a desk, a couple of armchairs, and a bathroom. A couple of suitcases stood by the closet. Fully dressed, Anastasia sat at the edge of the bed, facing me. She was ghostly pale, her skin grayish, lips thin, eyes half-lidded. She looked like a wax figure. Like a corpse.

"Something's happened," Anastasia said.

I swallowed. My eyes teared up again. "It's Dorian."

She bowed her head and nodded. "I could tell. Something woke me—I could just tell."

"He fell when the porch railing gave way. It looks like . . . Odysseus thinks it was rigged. Anastasia, I'm so sorry."

She sat very still. After a long pause, she said, "Stupid, fragile mortals." A trembling hand wiped her cheek, though nothing was there. She took a deep breath, which was odd, because vampires didn't need to breathe. They only drew air to speak. But she seemed to need to gather herself. The breath seemed to help her straighten and regain control.

She looked over her shoulder to Gemma, who was asleep, a still, waxen figure under the covers.

"Are you going to wake her up?" I asked.

"No," Anastasia said. "Let her have a few more hours of peace. She'll find out soon enough. The railing—you said it was rigged?"

"The power's gone out, Provost has vanished, and—and part of the crew's been murdered. The airplane's sabotaged. We're isolated here. Worst-case scenario—"

"Conspiracy," she said. "Someone wishing to get at me

would do very well to strike at Dorian. I always kept him close because of that. Do you understand?"

We could all probably agree that some conspiracy was afoot. But it was amazing how different such a conspiracy could look depending on your perspective.

"You think this is all about you?" I said.

"I think someone may be taking advantage of an opportunity, yes. Your magician friend, for instance. He's taking charge, isn't he? He's guiding the actions of the group now."

I shook my head. "I know him. He doesn't work like that."

"Do you know him, *really?*"

And I couldn't say that I did.

She turned to look at Gemma again and said, "If you could please leave us alone. We'll be up at nightfall, as usual. There's nothing I can do until then." I turned to leave, when she called. "Kitty. Come nightfall, we'll have to face the issue of sustenance."

"Thanks for the warning."

"It doesn't have to be difficult."

I couldn't think about it. We'd have to cross that bridge tonight. "Yeah. I'll see you in a few hours."

She was still sitting at the edge of the bed, unmoving, when I went back upstairs.

I got back to the living room the same time Grant and Jerome did.

"We checked on the generator and batteries," Jerome said. "The fuel's been drained and the wiring cut."

"Someone should go for help. Didn't someone say that?" Jeffrey said.

The sooner the better, in my opinion. I said, "Jerome and I can travel fast. We won't have to stop."

Jerome said, "If we shifted—"

I shook my head. "We need to be conscious and able to speak when we get there. This may be slower, but it'll be fast enough. If we leave now, we can be there by dusk."

"But it's thirty miles!" Conrad said. "That's impossible."

"They're werewolves," Lee said. "It's not impossible. I wish we were on the coast. I feel useless here."

"Just keep your eyes open," I said. "Use your nose. You can be lookout."

"We should get going," Jerome said, already at the door. I went to join him. Hesitating a moment, I took off my shoes and socks. Jerome was already barefoot.

Grant studied me. "Are you sure you'll be all right?"

I smiled thinly. "This is simple. We run to the next lodge and call for help. With any luck we'll be back here by morning."

"It's a plan, then," he said. "Be careful."

"Likewise."

We went outside. I could feel the others gathering by the window, watching us. The wreckage of the porch railing still lay scattered on the ground, along with the stain where Dorian's blood had soaked into the ground. It smelled ripe and rotten in the morning sun, and a few flies buzzed over it. Apart from that, the area was still, quiet.

Jerome wasn't close to shifting, but something wolfish looked out of his eyes. His breaths came slow and deep, and his attention turned outward, far outward, searching the farthest range of sight and hearing for danger. I knew how he felt—I wanted to get away from here, to run off some of this anxiety.

"You ready to do this?" I said.

"Yeah. You think you can keep up with me?"

"Probably not. But I don't think anyone should be alone right now."

His expression turned wry. "You might convince me to start liking this pack thing."

"I told you, it's all about having someone watch your back."

He pulled off his T-shirt and tossed it to the porch. His body was sleek, molded with well-defined, powerful muscles under smooth, dark skin. The guy worked out, but more than that, his body rippled with power. His muscles were natural, hard-earned, and he knew how to use them. He rolled his shoulders, flexed for a moment, then set off, from stop to run.

I bounced, testing my feet against the gravel, feeling earth under me and air around me. Then I set off after him. We took the hiking trail that led from the lodge and to wilderness—thirty miles to the next bit of civilization.

chapter 12

The Wolf had strength, agility, and stamina that the human side didn't. The Wolf could run all night when she Changed under a full moon. I wasn't as strong as that right now, but I didn't stumble when a normal human would have. My lungs didn't sear with hard breathing, I didn't fall over after a mile. I found a rhythm, and my muscles flowed. My strides were long, steady, smooth, and my breath came easily. Letting the animal side fill me, I could keep this up for hours.

I became as much Wolf as I could without shifting entirely. If someone had spoken to me then, I wouldn't have been able to answer. I'd have had to pull myself back from that edge first.

Jerome was stronger and faster than I. He pulled ahead, but only by a few strides, then adjusted so that he could see me by looking over his shoulder. We kept to the edge of the trail; the ground was softer and trees offered some shade. We probably couldn't continue this all day, but we could slow to a trot during the heat of the afternoon, pick up the pace again after resting, and still make good time. My vision collapsed, focused on the way ahead of me, while my other senses expanded. I tasted the air, which was filled with scents of pine sap, insects, heat; and sounds roared around me—wind in trees, birdsong, our steps padding on the road.

I was still in that zone when Jerome pulled up suddenly, backpedaling to get away from something ahead. I nearly collided with him, but stopped myself and knelt. He also ducked to a defensive crouch and stared ahead, as if making a challenge. I took a breath through flaring nostrils, and smelled something out of place, metallic.

Crossing the trail a few yards ahead of us, a shiny object. I focused on it as a human rather than a wolf.

"Is that what it looks like?" Jerome said.

It looked like three coils of razor wire strung on hastily planted steel T-bar fence posts. Like someone had tried to rope in a prison in a hurry. I crept closer for a better look. The stuff was so shiny it gleamed, even in the shaded forest.

I put my finger on a section of wire, well away from the protruding sharpened spikes. In a few seconds, my finger started itching. A few more seconds, the itching was painful enough I had to pull my hand away. An allergic rash reddened my fingertip.

"You've got to be kidding me," I muttered. "Silver," I said, glancing back at Jerome.

"Shit."

Someone hadn't just wanted to rope in a prison—they'd wanted to make a prison for lycanthropes. We couldn't make our way over or through the fence without risking cuts and scrapes, and if the silver taint entered our bloodstream, we were dead. I looked one way and the other, trying to see how far the fence went. From here, I couldn't see the end of it.

"It can't go on that long," Jerome said. "You know how expensive that would be, stringing this whole place up with silver wire? Someone's just trying to keep us off the path."

That mysterious someone again. When I got my claws on that someone . . .

"Which way?" I said. "Left or right?"

Jerome considered, then started walking to the right. Right was downhill, a little easier. I followed him. Even though we followed the silver fence line, we kept a respectable distance between it and us.

Vagrant breezes carry information to a wolf's nose: what's going, what's coming, what passed this way before and how long ago. How to find food, water, friends; how to find your way home. A sudden, intrusive smell can cut across the normal tapestry like a razor, sharp and sudden. Destructive and wrong.

I stopped cold and turned into the slight breeze, trying to catch hold of what I'd sensed for only a second. I turned in place. My feet throbbed; my muscles ached at being wrenched out of their rhythm. I'd lost track of time, but the sun was high, probably well past noon. Several hours at least had passed. We'd run maybe half the distance.

Jerome stopped a few paces ahead of me and looked back. His body heaved with deep, steady breaths. He didn't speak, just gave me a focused look, then turned his own nose to the air, looking for what I searched for.

Skin, sweat, clothing, rubber—human. Just a glimpse. Maybe hikers, maybe a mountain biker. I'd caught only a hint. It was gone now. Maybe moving away, maybe gone downwind.

I looked at Jerome. He shook his head.

A sound like a whip cracked past us; Jerome twisted, dropped to one knee, and clapped a hand over his shoulder, where a rod, maybe ten inches, protruded. Blood dripped in a thin line from the puncture wound.

Breath left me in a gasp. I knelt beside him and touched his arm. At the same time I looked out, toward the direction the arrow had come from. Where I'd sensed a trace of human hunter. When would the next one strike?

Jerome's breaths heaved, and his face twisted with pain.

"Jerome?"

"Get it out, get it out—Jesus, get it out!" He bared his teeth, and his skin prickled under my hand, rippling with newly sprouting fur. His face was changing, stretching. Pain was pushing him over the edge, making him shift.

"Jerome! Hold on, keep it together!"

"Get . . . it . . . out!" He screamed.

I braced my hand on his shoulder, grabbed the arrow, and yanked. Jerome arced his back and howled—part human shout, part wolf cry of anger.

The wound was shallow, the arrow stuck in the outer layer of muscle. It wasn't even bleeding much. But Jerome was shivering, wracked with pain. I looked at the arrow in my hand, short and sleek—a bolt for a crossbow. The tip—smooth, not barbed—gleamed, even through the sheen of blood. I touched it, held my finger against the metal—and my skin started itching, burning, in an allergic reaction.

Silver. The point was silver.

When a silver weapon struck lycanthropes, the wound didn't kill them. The silver poisoning the blood did. Jerome was dying. His wolf was trying to take over, trying to battle it. As if it would help.

"Jerome!" I cried, clinging to his arms, trying to meet his gaze. My heart was racing, a howl building in my throat.

Another arrow ripped through the air. Jerome lunged into its path—between it and me. It struck his back.

"No!" I gave a full-throated scream.

He looked at me. He was trembling, his eyes wide, glazed, inhuman. Black streaks marked his veins, crawling from the wound in his shoulder, poisoned blood flowing through his body.

"Kitty. Run," he said through gritted teeth. He had fangs now, in a long mouth.

"Jerome." My voice was thick with despair.

"Run!" he said, and it was a growl. He twitched, convulsed, pushed me away.

I ran.

I took off through the trees, hoping to get some cover. Didn't look back, sure that the next silver-tipped bolt would strike me. The thought pushed me over an edge— I couldn't handle this situation, not like this. Not as a human. I could run fast on two legs. I could run faster on four, I could hide better, and right now that was all I cared about.

I pulled off my T-shirt, my bra, and didn't fight it. When I wanted it, when it came fast like this, it didn't hurt so much. I leaned into it because this time, it could save my life. My back rounded, a wave passed through me, my body turned liquid, bones and skin melting, re-forming, fur prickling. Shoved my sweats and panties down in the same moment—

She shakes herself and keeps going, can't stop. A hunter has attacked and she's alone now. Run, that's all she thinks of, legs pumping, taking deep breaths, scenting for danger. Catches traces of an enemy and moves away.

She tastes the air and feels the wind like fingers through her fur. Nothing can catch her like this. Nothing. But she keeps running, trying to outrun fear. At this moment, speed is the greatest strength she has, and she uses it.

But she can't keep running forever. She has to go somewhere, so she heads toward safety. She knows that smell, where she's been sleeping, where she has friends. She has no place else to go. Too far away from her own pack, this will have to do. Though she would run to her pack if she could.

Time passes.

She slows to a trot as she approaches the den where she hopes to find safety. Strange smells—too many people, the two-legged ones, have passed here. Some of them may be hunting her. She whines, because she can't trust where she is. Can't trust any of these smells. But the human side, the two-legged self, nudges her. There are friends here. At least, there should be. She has to hope.

The trees end, opening to a wide, exposed clearing, and the large human structure in the middle of it. Full of danger. Her fur bristles, her tail is stiff, her head hangs low. She circles, tracking every smell, every hint of danger. Searches her memory, finds the area smells much

*like it did when she left. Nothing has changed; the hunter
has not followed her. The blood in front of the structure
is old, from this morning.*

*She paces slowly, carefully around the building, spiral-
ing closer. Ready to flee the moment the air feels wrong.*

*The den draws her in. A noise startles her—she flicks
her ear. Footsteps sound hollow, and a two-legged figure stands before her, looking out. She stops, stares. He
doesn't stare back. Drops his gaze, doesn't offer challenge, and she feels better. He smells familiar. A friend.
He has helped her before. She remembers. Her throat
whines, because she's been afraid for a long time now
and wants to rest.*

*More footsteps, more people, too many, and her ears
pin back, her hackles go rigid, and she braces, ready to
run, ready to fight.*

"Stay back. Go back inside, all of you," *the first man
says. The one she wants to trust.*

"What is it? Oh my God—is that—"

"It's Kitty," *he says.*

"You've got to be kidding me, you don't seriously
expect—"

"Conrad, shut up!"

"What happened?" *another says. A female.*

"I don't know. We won't know until she turns back. We
need to get her inside, to safety."

"And how do you propose we do that? It looks . . . she
looks . . . I mean . . ."

The first one, the male, acts like an alpha. "Everyone needs to get back inside and give her space. She's
spooked. Go upstairs. I'll take care of this."

"Odysseus, are you sure?" *Another male, an odd-*

smelling one—he smells like fish and rivers—says this. "If she bites you—"

"She won't. I'll be fine."

Then the doorway, the whole front of the den, is empty, and he turns his back to her and walks inside, leading her in. Head low, hesitating, she follows. The hard, artificial ground feels wrong, harsh against her feet. Her claws click. If she goes inside, she'll be trapped, no way to get out, no wide spaces to run in. But to her other side, it smells safe. Her other side trusts.

She slips inside and keeps to the wall so nothing can sneak up on her, surround her. She stays by the entrance, just in case. She keeps her eyes on the man, who sits nearby, quietly, watching.

Then, because she's been running all day, she folds her legs under her, curls up tight so her tail brushes her nose. She hopes the world is safer when she wakes up.

The bed was hard, but I was warm. My mouth was sticky. I'd had nightmares.

Not nightmares. Memories.

I gasped a breath and sat up. I had a blanket over me— someone's kind thought. I was against the wall, right next to the front door. This was how far they'd been able to coax me inside. I was amazed I managed to make it this far. Part of me thought I should have just kept running until I made it back to Colorado. Except for that fence, trapping us.

I pulled the blanket tighter around me and scrubbed my face, trying to wake up. My muscles ached, my head throbbed. I wanted to go home. I glanced out the window; the sky was dark. I didn't want it to be night. Inside, several candles burned, on the coffee table and the kitchen counter. A low fire flickered in the fireplace. The light was warm, full of rippling shadows. Terrible, terrifying.

"Kitty." Odysseus Grant sat on a sofa, watching me.

"Déjà vu, huh?" I said, smiling weakly.

"Are you all right?"

Screwing my face up to keep from crying, I shook my head.

"What happened?" Grant asked.

I swallowed, to clear the tightness in my throat. "Jerome is dead. We're being hunted."

chapter 13

I went to my room so I could wash and change while Grant gathered the others in the kitchen to try to figure out what to do next. I took a quick shower, enough to rinse off and wake up, but I wanted a longer one. I could have stayed under the spray all night, as long as the remaining dregs of hot water lasted, hoping it would wash away all that had happened. But standing still made me feel like a target. Whoever had shot Jerome would come after the rest of us. I couldn't just stand here waiting for it.

After putting on a shirt and jeans, I felt mostly human again. But my shoulders were stiff, the shadow of rigid hackles, and the part of me that had claws still glared out of my eyes. I went barefoot, in case I had to run again.

Before my shower, Grant told me that they'd dismantled all the cameras around the house. I still felt like someone was watching me.

The others were waiting for me, gathered around the kitchen table, pensive. In the wavering light of candles and the fire in the fireplace, their faces looked long, skeletal. Grant presided, arms crossed. He might have been a

wizard from a fairy tale. I shook my head of the vision.
He nodded to me in greeting.

The rest stared at me, and I knew they had seen me
as Wolf. They looked at me differently now. They might
have known what I was intellectually, they might have
seen the video clip from Washington and thought they
knew the story, thought they were ready for it. But to see
the actual wolf, large for a wolf and gazing with a strange
intelligence—then to see the woman lying where the animal had fallen asleep. The most open-minded person in
the world would still have to think about it. I'd still look
different, somehow. Tina, Jeffrey, Ariel—they looked a
little bit afraid.

But Lee—he looked on me with pity.

I couldn't blame them. But it made me sad, self-
conscious. I crossed my arms to match Grant, tried to put
out a little alpha attitude.

We were missing people. Besides Dorian and Jerome.
The vampires hadn't yet emerged, but there was one
more.

"Where's Conrad?" I said.

That broke whatever tension had held us all rigid. Ariel
giggled—nervously, but still. Even Grant smiled a little.

Tina said, "He watched you change back. He hasn't
come out of his room since."

I held my forehead and winced. "Finally got through to
him, did we? I'm sorry I missed it."

"No, you're not," Jeffrey said. "Grant had to knock him
out to get him to quit yelling."

No, really, I was. All that buildup and I didn't get to
see the denouement. I wouldn't even get to watch it when
the show aired. Because this show was *never* going to air,

not if I could help it. "Should someone go get him? I don't think any of us are safe alone."

"Kitty—what happened to you? What happened to Jerome?"

I took a deep breath; I could do this calmly. "About twelve miles out, someone put up a fence. Silver-alloy razor wire across the trail. It was a trap, enough of a barrier to slow us down. Jerome was shot with a silver-tipped crossbow bolt."

The reactions were various: Ariel covered her mouth and looked away, Lee hissed in sympathy. Tina stared, Jeffrey bowed his head. Grant just looked colder than ever.

"How did you get away?" Grant said.

"Jerome bought me time. Stayed between me and the shooter and bought me time." And I couldn't even thank him for it. I shook my head. I could thank him by not succumbing to panic now.

"But why?" Ariel blurted. "Why kill any of us?"

"Do you really have to ask?" Anastasia said, standing by the basement door. She was pale, chalk-white. She hadn't fed yet and was standing here under sheer willpower. In the candlelight, she looked like a ghost. A couple of us gasped. I wanted to look away, but I didn't. I moved toward her, but she gestured and shook her head, to convince me she was all right.

"Whoever did this was watching the way out. They expected at least some of us to run. They were waiting," I said.

"There are more than one?" Grant said.

"I don't know. The smells outside are mixed up. There've been so many people running around here over the last few days, it's hard to pick out individuals. And it's hard to know who's involved and who isn't."

Lee leaned forward. "So you think Provost and the production crew are in on it?"

"I knew it," Tina said. "I've been feeling weird about this since we got here."

"I don't know," I said. "Three of the PAs are dead. Provost, Valenti, and Cabe are missing. They may have been kidnapped, killed, bribed away, anything. I just don't know. But I know it isn't over."

"What do we do?" Ariel said, her voice small.

Grant didn't say anything. Then everyone was looking at me. Like I was more likely to have answers.

"I don't know, I need to think." I chuckled harshly, looked away. "Part of me didn't want to come back. Part of me wanted to just keep running. But the only way I can pay Jerome back for saving me is to figure out what happened, who did this, and stop them."

"Easier said than done," Grant said.

"Oh, come on," I said. "We're all smart people here—we can handle this, right? It's not like we're stuck in a horror movie or something." Except we were. We were a bunch of horror-story monsters and characters stuck in our very own horror story. I put a hand over my mouth to keep from laughing again. "Oh, the irony," I whispered. I'd have appreciated it if it wasn't me in the middle of it.

I started pacing, my nerves finally getting the better of me. "Okay. Fine. You know why horror-movie characters always get killed? Because they've never seen horror movies. They don't know how it works. Right? But we do. So no one go into the basement alone. No one go screaming off into the woods alone. No one has any sex."

Tina and Jeffrey actually looked at each other sadly. Oh my God, we had to get out of this.

Thankfully, Ariel diverted my ranting before I could get really hysterical. "Anastasia. How's Gemma doing?"

After a pause, the vampire said, "She's weak. She needs to feed. We both do."

The expressions on the humans in the room grew even more wary. "And how exactly are you going to manage that?" Tina said.

We were too screwed to be worrying about petty crap like this. "I'll do it," I said. "It's okay. I've done it before. I heal fast."

"Thank you," Anastasia said, ignoring the stares of the others. "I'll bring Gemma up."

As soon as she was gone, Tina leaned forward, demanding, "Kitty, what are you doing? Are you serious?"

"They're targets just as much as the rest of us. We need to help each other if we're going to get out of this."

"But they're . . . they're . . ."

My grin turned bitter. "What's the matter? Some of my best friends are vampires." Nobody was happy, and the situation was getting worse. "If it upsets you that much, you don't have to watch."

"Jeffrey, have you sensed anything?" Grant said, moving forward and back into the conversation. "Do you think Dorian or Jerome might try to communicate with us?" Jeffrey could channel the dead. Could our dead tell us anything?

I expected Jeffrey's answer. He shook his head. "It's not so simple. Not everyone who's passed on can communicate. I can't just summon them. They may not have anything to say."

"Can you try? Both of you?" the magician said, including Tina in the question. I understood the logic: at least they'd be doing something. They'd keep busy, distracted. And we might even get some answers.

I went toward the stairs.

"Kitty?" Grant said.

"I'm going to check on Conrad." I headed upstairs.

Conrad's room was in the back of the house, near the stairs. I knocked softly and got no answer. Big shock there.

"Conrad?" I said. "It's Kitty. Can we talk?"

"I've barricaded the door! Stay away from me!" His voice was rough with panic. Now, here was someone acting like a character in a horror movie.

"Conrad, I think you need to come downstairs with the rest of us. We need to come up with a plan for how we're going to get out of here."

"I'm not leaving this room!"

Sighing, I tried to imagine how I'd deal with a two-year-old. "I don't know if they told you, but Jerome's dead. And I don't think this is going to stop. I think we're all in danger."

"Of course we're in danger! I'm trapped in a house with a bunch of monsters!"

"Monster is in the eye of the beholder, Conrad," I said tiredly.

"You. I saw you. That's . . . that's not . . ."

"I warned you," I said. "And you had to be all smug about it."

There was a long pause. I didn't hear anything inside. I could imagine what the room looked like: the bureau pulled across the front door, the shades drawn, Conrad huddled in the middle of the floor with a sputtering flashlight, trembling in the dark. Poor guy. Not.

"That's it," I said. "I'm sending Ariel to get you. You can deal with her, can't you? She's human."

"How do you know that? I don't know anything about any of you!"

I walked away.

Back downstairs, everyone else was still huddled in the kitchen, bent over candles and looking grim. Grant stood by the kitchen window and gazed out, either standing watch or searching. He looked like a sentinel carved from stone, and for my part I felt a little safer with him on duty.

Anastasia and Gemma were in the living room. The younger vampire was curled up on the sofa, her knees pulled to her chin, her brown hair hanging loose and limp around her face, like she'd been pulling at it. I didn't think it was possible, but she seemed even more pale than Anastasia. More than that, she was listless, glassy-eyed. Grief-stricken, I wanted to say. Except that she smelled cold, didn't breathe, didn't blink, didn't move at all—so she looked dead.

Anastasia had laid out equipment on the coffee table: gauze, blood collection tubes, a sterile pack with a brand-new hypodermic syringe inside. I was a little relieved.

I sat across from her. "I admit, I think I like this a little better than teeth. It's a little cleaner."

"If you didn't like the teeth, your host was doing it wrong."

"Oh, no, no. She was doing it just right. That's kind of the problem." I winced.

That was the secret behind vampire seductions. They

could hypnotize their victims, arouse them, bring them to ecstasy even as they drank blood from them. They didn't have to kill their prey. Why would they, when they could make their victims keep coming back for more? Blood was a renewable resource.

Anastasia gave a knowing smile.

She opened the package and prepared the syringe. Just a pinprick and a little blood. I could handle it. And we needed the vampires at full strength. We were all in this together.

"Are you right or left handed?" she asked, and I told her right. She sat on my left side and took that arm. Polite vampires always asked for the off hand.

I looked away and tried not to pay attention. Grant had shifted so he could see us and watched the proceedings, frowning. I looked back, almost challenging. *What did you expect me to do, let them starve?*

I hissed when I felt the prick in my elbow. A moment later, Anastasia said, "Hold this." She left the needle in place and held a square of gauze over it. Her hands were perfectly steady. I put my fingers on the spot and tried not to move.

She popped out the tube of fresh blood and took it straight to Gemma. "Gemma, here. Drink this."

She had to hold the tube under her nose a moment before Gemma reacted. Slowly, she shifted, blinked, came to awareness. She gripped Anastasia's hand, clutching at the tube, and Anastasia guided it to her mouth. Gemma tipped her head back and pulled the tube between her lips, letting the contents pour in. She didn't even swallow. Just let the blood stream down her throat.

Anastasia drew the empty tube away, and Gemma sat,

head tipped back, hands covering her mouth. Some color came back; she went from looking corpselike to merely pale. I could almost see energy returning to her as she straightened, her muscles tensed, and she came back to life.

Then she let out a sob. "Ani, he's gone, he's gone!"

Anastasia drew her in an embrace. "Shh, I know, I know." The older vampire held her, curled in her arms, like a mother with her child. Gemma cried, but they were dry sobs, shedding no tears.

I kept holding the needle in my vein and waited.

After a minute, Anastasia pulled away and held Gemma's face to look at her. "We must be strong. He would want us to fight, yes?" Gemma nodded but still looked forlorn. She watched as Anastasia returned to me and drew a second vial, staring at the blood spilling into the tube.

This one Anastasia drank quickly and without drama. Discreetly, she withdrew and capped the needle, wrapped up the equipment for disposal, and put it in a small vinyl pouch. It was all very clinical. Made it easier for me. Which might have been the point.

"That's all we need for now," Anastasia said. "You need your strength, as well. But I may ask for more later."

I rubbed my elbow; the needle-sized hole in my arm was already healed.

I was still sitting there when Ariel brought me a glass of warm orange juice and a couple of cookies. "When people give blood they're supposed to drink a lot of fluids, right?" She shrugged, looking sheepish.

"Thanks," I said.

"So," Anastasia said, standing at one end of the room,

arms crossed, and gazing across it. Grant regarded her from the other side of the room. I couldn't help but think: the two most powerful people here were facing off. "Now that that's taken care of, do we have a plan?"

No one answered.

I stared at the picture window and to the big bad world outside, where someone was waiting to kill us. The first response was always: turn Wolf and run. But the hunter was waiting and had silver. Had to use brains, not instinct. The brain clicked.

I knew someone who would know exactly how to get out of this situation. Not that I could call him. Not that he could come and help even if I could call him.

So I had to figure out how to think like Cormac.

chapter **14**

The first time I met Cormac Bennett he wanted to kill me, because that was what he did. He hunted monsters. I talked him out of it, and ever since then our friendship had the undertone of an ironic running joke. He'd introduced me to Ben, who was his cousin, and who I ended up marrying. Cormac had saved my life. He represented possibilities. Roads not taken. But that was another story.

He also gave me access to a perspective, to a way of thinking, that I otherwise never would have had experience with. I hunted under duress because I was a werewolf, and I limited myself to far wilderness where I wouldn't hurt anyone. But people like Cormac, who did it on purpose, who made it a profession, who honed their skills—

That was the kind of person who was after us now.

I found myself asking, what would Cormac do? If it were Cormac out there, what could I expect? If I could call Cormac for help, what would he say?

The funny thing? I could hear the answer.

The hunter would try to draw us out. He'd try to separate us. Right now, we were a pack with our own territory,

and we had a defensive advantage. Hunting other predators is different than hunting prey, Cormac said. We were
predators.

If it were Cormac out there and he'd had time to prepare, he'd have trapped the house. He wouldn't give us an
escape route. He'd have studied us, he'd know our weaknesses. He'd use silver on the lycanthropes, stakes and
sunlight on the vampires. He'd have a plan for each one
of us.

We just had to figure out what those plans were, and
how to turn them around. Use them against him. And
even more importantly, we had to figure out how to get
back in contact with the outside world. Get the power
working, find a phone, call in the cavalry.

Our hunter had had time to prepare. We hadn't. We'd
have to move fast if we were going to make up the
difference.

I turned from the window. Everyone was doing something different, all of them stuck in their own worlds. Jeffrey and Tina were on one sofa; Jeffrey looked like he was
meditating, Tina was tapping a pen on a piece of paper
but not writing. On the other sofa, Anastasia was still
comforting Gemma, who through her grief was showing her youth, her inexperience as a vampire. She might
never have lost anyone she loved before. Ariel was pacing,
wringing her hands. Lee was on a chair, drinking a beer.
Grant was staring at the window, searching the darkness,
like me.

We were sitting ducks, waiting to be picked off. We all
knew better than that.

"I think we should post a watch," I said. Everyone
looked toward me, a group of stark faces. I wanted to

duck, apologetic for breaking the quiet, but I didn't. I was an alpha wolf, and I could do this. "Probably from upstairs. It'll be easier to stay out of sight of anyone with a rifle. Then we need to check the house. It might be rigged with explosives, traps. Anything like that. We should also look for weapons we can use."

After a moment of stunned silence, Ariel said, voice wavering, "Are you serious? *Explosives?*"

Lee chuckled. His face flushed, and I wondered if maybe that wasn't his first beer of the evening. "What are you going to do, wage some kind of war?"

"Yes," I said. "Damn straight."

Anastasia stood, and all gazes turned to her. She drew the eye with her poise, her bearing, chin tipped up, gaze like iron. I suddenly felt like we couldn't do half badly with her on our side.

"I'm less interested in the war than I am in the conspiracy," she said. "I want to know how this happened. How it was possible for this . . . situation . . . to arise. I want to know who made it possible." She looked at Odysseus Grant.

An epic stare-down between them began. I looked back and forth between the two.

"You want to explain what you're talking about?" I said to Anastasia.

"You know what I'm talking about," she said. "You know what he's capable of."

Grant hadn't reacted. Not a muscle on his face twitched. Gazing at him, Anastasia looked like she could raise a hand and summon storms. At the moment, I was thinking they were both capable of a hell of a lot. I didn't particularly want to see what.

"I do know," I said, my voice low, steady. The talking-down-a-hostage-situation voice. "And I think that if he wanted to act against any of us, he'd do it a lot more elegantly and discreetly."

Grant was near the top of my "people never to piss off" list. Because if he ever decided he had it in for me, I would just . . . vanish.

"I'll take that as a compliment," Grant said.

Anastasia scowled at me. "Then what do you think is happening here?"

I didn't snap back like I wanted to, because I was still thinking like Cormac, and Anastasia didn't have that benefit. Hell, for all her experience she might never have met anyone like Cormac. I explained carefully, thinking out loud, formulating my own hypothesis. "I think it's pretty simple. There are people out there—bounty hunters, hit men, assassins—who want people like us dead. I think maybe one or more of them got wind of what was happening here. That they'd have a whole group of juicy targets in one place, just waiting to be picked off. They made plans, they camped out—maybe at that campsite Jerome and I found during the treasure hunt. They waited for the chance, got rid of witnesses. Now they can pick us off one by one, and that's all they want to do. I think they hit Dorian first because they knew it would weaken you and Gemma. That means they're smart. They know our weaknesses. So we have to pay attention. And I think we have to go after them before they get to us."

The others took time absorbing all that. I studied them in turn, sizing them up, guessing how they'd do under pressure—assessing my pack, I realized. Most of them probably had never been hunted before. They might never have been in danger like this. Grant and Tina had, I knew. They could fight. Anastasia, probably. The old vampires didn't survive so long without developing a few survival skills. Lee was a hunter, but he was used to being top of the food chain. Jeffrey, Ariel—I had no idea. I hated this, because Jeffrey and Ariel at least were too darned nice to be stuck in a situation like this.

That was why I was starting to throw down the alpha attitude: I felt like I had to protect them.

Lee finally broke the silence. "How do you do that? How do you just put yourself inside their heads like that?"

I looked away, trying not to laugh, because this wasn't funny. But God, I wished Cormac could hear this.

"I have this friend," I said. "He's good at this sort of thing."

"Any chance you could get him to come out here and help?"

My throat tightened, and I shook my head. "No chance at all, even if we had a working phone."

"Too bad," he said.

Yeah. Too bad.

Straightening, I pulled from the window. Reminded myself I was supposed to be badass. "Tell you what. There's a locked room upstairs. Anyone else want to check it out? See what Provost decided to keep out of sight?"

I trooped upstairs, leading the others.

"Maybe this is all some kind of mistake," Lee said. "Dorian was an accident, Jerome was the only target—he had enemies, right? Maybe from his boxing days?"

"Except there's still that prickling on the back of my neck," I said.

"What do you think we'll find in there?" Tina said.

"If I knew that, I wouldn't need to look."

Ariel split off to knock on Conrad's door. "Hey, Conrad. You okay?"

"I'm not coming out, so don't ask," came the muffled voice from within. Ariel stepped back, a startled look on her face.

"I'd have thought he'd start adjusting by now," she said.

I gave her a wry grin. "The trouble is, there's no way he can save face. He looks like an idiot, and he knows it."

The door to the mystery room was still locked. I rattled the knob again and wondered if I was strong enough to kick it in. That always worked so well in the movies, right? "Maybe there's an ax in the toolshed," I said.

"May I try?" Grant stepped forward, holding a couple of small, thin tools. Lock picks. The magician had everything.

"Be my guest," I said, stepping aside. I liked having Grant on my team, which made me even crankier when Anastasia whispered to me, "He has us all where he wants us."

I didn't want to have that argument right now. I didn't want to have that argument at all.

Grant got to work on the lock, using the pick smoothly, making minute adjustments. In a moment, the lock clicked and the door cracked open. Grant pushed inside the room.

I could see pretty well in the dark. So could Anastasia, and she was at my shoulder, looking in. The room had been cleared of furniture, and a dozen or so plastic storage crates were shoved up against walls, among other random bits of equipment. A storage room, as I'd suspected. I took a deep breath and tried to sort out the tangle of smells. Lots of metal, plastic, rubber, along with the smells inherent in the lodge. Familiar smells of technology and civilization. It didn't mean anything.

Grant was studying the room by the glow from a cigarette lighter. Tina and Jeffrey carried flashlights and panned the beams over the interior. I started looking in boxes.

One held a few extra remote cameras nestled among coils of coaxial cable. Microphones, wire, electrical tape, packing foam, forms listing inventory. All the odds and ends I'd have expected to find tucked away on a film production like this.

Then I found the box with stuff in it I couldn't identify.

"Grant?" I said. He and Anastasia came to look over my shoulder.

In this box we found coils of very thin wire, an almost clear filament that certainly wasn't meant for anything electrical. Sleek black boxes with tiny lenses. Batteries. Gun cases—empty.

"Trip wire," Grant said. "Motion detectors."

"Stuff you'd use for a security system?" I said.

"Or for a trap," he said.

I was almost afraid to dig looking for more, but I did, and found the canisters, steel and heavy, the size of grenades. Not that I'd ever seen a grenade. But I could tell. My skin was prickling. When I lifted it, my hand seemed to tingle at the feel of it. The sheer sinister aura leaking from it. I smelled it, a quick sniff, and quickly turned away because it smelled sour, chemical. Just a faint odor, suggestive of pain. My eyes watered from it.

"Tear gas," Grant said.

"Are you kidding?" I said, quickly setting the thing down. "What's a film crew need with tear gas?" And I knew. Cormac's voice whispering. All I had to do was think of what *he* would do with tear gas. "They could get us to panic. To scatter, if they wanted to separate us."

Jeffrey stared at the box, encompassed by his flashlight beam. "What does this mean? That Provost and the production company are in on it?"

"Not necessarily," I said. "I'd love to find out who owns the lodge. It might be that someone was able to get in here ahead of time and set up shop. We still don't know enough to go pointing fingers."

"But we can assume there may be some kind of booby trap out there rigged with tear gas?" Lee said. "This is fucked up."

"Yeah," I breathed.

"We need to check over the house. Carefully," Grant said.

"I'll search with you," Anastasia said to Grant.

"Don't want to let me out of your sight?" he said.

"That's right."

We scoured the house top to bottom. I wasn't even sure what we were looking for, but we brainstormed and made up a list: wires, cameras, or other bits of electronics in odd places. Places where recent construction might have been done: odd seams in the walls, sawdust on the floor. Any trace of anything that didn't belong. We checked windows, doors, roof beams, vents. Lee and I hunted by smell, though he said that out of the water he wasn't much good.

Just because we didn't find anything didn't mean nothing was there. That was the worst part. It felt futile.

I slumped into the kitchen, looking for something to eat and drink, and found Ariel. She'd taken a drawer full of butter knives and was lashing them together with a coil of wire from the secret stash upstairs. She'd made a half-dozen crosses.

"It's curandera magic," she said. "I was never very good at it. I tried, but I didn't have the patience like I should have. Grandma was always telling me to slow down, not to try to learn everything at once, that there'd be time. Then she was gone, and I wished I'd learned better. I don't have her talent, but this should work."

"I know," I said softly. "I've seen something like this work before."

"I had to do something," she said. "It's not much. But . . . it's something."

I helped her start hanging them above the doors and windows. It was protective magic, supposed to keep evil outside. It certainly couldn't hurt, could it?

Except when Anastasia and Gemma returned from searching the basement. Anastasia stopped in the doorway and glared. Not looking scared, but angry.

"Kitty?" she called. "What are those?"

I was standing on a chair, using duct tape to secure one of the impromptu crosses above the kitchen window. Crosses. Vampires. Oops.

"Crosses. Protective magic," I explained. Ariel held another cross to her chest and looked stricken.

"Was this Grant's idea?" she said. If I'd looked at her

eyes, they would be flashing with rage, but I knew better than to look at her eyes. Grant wasn't around at the moment—Anastasia wouldn't let him accompany her into their basement lair.

"No," Ariel said, quickly—bravely—stepping forward. "It was my idea. It's something my grandmother did. I thought—I thought it might help. I'm sorry. I wasn't thinking, we'll take them down."

Anastasia couldn't say anything to that, and my estimation of her went up a bit when she didn't try. She could see that Ariel was only trying to help.

"Can I ask a stupid question?" I said to Anastasia.

"I don't know why you bother asking permission," she said.

I ignored that. "What were vampires afraid of before Christianity and crosses and all that?"

"Crosses have been around in one form or another since before Christianity. It's a powerful symbol."

"And?"

She didn't continue. Ah well.

The vampires waited in the doorway until we'd removed the several crosses we'd put up. Ariel kept them, though, stashing them out of sight in an old grocery bag.

"They may not have worked anyway," I told her. "They're magical. I'm afraid we may be up against something entirely mundane."

"It's okay," Ariel said. Out of the blue, she gave me a hug. Quick, spontaneous. More comfort. "I'm glad you're here. I mean, I'm not glad you're stuck. But I'm glad you're here, because I know you'll figure this out."

"I elect you morale officer," I said. That got her to smile. My work here is done.

Lee and Grant collected weapons. They went through the kitchen, the closets, the utility shed, equipment left behind from the show, and the attic, gathering an arsenal that they spread on the living room floor. Along with the tear gas and motion detectors from the secret stash, we had a set of mean-looking carving knives from the kitchen; vinegar, ammonia, bleach, and other chemicals we could turn into some wicked cocktails; and from the toolshed, a shovel, an ax, and a set of surveying stakes.

Every minute they spent outside collecting the stuff, I had my heart in my throat, waiting for something to happen. Nothing did. However much I'd have loved to entertain the thought that maybe this was over, and that what happened to Dorian and Jerome were isolated and unrelated events and nothing else was going to happen, I couldn't.

"I wouldn't normally bother with the stakes, but considering the company, I thought we ought to keep an eye on them." Grant seemed pleased with the haul. I wasn't so sure we weren't just spitting into the wind.

"I don't see how this crap is going to do us any good," Lee said. Like me, he was looking over his shoulder. I wondered if he felt the same weird vibes I did, like someone was watching us, even though the cameras following us around were long gone.

"If we have it all together and locked up, it means no one else can get to it, either," I said. "How about that?"

He scowled and went away to look out the window. Making himself a target for someone outside, I observed. So how did we keep a lookout without giving the bad guys a perfect view of us? You have an answer for that, Cormac?

Anastasia regarded the armory with about as much confidence as I did, her frown revealing contempt. "Stakes are overrated as a weapon against vampires. You have to get close enough to use them, and that's always problematic, isn't it?"

"If you act stupid enough around vampires, they let their guard down," I said. "Then you can get close. They tend to get this look of shock on their faces, like getting staked was the last thing they expected even though they saw you coming at them with the thing in your hand."

"And you know this *how?*" Anastasia said, and I couldn't tell if it was astonishment or a newfound respect in her startled tone of voice.

"Long story," I said, blushing. "Never mind. Really."

"What next?" Grant said, changing the subject, lucky for me. "I don't relish sitting here waiting for this hunter to show himself."

"But how do we act without exposing ourselves?" I said.

"We may not have a choice," he said. "We'll just have to be careful."

"I still think the answer is under our noses," Anastasia said, glaring at Grant. "This is an inside job, it has to be. You—you've barely flinched through all of this. Like none of this has surprised you."

"He never flinches," I said. "He sees a human sacrifice in a flaming pseudo-Babylonian temple and he doesn't flinch, trust me."

"What are you talking about?" Anastasia said.

"Never mind. But you want to know who I want to talk to?" I had their attention then, which was good, because keeping us all from arguing was going to be half the battle. "Conrad. He may be putting on a good act, but the minute the shit hit the fan, he locked himself up and won't have anything to do with the rest of us. Now, is he really having a nervous breakdown, or is he keeping himself out of the way for whatever's next?" I paused, then shook my head. "You know what? That's paranoid even for me, forget I said that."

Grant said, "Kitty. Do you think you should try to get some sleep? You've had a busy day."

By any sane reckoning, I did need some sleep. I hadn't slept nearly enough to recover from shifting, not to mention all the running I'd done. I was exhausted. My brain hurt. I couldn't think straight. But I also couldn't imagine trying to sleep. I'd sit straight up every time someone in the house coughed.

"This doesn't exactly seem like the best time to be sleeping."

"This may be all the time you get," Anastasia said. "I think he's right."

Anastasia and Grant agreeing on anything was enough to convince me that maybe I really should try to get some sleep. But I wasn't going to go to my room to do it. I wasn't going to be alone. I may not have been with my pack, but I needed someone around. I found a blanket and curled up on the sofa, thinking I'd at least rest my eyes, thinking no way would I ever fall asleep when I was this keyed up.

But wonder of wonders, I did.

chapter **15**

No. I'm sorry, I'm not doing this anymore. I'm not getting anything but nastiness. There's something out there, and it doesn't like us. We knew that already."

I opened my eyes in time to see Tina get up from the dining room table and walk away. Sitting up, I saw that she'd left behind Jeffrey and the Ouija board. I could infer: they'd been trying another séance, and it wasn't going well.

"Hey. You okay?" I said to Tina when she came within range.

She jumped, making me feel guilty. We were all on edge. Seeing me, she sighed. "Oh, yeah. We just thought we might find something out. It's not working."

"I'm not surprised. We're all really keyed up."

We were all awake. Some of the others—Lee, Ariel—looked like they'd been trying to sleep, too, curled up in armchairs, sprawled on a sofa. But no one was asleep. Everyone looked up at the sound of voices. Grant and Anastasia had been by the table, watching the psychics. Now they watched me.

Tina was pacing in front of the fireplace. "They won't have to do anything to get us. We'll all go stir-crazy at this rate. Then we'll all go screaming into the woods—"

"They're waiting for us to panic," I said. "All we have to do is not panic."

She rolled her eyes, evidently not too confident of our chances of doing that.

Thinking like Cormac again: he wouldn't sit around waiting. I said, "We're not going to find out anything about these guys until we can draw them out. Get a look at them, see what their resources are."

Grant said thoughtfully, "Actually go outside and take a look around."

"Are you crazy?" Tina said. "They're out there with arrows, guns probably—"

"So we'll have to be careful. Stay out of sight," Grant said. "Get the lay of the land, find out what's really out there, then formulate a strategy. Reconnaissance."

"We're in the army now," Lee said, shaking his head.

"Yo Joe," I muttered. "What do you say? Want to go hunt some bad guys?"

"I'll go," Ariel said.

"You don't have to," I said. "It's my stupid idea. I'll volunteer."

Anastasia said, "I'll go. Some of us are better equipped for this sort of situation."

"But I want to help," Ariel said. She sounded so earnest. She wasn't a supernatural creature; she didn't have otherworldly powers. She was just a person with a few folk spells. And she wanted to help. I wanted to hug her.

"We'll need someone to keep watch while the three of

us search," Grant said. "We can keep an eye on each other that way."

He made it sound sinister.

So Grant, Anastasia, and I stepped out to the front porch, but I was sure they were watching each other as much as they looked out to the dark, searching for an attack. Ariel, joined by Jeffrey, waited by the door, and their job was to look to the forest for anything suspicious. Grant held a flashlight; Anastasia and I didn't. A faint glow from candles leaked to the outside, but otherwise, nothing intruded on my night vision. I could see individual trees and the stripe of sand along the lake shore. Above, the Milky Way was a visible band, a cloud of stars. I had my ears and nose tuned to the air, listening for footsteps, voices.

What I needed were a bunch of the guys from a police procedural TV show. Then I needed the world to act like the world in a police procedural TV show so that they could actually figure out what was going on by the scraps of clues lying around. They had to be lying around, right? A little piece of fabric that would light up under a UV light with a complete description of what was happening?

Didn't think so.

Anastasia ran her fingers along the wood post where the railing had broken off, studying the sabotage that had killed Dorian.

"Are you okay?" I said softly.

"Fine." She turned her attention to the clearing in front of the porch and walked away.

We went along the porch, searching for anomalies. Then, reluctantly, I moved off the porch, to the steps. Every third second I glanced to the trees, sure that something was watching us. Maybe it was the paranoia talking.

I stopped on the last step.

A stripe of gravel in front of the steps was different. I hadn't noticed it before because I hadn't been looking. The brain glosses over a thousand anomalies a day—someone had been fixing the wiring or the pipes, or putting in a sprinkler system, or making a repair. There were a hundred reasons why there'd be a stretch of off-color ground near a house like this. But now, when I looked on everything with suspicion—what was the reason? A mound of dirt, raised fractionally, as if something was buried.

Grant saw me staring and said, "I'll get a shovel."

Ariel shone the flashlight on the spot while we dug. We didn't have to dig deep, only a few inches. There, just under the surface, we found a steel rod sprouting a dozen spikes, maybe a couple inches each. Again, I could come up with a dozen reasons why something like this might be here: some arcane piece of construction left over from a remodeling job and accidentally buried, some unknown bit of landscaping. But digging out to either side, we found the rod was attached to a motor, and the motor protruded above ground, just a little, in a spot sheltered by the porch steps. There, a tiny antenna suggested some kind of radio transmitter or receiver.

Grant demonstrated: when the signal arrived, the motor would turn the rod, and the spikes would spring to vertical, emerging from the ground like some parking lot tire-killing defense barrier.

"Oh, my God," Ariel said, wincing.

The spikes were a razor-sharp steel and silver plate. If Lee, Jerome, or I had been standing here or passing over this spot when the signal came, the spikes would have launched, torn through our shoes, and cut our feet. Silver poisoning would do the rest. It would be slow and agonizing, as silver-poisoned blood climbed from the feet to the heart.

The trap was sneaky, clever, and cruel. Standing outside, my back suddenly felt exposed. There wasn't any kind of trip wire. It wasn't automatic, which meant someone had to be watching to know the right moment to spring the trap. Maybe our hunter was out there right now, watching us. Peering through the scope of some high-powered sniper rifle. With silver bullets. I took a deep breath but couldn't scent anything on the breeze, and the smells of the others around me were too strong. But he was out there.

Grant completely excavated the trap, found where the motors on each side were anchored to the ground with stakes, and dug them out. He shoved the whole thing under the porch, out of the way. My skin was still prickling with nerves.

When the crack came, I thought it was a tree branch breaking. I didn't make the connection, because it didn't sound like gunfire—it was too small, sharp, and focused. A silencer, I realized. But stuff like that only happened in the movies, right? I waited for the rip of pain that was sure to follow the gunshot.

Jeffrey caught Ariel as she fell. She dropped the flashlight.

"Inside! Now!" Grant hollered. I was already on the porch, opening the door and helping pull Ariel inside. We laid her down on the floor, and I slammed the door shut. The big picture window in front didn't have drapes. I wished I could draw drapes and shut out the world.

"What is it? What's going on?" Tina said.

"Oh, no," Jeffrey breathed.

Ariel wasn't moving. I dropped beside her, touched her forehead. Her eyes stared. "Ariel?"

I couldn't hear her heart, but her skin was still warm. She was just standing there a second ago—

Kneeling beside me, Grant felt her neck, then turned her face. He smoothed back the hair over her ear and pointed to the bullet hole. A tiny little thing, maybe the width of a pencil, with just a tiny trickle of blood leaking from it. But it went right through the middle of her brain.

I bent over until my face was next to hers and tried not to scream. I held her, pressed my forehead to hers, and clenched my hands. A howl was building in my throat, but if I let it go, I wouldn't stop. I'd have to shift. I'd have to go running, to find the person who did this and rip his throat out. And if I tried to do that in a fit of rage, I'd fail.

"Kitty," Grant said. I expected to feel a hand on my shoulder, a comforting touch, but I didn't, which was good. I'd snap at anyone who offered such a meaningless, stupid gesture.

I took a long, snuffling breath and realized I was crying. My head was going to explode. My hands were going to turn into claws. I wanted to know if the bullet was silver. I wanted to know if it had been meant for me. It should have been me.

Sitting back, I idly smoothed Ariel's hair. I hadn't gotten to know her well enough. She was too young and pretty for this. That scream built up again. Despairing, I looked at Grant.

His expression was long, mournful. I'd never seen him look so sad.

"We have to get whoever did this," I murmured. Grant nodded once.

Wolf was close to the surface. I felt myself walking around with a hooded gaze, my head low, watchful, my body stiff, my fingers curled. Not just Wolf, but Wolf on the hunt. A Wolf who wanted blood.

I tried to relax and take a deep breath, because I didn't want to shift right now. Because I had a feeling that was what the hunter expected me to do. Grant watched me; he'd seen this before, and he knew the signs.

I shook my head. "I'm okay." I wasn't, not really, but I wasn't going to shift. Not right now.

The others watched us: Gemma with her hand over her face, like she couldn't believe it; Tina looking away, holding Jeffrey's arm. Jeffrey facing us, but with his eyes closed. Lee, staring out the window, hands clenched by his sides.

"Get away from the window," Anastasia said, moving up to him, displacing him from the spot that gave whoever shot Ariel a perfect view. Lee curled his lips, a silent snarl. I wondered if he felt the same way I did. Or worse—his escape routes required open ocean. He had to be going crazy.

"Kitty, Lee," Anastasia said, urgent, with a commander's voice and not the urbane vampire voice I'd always heard from her. "I need your help. Leave out the back. I'll draw him out. Be ready."

"What?" Lee said. "What do you—"

But I knew. This plan was familiar, and I knew it without even hearing it. Lee didn't recognize it because he didn't hunt with a pack.

"Be ready," she said.

I took Lee's shoulder and guided him to the kitchen as

Anastasia left through the front door. I pulled Lee out the back door in the kitchen.

"What does she expect us to do?" he said harshly, the anger of helplessness showing through.

"We have the best noses," I whispered. I waited for the sound of a gunshot, for the sign that the sniper was still there and waiting for the next target—the bullet wouldn't have done anything to Anastasia. She'd walk right through it, but maybe the shooter didn't know that.

Who was I kidding? The arrow that killed Jerome was silver-tipped. The shooter knew what he was doing and wouldn't waste a bullet on the vampire. No, his bullets were most likely silver, and he'd save them for me and Lee. I wondered if Lee had figured that out.

I wasn't a vampire. My senses were not so fine that I could follow the path of a bullet, but I could tell when something didn't fit, when something was wrong. I could smell the gunpowder and sense that we'd been invaded. Anastasia was moving toward that wrongness; she needed our help.

"You flank left," I said. "I'll move ahead and flank right."

He must have figured it all out, because he nodded. We ran, jogging behind the lodge and toward the trees, arcing in opposite directions, keeping low and quiet. At every moment, I expected to hear a bullet whine toward me. Or a mine to explode under my feet. As a werewolf, I was tough and healed fast, but I didn't know what an explosion would do to me. It didn't matter, I understood what Anastasia was asking: she would flush the quarry, and then we would strike.

This was when Wolf could be an asset. I used her

senses to range much farther ahead and around me than I could see. I moved quietly and knew where all the shadows were to hide in. Quickly, I reached the trees, entering the woods, gaining as much ground as I could to be in position. A prickling in my neck made me pause and look back toward the lodge. I spotted the vampire. To Wolf's eyes, night wasn't dark. It was filled with nuance, shadow, moments of light, spots of movement. Anastasia wasn't moving, but she was incongruous, a poised figure in her tailored black clothes. Her face was pale, brilliant, like ivory. Her gaze focused on a spot. Something had been hidden before, but now she studied it, her chin tilted up slightly. Her figure was entrancing, beautiful; I could have just watched her. Instead, I looked to where she did, tried to find what had caught her attention. My nose flared, trying to detect it by scent. Finally, I saw it, well masked in the shadows: a man perched fifteen feet off the ground, on a branch of a pine with a view of the front porch a hundred yards away, where the picture window shone with light from the candles inside. Ariel had been backlit, a perfect shadow, a perfect target.

I couldn't scent him because he smelled richly of pine, maybe sap from rubbing against the branches as he'd been sitting there. The extra-straight branch near him was his rifle, which smelled of burned gunpowder.

He saw Anastasia. He was quickly loading something into the rifle—and what kind of special bullet would you use on a vampire? Could you make a bullet with holy water or garlic in it? No doubt someone had tried somewhere along the way. What was Anastasia doing? Just waiting there for him to load and fire?

But she was gone, suddenly as mist, moving almost

too quickly to see. Then she was climbing the tree—even though the lowest branches were a dozen feet up. Somehow, she must have found fingerholds in the bark. Or her hands were made of glue. Didn't matter. She would need help; this was the time. I loped around, putting myself on the far side of the tree. I caught a whiff of sea and salt—Lee. He crouched between the tree and the path. All escape routes covered.

The guy was moving but not panicking at Anastasia's rapid approach. He finished loading the gun, then stood, bracing himself against the trunk so he could look down on her, sighting along the barrel. Anastasia shifted, rotating along the trunk—I had no idea how. The sniper followed but had trouble; the branch he stood on got in the way.

I had to distract him. Anastasia had flushed him—time to overwhelm. Dropping to my knees, I grabbed a pinecone and threw. I didn't have great aim, but this just had to make noise. Get him to look somewhere else. But I did better than I thought—the pinecone struck the tree above his head, rained a few needles on him, made him look up, then out to where the projectile had come from. At me, in other words.

And Anastasia was standing on the branch in front of him, perfectly balanced on her high heels, hands on her hips, staring him down. She might have said, "Boo."

He fell—and his safety harness and line secured to the branch caught him. He'd probably used it to haul himself into the tree in the first place. Recovering quickly, he righted himself, planted his feet on the trunk, and used the rappelling gear to lower himself the rest of the way down. Man, this guy was *good*.

He unclipped from the line, started running—and this was my game, now. He was human, and whatever else I smelled, whatever confusion my senses were going through, I didn't doubt that he was a regular human with no other superpowers than what his fancy equipment gave him. Flat out, I could run faster than him.

I didn't run straight at him but parallel to him, flanking him. He spotted me—that was the idea. As I'd hoped, he veered away from me—toward Lee. He still held the rifle, which was worrying. But he didn't aim and fire, which made me think that whatever ammunition he'd switched into it wouldn't kill werewolves. A small bit of luck.

Then he switched the rifle to his left hand and drew a handgun from a belt holster. Shit.

Two instinctive reactions vied against each other: I could dodge, drop, hide out, and let him get away—some prey wasn't worth the effort; or I could charge him and maybe surprise him out of any meaningful action. In either case, I had to hope he didn't get a good shot off. The decision happened in half a second. This was the guy who killed Ariel, Jerome, and Dorian. I couldn't let him get away.

I charged.

Ignoring the repetitive chorus of *Holy crap, I'm gonna die* playing in my head, I ducked and wove, hoping to mess up his aim. I wasn't much watching, thinking only of tackling him before he could fire the gun. Like maybe he'd be so surprised he'd just stand there. He didn't. He kept running, too, gun in hand, raising his arm to shoot. But I ran faster.

Lee tackled him from behind.

Lee wasn't a runner, not like me. I had wolf in my

blood, and he had seal. But seals *are* master ambushers. He'd been waiting for the chance, and I slowed down the sniper enough to give him his opening. He knocked the sniper to the ground and held him there. They writhed, the gunman struggling to escape and Lee struggling to stay on top of him, digging his elbow into the man's back, pinning him with his legs. Lee's teeth were bared, and they may have been a little more pointy than normal.

I grabbed the rifle, threw it, and kicked the handgun away. The guy wasn't even screaming. Up close, I saw details: he wore black commando gear, close-fitting fatigues, utility belt, leather gloves, combat boots, even a full-face stocking cap, and black paint shaded the skin around his eyes. Hard-core.

"Let him up," Anastasia commanded. She stood before us, at the sniper's head, in perfect position to stomp one of her heels through his skull. Not a hair or fold of clothing ruffled, she didn't look like she'd been climbing trees.

Lee growled, a gruff noise between a bark and a sigh, and the vampire said, "Let go. I'll handle this."

Lee leaned away from the sniper, who jumped to his feet as soon as the pressure was off him. The guy was patting down pockets like he was searching for something he'd misplaced—the first sign of panic he'd shown. Maybe he had stakes or crosses stashed somewhere.

Anastasia didn't give him time. She grabbed his neck with a hand, fingers bent like claws, stepped around him like they were part of some strange tango. He clutched her arm and screamed, a noise of gruff, primal fear. From behind now, she wrapped her arm around his face and snapped. It all happened in a second. He crumpled in her arms.

I looked away. Lee was panting, crouched on the ground, head bent. His skin had taken on a sickly, grayish tone. Blood draining in fear—or near to shifting?

"Lee?" I murmured.

"I'm okay," he said, his voice rough. He pulled himself back from the edge. His breathing slowed, and his skin returned to its brown human tone.

Anastasia wasn't breathing at all. She knelt, the sniper still in her arms, holding his body close, his head cradled on her shoulder. I took a deep breath, collecting scents, gathering information. The sniper—he was still warm. He hadn't started cooling in death—because his heart was still beating. Anastasia had broken his neck without killing him. She'd known exactly what she was doing.

If I'd had the chance, I probably would have just beaten the guy's head in or ripped his throat out, depending on how far I was gone. Anastasia's calculating action left a chill in my gut. I didn't want to have to look in his eyes and see the knowledge of his impending death. I was a coward. I just wanted a normal life, and this was more proof that I wasn't cut out for a life so red in tooth and claw.

She was murmuring to him, in mocking seductive tones. "Hush there, darling. You played the game and lost. That's all. You'll be able to sleep soon enough, so relax."

The sniper's body was limp, still. But his eyes were wide, shining, unblinking. Terrified. I gagged on the lump in my throat.

Gently, careful to keep his head and neck still, to keep

him alive for the next few moments at least, she peeled off the knit mask, sliding it up his face, then letting it fall off the top of his head.

"Oh my God," I said, stepping back, hand over my mouth.

It was Ron Valenti. One of the producers of this horror show.

chapter **16**

He'd covered his clothing with pine sap to mask his scent. Until we were nearly under him, he didn't even smell like a person, much less one we knew. If I'd caught his scent moving back and forth earlier, it was because he'd been here all week.

Anastasia took the news without a reaction. She stroked his hair, crooning at him like he was a babe in arms.

Lee snarled, which almost sounded like the hiss and bark of an attacking seal. He started toward the prone figure, but Anastasia turned a sharp, commanding glance to him, and I dared to put a hand on his shoulder. His muscles were hard, like wood.

"So nice to see you again, Mr. Valenti," Anastasia murmured. "But I must say, Armani suits you better than this look." Her voice was honey and razors at the same time. A hundred clichés about vampires had their origin in a scene like this.

Valenti groaned, his pain and despair clear.

Anastasia shushed him again, low and purring. "I assume your friend Provost is part of this. Who else? Our dear Mr. Cabe? Was the entire company involved? Did you bring in other hunters? Sell tickets for the chance to bag the prize of a lifetime?"

Valenti's voice came out a whisper. I could barely hear it. He was struggling to breathe. "No . . . no . . . no one . . . else. No . . ." Tears leaked from his eyes.

"How many more are out here, Mr. Valenti? How many more are waiting to kill us?"

He tried to swallow. Failed, and a line of saliva spilled out of his mouth. He was dying. I could hear his heart fluttering with effort.

Every breath was a failed gasp. "Two . . . two . . ." He answered, because no one denied Anastasia.

"Do they have help from the inside? One of the residents? Odysseus Grant, perhaps?"

"Now wait a minute," I said, and the vampire threw me that look. I clenched my jaw.

Valenti actually chuckled, or tried to, but he wheezed, then choked, probably on spit pulled into his lungs. He coughed, which made the choking worse. Now he wasn't breathing at all. Terror pulled his whole face taut; his eyes gleamed.

"Shh, shh there." Anastasia touched his cheek, murmured comforts, but she couldn't stop the inevitable. She shifted his body, bent over his neck. Valenti was whining now, a high note of desperation. He had to know what was coming. He probably hadn't seen himself going this way.

Fangs bared, Anastasia bit into him.

I closed my eyes. Lee made a noise of denial and turned away. The light of the moon shone. Long, straight shadows of pine trees fell over us. The lodge, dark except for the candles and flashlights in the front room, hunched like the cottage in a fairy tale. And somewhere out there, two more just like Valenti were waiting to strike.

Valenti had stopped crying. Anastasia's quiet swallowing was the only sound. When vampires feed solely for sustenance, they don't need to kill their victims. A few swallows of blood sustain them, and the victim is none the worse for wear. Anastasia drained Valenti. It took a lot longer than drinking a few swallows.

When she dropped the body, I turned to look. *Now* he was dead, cooling quickly. His skin was white, ghostly. He wasn't just dead, but a husk. On the other hand, Anastasia glowed, flush and strong. She straightened, and behind closed lips her tongue ran over her teeth.

Lee said, "He's not going to come back, is he? He's not going to turn into . . . into one of you."

"No," she said, the repulsed look on her face telling exactly what she thought of that idea. She glanced at me, scowl still locked in place. I had been staring at her. I couldn't stop. I would never be able to turn my back to this woman again.

The air smelled sharply of blood; it hadn't before. I wanted to get away from the odor. "We should get inside," I said lamely.

"Help me with him," she said, pulling on the body's arm.

I paused, then said, "What?"

"His friends are out there, and we're not leaving him here for them to find. Kitty, get his weapons."

"But—" I stopped. What could I say? I wanted to get out of here so badly. My senses were on trip wires, turned out to the trees, the clearing in front of the lodge, the wide-open sky and silvery light of the thin, waning moon. Provost and Cabe were out there, probably armed just like Valenti.

Lee went to take charge of the other arm. Together, they hauled the body upright, its arms over their shoulders. The head flopped. I found the handgun, then the rifle, lying where I'd tossed them away, and followed them back to the lodge, looking over my shoulders for whoever else was out there.

They entered the front door, and I followed, closing and locking the door behind me, just as Tina screamed, a short burst of shock.

"Oh, my God," Jeffrey said at the same time.

Anastasia dropped the body in a heap, startling Lee into dropping his half, leaving it in a lopsided heap on the floor. Not very delicate.

There was a sound of retching—Conrad, it seemed, had rejoined the group just in time to see this presentation. He'd turned away, both hands covering his mouth.

"Is that—" Gemma started the question. Didn't have to finish.

"Now we know it's an inside job," Anastasia said, with false brightness. "Sorry I couldn't save you any, dear. You'll get the next."

"I think I've lost my appetite," Gemma said, grimacing.

Conrad had turned back around and looked as bloodless as the corpse. "Do you mean . . . does that mean . . . you didn't . . . oh, my *God!*" He stumbled away from Anastasia, even though he was already across the room from her. Couldn't say I blamed him, but it was still pathetic. Anastasia just rolled her eyes at him. She knelt and started patting down the body, searching all those pockets and pouches.

Odysseus Grant was the only one to regard the corpse without horror. Instead, he wore the pursed lips and creased brow of concentration.

"Can you shed any light on this?" Anastasia asked him, the pointed lilt to her voice even more pronounced.

He said, "Only that it confirms what we already suspected. Though I'm almost impressed. I had assumed they set this up on behalf of someone else. But it's all them."

Anastasia collected a pile of odds and ends from Valenti's person: a box of bullets, a rolled-up wire, a vial of clear liquid—Anastasia put this quickly away from her—and a walkie-talkie the size of a cell phone, turned off.

"Where's Ariel?" I said to Tina.

"We put her with Dorian."

I nodded. Wiped my eyes before the stinging got too bad.

"What do we do now?" Jeffrey said.

A horror movie was well under way, and I wanted it over and done with. But no end was in sight. They'd get us all if we didn't do something. Other than run screaming into the night, at least.

I regarded the group gathered around the crumpled body of Ron Valenti. "The show was a trap. That's clear. But they're not just hunting us to kill us. They could have just blown up the house, or fired at us all when we went outside. This is a game. A challenge. They're setting traps, a different one for each of us. I think they're going to draw this out, killing us one at a time, because they think we can't get away. And they think we won't fight back. But this is a war now. When the others figure out what happened to him, they'll hit us hard."

"So what are we going to do?" Tina said.

"I'm getting out of here," Conrad said. The look on his face was a bit—if I had to put a word to it—feral. Wide eyes, tight jaw, teeth nearly bared. Grant raised an inquiring brow. The rest of us were dumbstruck and silent. "I'm not putting up with this anymore. I'm out of here."

He grabbed a flashlight and headed for the door. I blocked him. "Are you crazy?"

He shook his head and smiled, but the expression was wild, trembling with terror. He was acting out of panic and desperation. Always a bad idea.

"No. Getting away from here is going to save me. You—you all are *monsters*. Those maniacs—they're hunting monsters. That's the whole point, isn't it? I shouldn't even be here. They won't go after me, don't you see? I'm just collateral damage. An accident. You all are the real targets. So the farther away from you I get, the better off I'll be."

I blocked the door with my arm, keeping him from reaching for the knob. "You want to talk about stories? You know what happens to the guy who runs out into the woods all by himself, don't you? We're safer together, Conrad."

His frown became a snarl. "Being together hasn't been safe so far, has it?"

"You don't know that they won't go after you, too. They've already proven they don't want witnesses," I said.

"I'll take my chances. Look, I've got my phone. I'll hike to someplace where there's a signal and call for help. Let me go." He raised the flashlight like he was going to use it as a weapon. Maybe he expected me to flinch back. To feel threatened by his panicked little body.

I didn't twitch a muscle. Stared him down like the monster I was. Between the two of us, I was the dominant one. I didn't even have to work for it. He cringed, and his eyes went wide, as if some primal part of his brain understood the exchange of body language. He understood that I wasn't going to let him past—but he didn't understand why he couldn't just barge through.

Anastasia touched my shoulder. I turned, drawing away from the door—and Conrad took his chance to swing it open and scramble out.

I called, "Hey—" But Anastasia held me back. And she was right—I really shouldn't go racing outside with snipers around. But Conrad was gone, into the wilderness, alone.

I turned on the vampire. "What—"

"We're better off not having to babysit him," she said.

"Well, that's damned cold."

Her lip curled. "You pack animals, always trying to take care of the children."

"Fuck you."

She turned on me, dark eyes shining, lips in a thin frown. This time, I had to work to keep my spine straight and not look away.

"We need information," Grant said, a calculated interruption.

"Too bad our only lead is dead," Lee said, nodding at the corpse.

Grant regarded the body a moment and seemed to come to a decision. "I need space. Move these chairs out of the way. Tina, there's a bag in my room. Like a briefcase, black, locked. Can you bring it to me? Don't look in it, just bring it."

She seemed like she was going to argue. Lips pursed, she hesitated. But Grant didn't acknowledge her and wasn't open to argument. She went upstairs. By the time she returned with the bag, we'd pushed back the chairs and coffee table, giving us a large space in the living room.

"Anastasia, help me with him." He went to Valenti's head and directed the vampire to his feet. Amazingly, she didn't argue but did as he asked. They arranged Valenti on the hardwood floor in the center of the space. Anastasia quickly backed out of the way.

"Grant, what are you doing?" I said.

"Just watch. Tina, Jeffrey, stay right there, inside the circle. Tell me everything you sense, everything you hear." He took the bag from Tina, and she seemed all too happy to get rid of it—she'd been holding it by her fingertips.

Pausing a moment, Grant looked at each of us in turn. "Don't say anything. No screams, no words, nothing. You won't like this. But we need information."

"What—" Tina started, but Grant silenced her with a single shake of his head.

"Do you have a better idea? Is his spirit forthcoming enough to talk to either one of you?" They shook their heads. Tina inched closer to Jeffrey and took hold of his hand. They stood shoulder to shoulder.

Grant got to work.

He pulled out a red votive candle, set it by Valenti's head, and lit it, bathing the body in gold light, giving it a false semblance of life. The dead eyes stared. Next he took a piece of chalk from the bag and drew a circle, starting at Valenti's head and moving clockwise. The chalk circle encompassed the body and about five feet all around it. He enclosed Jeffrey and Tina within the circle, as well.

Next he sprinkled some powder over the candle, and a sharp smell, burning sage, drifted out. My nose itched, and I sneezed. I tried to hold it back. But it didn't seem to interrupt the proceedings.

Chalk in hand, Grant drew symbols—at the body's head, feet, left and right hands. This was ceremonial magic. I knew the signs, had seen similar rituals—a circle often meant protection or a barrier. Symbols, light, incense. I had a very bad feeling about this. I was standing at the wall; I couldn't back up any farther.

The last item Grant drew from his bag was a round mirror. This he set on the floor by the candle. Light from the candle reflected off it, a spot of brightness.

Grant knelt by Valenti's head and said, "Ronald Valenti. I need to speak with you." A few moments passed, a few quickly thudding heartbeats. "Valenti. Hear me. You've been a very bad man, but here's your chance to do something right. Speak to me, Ronald Valenti."

Grant was right. I didn't like this. But I didn't interrupt. The mirror fogged over. The light dimmed.

"Tell me what I need to know," Grant said in a whisper.

The body's eyes blinked.

Jeffrey drew a sharp breath. "It's back. His aura's back," he whispered.

"What color?" Grant said.

"Dark. Muddy."

"Ronald Valenti," Grant hissed at the body. "Who else is working with you? Where are they? What is your plan? Show me in the mirror." The magician looked at the fogged mirror. I couldn't tell what he saw in it, if anything.

The body blinked but otherwise didn't move at all. If it had started speaking, I probably would have run. Grant must have seen something, because he studied the mirror, jaw set.

Then his gaze shifted back to the body. "Just one more thing. Why? Why do this?"

Again, I couldn't see what the mirror showed, but Grant seemed to be fascinated by what he saw in it.

Grant didn't ask anything else. When he was satisfied, he put his hand over the corpse's face, closing the eyes. "Ronald Valenti, I'm finished with you. Rest now. Depart this place. Finish your journey onward. And may you rot in a fitting hell."

A breath sighed through the room, as if a window had blown open, and the candle went out, all on its own. Tina gasped—she and Jeffrey were holding each other tightly now.

"It's gone now," Jeffrey said. "He's dark again."

Grant pulled a white handkerchief from his pocket, wiped away the symbols he'd drawn, and scrubbed the chalk circle until it was a blurred, formless mess. The mirror was bright and clear.

"I'm done with it," he said, nodding at the body. "We should put it with the others."

Or drop it in the lake. But that would feel like poisoning the lake.

"I think I need to take a shower," Tina said.

Nobody moved except Grant, who was packing items back in his case. The magician finishing his work. And I didn't know why anything Grant did surprised me anymore.

"That was sick," Lee said, harsh, frowning.

Grant stood, glared. "What that man did to Ariel, Jerome, Dorian, and the production assistants was sick. He and the others did what they did for sport. I do it out of necessity. And I don't do it lightly."

Cormac would have understood. Cormac would have approved, so I couldn't argue.

Grant paused in front of me. I'd been staring at the body, and I turned to him reluctantly. "You look like you want to say something."

I shook my head. "I don't have anything to say."

His expression didn't change. It hardly ever did. But he put his hand on my shoulder, a brief touch, a faint comfort.

Anastasia was the one to finally ask, "What did you learn?"

"They're still filming us," he said. "They're planning on selling the footage as proof that monsters can be killed. That they ought to be killed."

"A snuff film?" I said, astounded.

Grant nodded. "Provost and Cabe are his partners. They're out there now. I saw two bases of operation, one near the lodge and one near the outgoing trail. They attacked Jerome and Kitty from that one. They have us trapped, and they have all the time in the world."

"Then we go after them," Lee said. "We know where they are now, we go get them, then get the hell out of here."

"They have weapons," Anastasia said. "They're entrenched. We're too vulnerable. That's exactly how they planned it."

"So we flush them out," I said, because that was what Cormac would say and how he'd have handled this. He sure as hell wouldn't sit here waiting for the bad guys to come to us. Get the upper hand. Startle them.

"How do we do that?" Lee said, anxious, frustrated. Sweat shone on his brow, and the ocean smell of him was stronger.

I picked up the walkie-talkie from the pile of Valenti's leavings, switched it on, and pressed talk. Everyone in the room cringed or lurched, making various noises of protest—what the hell was I doing?

Poking the wasp nest. I was good at that sort of thing.

"Hell-lo-ooooo," I said, singsong, into the speaker. Moving to the front door, I cracked it, turning my car to the great outdoors to hear what I could. I let my finger off the button and waited, listening through the static hiss for something more meaningful. And waited. My heart was thumping hard, but I didn't let on. I was in the middle of a practical joke, and I was determined to find this little piece of it funny. I grinned while the others watched, horrified. Except for Grant, who smiled, just a little.

Then the static clicked and shifted, and words came through. "Hello? Valenti?"

And that was Joey Provost's voice, with the show business veneer rubbed off. What was left was backstabbing manipulator. Such a fine line between the two. I didn't hear anything outside; he wasn't close, which was something.

"'Fraid not. It's Kitty Norville. Thanks for calling *The Midnight Hour*. Do you have a problem you'd like to talk about?"

I waited through another few moments of poignant static before hearing, "Where's Valenti?"

"Ooh, that's a really tough question. How religiously inclined are you?"

"Bitch," he hissed.

"I love it when people call me that, it's so meta. Just tell me one thing—what made you think you could get away with this? Get away with *murder?*"

He didn't answer. I waited, listening through static for a long time. For all I knew, he'd shut his device off. I'd hoped Provost would be stupider than that. I'd hoped he'd have to talk, then give something away, like an undefended location. I threw the walkie-talkie down. Which Cormac probably wouldn't have done.

"Consider them flushed," I said.

"Then we have the offensive, at least for a little while," Anastasia said. "What do you think they'll do?"

I took a deep breath. Took a flyer. "I think they'll come here. They'll want to find out what happened to Valenti, and then they'll want to take us down fast. They may not bother with the horror show anymore."

"Agreed," Grant said. "Then we should move fast. Get out there and find their hunting blinds. Clear them out, leave them without equipment. Then we go back to our original plan to get out and call the police."

"It'll be dawn soon," Gemma said. She sounded small, like a scared kid. Did Valenti and his crew even think of her as a kid? Or just as a monster?

Anastasia said, "We have a few hours. We'll be fine, Gemma." An unspoken *trust me* finished the sentence. Gemma pretty much had to trust her, didn't she?

"Lee, you're a hunter. You can use this?" Grant handed him Valenti's sniper rifle. He took it, and he smiled a little. A fire lit his eyes.

"Did your voodoo magic show tell you where these blinds are?" I said to Grant. "*Exactly* where?"

He didn't answer right away, but Tina said, "I saw them. We both did." Jeffrey nodded.

Grant's lips thinned to a line. "I was hoping you had."

We broke into teams. Lee, Tina, and I would go after the blind by the outgoing trail. Tina would help guide us, based on the images Grant had produced. After destroying what we could of the blind and the weapons we assumed we'd find there, we'd continue on to get help. If we encountered more silver-tainted barriers, like the razor wire, Tina could help clear the way. If need be, I could run ahead while Tina and Lee waited. Jeffrey, Anastasia, and Gemma would look for the blind closer to the lodge. Anastasia took the handgun so both parties went armed. Originally, Grant wanted Gemma to stay inside. She refused, wanting to stay with Anastasia. So Grant would wait at the lodge in case the remaining hunters came back.

"Are you sure you'll be okay by yourself?" I asked him. It was a stupid question. Of course Grant could take care of himself.

"I'll be fine," he said.

Were there really only seven of us left? Maybe Conrad had gotten away okay. Maybe he'd found help.

We stood on the porch, getting ready to head out. I felt the need to add instructions. "Remember, we're not going after Cabe and Provost. We're going after their *stuff*. It's probably best if we avoid them entirely."

"But, you know, if you get a shot off," Lee said.

"Kitty's right," Grant said. "Don't take stupid chances. And there are probably still traps out there. Be careful."

Words of the day, really.

chapter 17

Tina walked close behind me, within arm's reach, because she didn't have good night vision and needed me to guide her. Lee walked a few paces to my right, carrying the sniper rifle in both hands, like a character out of a Vietnam War movie.

I concentrated on listening, smelling—spotting anything out of the ordinary. A place in the shadows with the wrong colors or an odor that didn't belong. So far, nothing. But I remembered the pine pitch Valenti had used to mask his scent. Any minute now, I'd hear the hiss of silver-tipped arrows flying.

We'd traveled maybe two miles from the lodge, but it had taken an hour, since we'd moved so carefully, soundlessly, and full of paranoia. I kept glancing at Tina, hoping for some sign that she knew where the site was, that she was leading us somewhere. And for part of the time she did look like she was searching, stopping and studying the landscape, as if trying to recognize a landmark. Mostly, though, she looked scared, her face tight, brow furrowed.

Even if we didn't find the hunters' shelter, that would be okay. If all we did was hike within cell phone range and call the cavalry, I'd be fine with that.

After another half hour of cautious walking, Tina put a hand on my arm.

"We're looking for a tent," she said. "Camouflaged, under a pair of trees. I think it's near here. This looks familiar."

We all looked outward, scanning the trees. I took in a long, slow breath—and smelled canvas.

I couldn't see it until we were almost standing next to it. Just like Tina had said, it was a low tent slung between trees, a darker shadow standing out against a natural backdrop. We waited outside it a long time, like we expected it to come to life and swallow us. Lee aimed the rifle.

"I don't hear anything," Lee said. "Do you?"

I didn't, and I couldn't smell anything living inside. I supposed it was time to get a closer look at what we were up against.

The tent was little more than a tarp slung over a rope tied between the trees and staked out to form walls. It was draped with camo netting, like a hunting blind. Lee pushed back the flap with the end of his rifle—the Vietnam War movie again. My heart raced, waiting for the screaming guy with the grenade to jump out. But nothing happened.

Inside was just enough room for a low camp cot and a small, collapsible metal table. Next to the cot was a steel cage, square, just big enough to hold a person. I didn't want to know what they planned to do with that. Under the table sat metal crates—ammo boxes and the like. On top of the table were a camp stove, a bottle of water, some packets of freeze-dried food, and a tiny portable TV showing a black-and-white image of the trail leading away from the lodge. I wondered how many other cameras were out there. They couldn't have had one in the lodge's interior, or they'd have known what had happened to Valenti. So they weren't omniscient. That was something.

Leaning against the ammunition cases was a crossbow, sleek steel and black, modern and dangerous, and a cylindrical container of bolts to go with it. Silver tips. This was the weapon that had killed Jerome.

Suddenly, I wanted to break something.

"What do we do now?" Lee said.

I didn't know. This was so big, so organized. I was just trying to live my life and do my thing, and suddenly I was furious that I kept getting interrupted by crap like this. I didn't just want to howl, I wanted to roar. The sound an animal made when it went rabid.

I took a deep breath and tried to push that feeling away.

Concentrating on calm and not on the knot in my gut, I said, "We need to get rid of this stuff so no one can use it anymore."

Tina shook her head. "I think we need to get out of here."

"What's wrong?" I said.

Lee said, "It's just nerves. This is what we came here to do."

"No. Nobody move," she said.

We all stood still. I held my breath, listening, waiting. A breeze shifted the trees outside, and the tent's canvas rippled. I tried not to jump. We were the hunters now, had to stay calm. Just keep telling myself that.

After a moment, she nodded toward a space at the edge of the table. "There," she said. "On the table, a trip wire."

"What?" Lee said. "I don't see anything."

He started toward the table when she said, "Don't! Don't move, don't touch anything."

Focusing, I could see it: a thin, clear filament, like a fishing line, running from the table to the ground. I pointed. "There. You see it?"

"If we move the table, something goes boom," Lee said.

I sighed. "I say we back up out of here the way we came and forget about plan A."

"Agreed," Tina breathed.

She backed up and out the tent entrance. I followed, stepping carefully, searching all around me for the least little anomaly that might be a booby trap. Lee followed on the same path. He paused at the entrance for one last look around inside.

Something exploded. A whoosh of red fire, then a *whoomp,* like the air sucking out of a room. I grabbed Tina and fell to the ground, sheltering her. She screamed.

I didn't see what caused it—I'd never learn exactly what Lee triggered, whether he tripped a line that Tina and I had missed or stepped on a pressure plate. Maybe the explosion had been on a timer. Maybe it would have gone off no matter what we'd done, and it was undoubtedly meant to catch all of us in the blast.

A searing, angry heat washed over us. Tina curled up, sheltering her head, and I did the same as debris rained. Ashes and burning filled my nose, and I choked back a howl. *Time to run,* Wolf said. This was dangerous, we had to get away.

No. Not without Tina. She was dead out here by herself.

I whined, shook, hugged myself to keep fur from sprouting, and finally looked up. Little fires had broken out around us, on the forest floor and in trees, but none of them seemed serious. Tongues of dancing flame flickered in a regular circle around what used to be the tent, now lying in burned, shredded pieces. Other debris remained: the charred stump of a table, flipped over and flung a dozen yards away; a mangled cot; the ammunition cases—made of metal, whatever explosives were inside them hadn't ignited—and other unidentifiable debris. And Lee.

He'd been thrown from what had been the entrance of the tent and lay sprawled, twisted into an inhuman shape. His clothes had burned away, along with his skin and hair. All of him was charred. He still had the rifle in his burned hands. He smelled cooked. I covered my face and gagged.

Tina clung to my arm with both hands. "Lycanthropes are tough—they can survive just about anything, right?" she said.

We could survive a lot of things, but not everything. If we were decapitated, if our hearts were destroyed, if the damage was too great—I didn't know all the limits of what we could survive. But I didn't think a lycanthrope could survive this.

I crept forward because I had to see. Heat rolled off the whole area, baking the air, making me itch. I tried to keep from smelling it and kept my gaze on Lee. He didn't move. When I got close enough, I could see he didn't have a face anymore. Nothing but a black crust. He wasn't breathing. I couldn't hear his heart. I waited for five minutes, to be sure. When I touched his neck, the skin broke, still hot, still smoking. I didn't feel a pulse. Too much damage, too much shock, with no chance to heal. So, high explosives could also kill a werewolf.

I hurried back to Tina, grabbed her, and kept moving. I didn't have to urge her along to keep up.

"What do we do now?" Her voice was stiff—forced calm.

"Keep going," I said. "We have to call someone. We have to get help."

"I don't know how long I can keep running."

"We don't have to run. We just have to keep moving." That explosion had probably been heard all over the valley. The hunters knew their trap had been sprung. They might come back to assess the damage. We had to move.

I wondered what the others would think had happened. But I couldn't worry about that. I hoped they wouldn't decide to come look.

A hundred yards farther on, we came close enough to the trail to hear shouting.

"Help! Help me! Oh, God, please!" The voice was rough, as if it had been screaming for a while. No tears, no sobbing, but the despair was plain. We stopped, listened.

"That's Conrad," I said.

The scent of blood on the air hit me. Part of me wanted to leave him, just pass on by and keep going—he wasn't one of us. This was probably another trap, with Conrad as bait, and we'd be better off moving on. But we didn't.

"No, go slow," Tina hissed, after I'd started to race forward. We crept forward more cautiously. I looked around, up into the trees, searching for the merest glint or hint of movement. Wondering where the next bullet was going to come from. And bombs, those guys were using *bombs*.

Tina clenched my arm and pointed ahead to a dark spot on the trail. A sinkhole, with debris scattered around the edges. Conrad clutched one side with an arm, bracing, trying to scramble out but unable to gain the leverage.

"Conrad?" I said, in as loud a whisper as I could manage.

"Kitty? Oh, my God, help me! Help!"

Tina and I rushed to the edge of the sinkhole and looked in. The bottom was lined with spears, a dozen rigid poles sticking straight up, tipped with shining metal—silver. A tiger trap. Conrad had sprung the trap and fallen in, and one of the spikes had impaled his leg through the calf, from ankle to knee. Blood dripped down the length of the spear.

He'd managed to keep himself from falling in and impaling himself on more sharp points. But he was clinging and unable to pull himself off the spear that did get him.

"Oh, shit," Tina murmured.

Yeah. That about covered it. Maybe because we couldn't save Lee, we worked hard to save Conrad.

I grabbed Conrad's arms, gave him an anchor, kept him from sliding in farther. He was pale, covered in sweat, his clothes soaking with it, and shivering, no doubt on the edge of shock. Tina lay flat, as far over the edge as she could and still keep her balance, which let her stretch just far enough forward to reach the spear that pinned Conrad. She grabbed it, maybe thinking to pull it out of its hole. Her hands slipped on the blood. She tried again, working to be careful, but she couldn't help but jerk it when she did. Every time, Conrad groaned, gritting his teeth, trying to keep from crying out. His fingers dug into me.

"I think it's set in concrete," Tina said. "I can't budge it."

Concrete? Overkill a little? Like I even had to ask at this point. I pursed my lips, bracing for the next few difficult minutes. I renewed my grip on Conrad, to make sure he knew I was there. He didn't seem quite aware.

"Conrad? We're going to have to slide your leg off." I had no idea if that was the right thing to do medically. We didn't really have a choice.

"Oh, God," he moaned. He was past thought, wrapped only in pain and fear.

"I need you to hold on," I said, making eye contact with Tina, trying to urge her to work quickly. She'd gone almost as pale as Conrad, but her expression was set, determined. She didn't hesitate but shifted her reach to Conrad's leg.

Now we had to lift at the same time.

I got a grip under Conrad's shoulders and pulled. He screamed. Would it be gauche of me to knock him unconscious to shut him up?

"They're going to find us," Tina muttered. "Between the bomb and his screaming, they'll find us." She lay stretched out beside me, clutching the fabric of his pants and guiding the limb off its skewer.

"As soon as he's up, we'll run," I said, gritting my teeth. At least, we'd run as well as we could. Conrad's grip was starting to hurt, but at least he wasn't thrashing. I thought he might thrash with panic, but maybe he was going limp from blood loss.

"Got it!" Tina called finally, and I fell back with my

final effort, Conrad secure in my arms. He was breathing fast, hyperventilating.

"Conrad, hush, breathe slow. Slower." I spoke softly, calmly, even though my own heart was racing in my ears, my hair standing on end, my own panic about to burst. This was just like talking down a panicking werewolf. I could handle this.

Tina pulled out a jackknife, cut away the lower half of his pants, and made two bandages of it, tying them tight around the entry and exit wounds.

"Conrad, can you stand?"

He was still gasping for breath, gulping for air. "I don't know, I don't know."

Tina and I didn't have to talk. She took one of his arms over her shoulder, I took the other, and we hauled him. He let out a yelp, and I hissed at him to shut up. Not that it mattered at this point.

"Where?" Tina asked.

I nodded toward the lake. So far, all the traps had been around the lodge and the trails leading to it. If we went somewhere else, yet stuck to the edge of the forest, we might find a safe place to hunker down. If we did, I'd leave these two there and go for help.

My night vision was good enough to lead the way. Moving among the trees, we put distance between us and the tiger trap. Conrad managed to pull himself together, keeping himself upright on one leg, hopping painfully on the other. That only meant we weren't dragging his feet behind us anymore. With every breath he whimpered, but he was obviously trying to keep quiet.

Ahead, a clearing opened up, a brighter space of open

sky and moonlight shining down. The pewter gray surface of the lake shone, maybe a dozen yards away.

"Let's rest for a minute," I whispered, coming to a stop by the trunk of a wide old pine tree. Tina and Conrad slumped against it beside me, and we lowered him to the ground. He pulled his legs close, hugging the injured one, rocking. The whimpers sounded deep in his chest, suppressed.

I squeezed his shoulder. "Conrad? Conrad? How are you?" *Really* stupid question. I didn't know how else to pull him out of himself. I needed him lucid.

He pushed himself up so he was almost sitting. He was shaking. Tina braced him, and he managed to stay upright.

"I'm sorry," he said, panting. "I'm sorry, I'm so sorry."

He'd entered the raving stage. Now we had to dodge the hunters *and* get an incapacitated man to safety.

Tina was crying. I hadn't even noticed, but tears streaked her face. She hadn't made a sound. Stress, or her own brand of panic, I didn't know what. I touched her hand.

"He thinks he's dying," she said. "He's praying."

I slouched against the tree, one hand on Tina's arm, the other on Conrad's shoulder. I looked through the last of the forest to the lake, so calm and beautiful in the crisp night air. Silver lined everything.

What had Anastasia said? Werewolves were pack animals. We were always banding together to fight, to take care of each other. I felt that now. We'd banded together, and now I felt like it was up to me to take care of these two. I didn't have a clue how to do that.

Part of me wanted to wait here for someone to find

us, to rescue us, but we couldn't do that, because Provost would likely find us first. We were dead just sitting here. That was what Cormac would say: keep moving.

The smell of blood from Conrad's wound was overpowering. This sent a blaze of warning to the Wolf side— that much blood was like a beacon to predators saying we were hurt, vulnerable, easy pickings—

But human hunters wouldn't be able to smell it. We had a little time. Settle down.

I'd brought my cell phone but still didn't get reception. Probably another ten to twenty miles before we'd get close. We couldn't haul Conrad that far, and if we didn't get him stationary and hydrated, he'd die of blood loss before that. The lodge was maybe three miles away. We could defend ourselves better there than we could in the open.

"We have to go back," I said.

Conrad looked up, focused a moment. So he was lucid and paying attention. Good. "Do we have to?"

"We can't stay in the open," I said.

"We're safer with the others," Tina said. Conrad nodded. Maybe he was ready to be a team player. "Should we try to wash his leg off in the lake?"

I shook my head. "Stuff's not clean enough. We'll use bottled water at the lodge." Be optimistic—we'd get back just fine. "Conrad, you ready?"

He made a sound, half sob, half chuckle. "No. But that's okay."

"That's the spirit," I said. Tina and I gathered ourselves, hoisted Conrad over our shoulders, and set off.

We made more noise than I was comfortable with, pushing around shrubs, shuffling through debris on the forest floor. Conrad couldn't stay quiet, and I couldn't force him to. He was doing well, considering. I tried to turn my hearing outward, searching for sounds and smells of approaching danger, and couldn't sense anything. I couldn't let it get to me. Just had to press forward. We'd take a break outside the lodge; I'd scout for Cabe and Provost and get in touch with the others.

Progress was slow. It would take us a couple of hours at least. We had to keep stopping to rearrange our grip on Conrad, to let him rest. Tina and I were both dripping sweat, despite the cool air. We had only just reached the edge of the lake when the hairs on my neck started prickling. Like fur, like hackles rising. The undeniable sense of being followed. Of walking into danger.

I pulled the others to a stop and waved her to silence when Tina started to speak. Conrad's head lolled; he'd been drifting in and out of consciousness. I propped them both against a tree and took a few steps away, to get a taste of air that didn't have so much blood, sweat, and fear in it.

A hint of breeze gave me a scent that bowled me over. I crouched, nose up, taking it in, trying to figure out what it meant. This was *wild*. Musk wild, without a hint of human to it. Wolf whined; my hands clenched.

The smell of blood *had* attracted predators.

A wolf stepped out of the trees in front of me. Tail stiff, head down, amber eyes glaring. Earthen gray and brown fur, standing on end. Lip curled, showing teeth.

And all I could think was, he looked so *small*. Because he wasn't a lycanthrope.

I knelt, face-to-face with a natural, wild wolf.

chapter 18

Montana had wild wolves. I knew that. I just hadn't *thought* about it. I hadn't thought that I would ever encounter one.

Make that five. Four more came into view, another one ahead, the others to each side of me. Two females, two more males. I could smell them, the differences—I recognized the scents, even though it seemed so *wrong*. They were various shades of brown and gray, pale on their bellies, tails tipped with black. They smelled like a pack. Like a family. But not mine.

I had never seen wolves in the wild before. I hadn't even seen one in a zoo since I'd become a lycanthrope. Zoo smells of musk and far too many creatures crammed into too small a space were more than my sensitive nose could handle. Kind of like this. So wild, and so alien. I almost howled for real, because I could feel the need to Change, Wolf writhing within me. Face wolves as a wolf, it was the only way. But I breathed slow, hugged myself, pulled the need inside.

"Kitty," Tina whispered. She'd spotted them, too.

I held my hand out, stopping her. "You two, stay up. Stay standing, stay tall, tall as you can."

Real, wild wolves. They seemed agitated—and who could blame them, with the recent explosion and all sorts of crazies tromping through their territory. They were looking at me. Circling me, studying me. I could read it—the body language was the same. The wary stance, hackles straight up, this waiting to see what I would do. The readiness to defend themselves. They weren't sure if we were prey or something else. They waited for me to reply.

My eyes were wide, my heart racing—I felt like prey, and they were sizing me up. But I didn't know what to do.

Yes, you do, the lupine voice within me whispered. Look away, don't stare at them, lower your head, slouch. Tell them you aren't a threat. On all fours now, I did that. Turned my shoulder to them. Held my back as if I had a lowered tail. Kept my gaze down. I whispered to Tina, "Don't look at them. Look down."

To a predator, a stare was a challenge. I didn't stare. I couldn't see what Tina was doing. Not panicking, I hoped.

I put myself between Tina, Conrad, and the wolves. They'd smelled blood—injured prey. They were just following instincts. They'd try to get around Tina and me and get to Conrad. If we were deer, that was what they'd do. I let Wolf seep into my being, as much as I could without shifting, until the world wavered to gray wolf-sight, and I smelled my own fur. Maybe they would smell it, too, and not think us so different than them. With every hair of Wolf's being, I tried to tell them, *We don't want trouble, we're not invading. Just passing through. But you can't have the sick one, he's ours, our pack. Mine. Let us pass. No trouble here.*

We were invaders. They'd have every right to attack. But maybe this was just odd enough that they'd pass us by.

The larger male, the one I'd first seen, stood front and center, watching me. The others had broken their stances, were padding back and forth, noses to ground, tails out like rudders. Waiting for the alpha male's signal. The leader stayed still. One of the females sidled up to him, bumped him, licked his chin. I could almost hear her saying to him, *This is too strange, not worth the trouble, let's leave.*

His mate. An old married couple working it out. God, I wanted to see Ben so badly.

I met the big male's gaze once, then lowered my face again. If that didn't offer him peace and ask him for safe passage, nothing would. He wasn't moving, and I knew what that meant.

"We have to leave," I said, slowly rising to my feet and joining the others. "He won't turn his back on us, so we need to be the ones to move."

"But what if they come after us?" Tina's voice was taut; she was right on the edge.

"They won't," I said.

"You can't actually talk to them, can you?"

I sort of could. I let her draw her own conclusion.

With Conrad over our shoulders again, we moved off, as quickly as we could, into the trees and back toward the lodge. I glanced over my shoulder once; the wolves were watching us, the male in the center of them all. But he was sitting now, his fur flat, relaxed almost. Not getting ready to run and launch an attack. One of them flopped to her side and started licking a paw. They weren't going to come after us. But this was definitely their space.

My nerves were tingling. Tina kept asking questions— "What was that? What the hell happened there?"—and I couldn't answer. I couldn't talk.

"Kitty!" she finally said, almost a shriek, and I looked at her. Her eyes widened in fear. I don't know what face I showed her, but it probably wasn't quite human. Something wolfish glared in my eyes.

I closed my eyes, shook my head, breathed slow. Told Wolf to settle.

We're in danger.

I know.

Must flee.

It's not that simple.

We kept moving.

chapter 19

We rested three more times. Conrad had fallen unconscious by the time we reached the clearing in front of the lodge. There, we stopped again. The house and everything around it looked quiet. I wanted to know what was going on before we moved any closer.

The shadows had changed, growing more washed-out, more surreal. The sky had paled—close to sunrise. Dawn had sneaked up on me. When was the last time I'd slept? After I'd shifted yesterday? I couldn't remember how long ago that had been. The gray predawn sky didn't improve the hazy fuzz I seemed to be moving through.

"I'm going to go to the house to find Grant," I said, leaving Tina and Conrad sitting at the edge of the clearing in front of the lodge. Not much cover here. I moved along the edge, slow and watchful, taking deep breaths. Nothing smelled out of the ordinary. I didn't dare call out to Grant, in case an enemy was close by and listening.

I felt like I had a target painted on my forehead. I scratched it, then felt like an idiot for doing so.

I'd reached the porch railing when Grant cracked the door and stepped outside. He'd been keeping watch.

"Kitty."

I didn't know where to start. "We've got Conrad. He's hurt, badly."

"I heard what sounded like an explosion—did you find the blind?"

I swallowed, a gulp of air, of courage. "We did. It was booby-trapped. We lost Lee."

He nodded and followed me out to where Tina waited with Conrad. The three of us brought him inside and lay him on one of the sofas. Tina and I collapsed. Grant handed us bottles of water, then looked at Conrad's wounds.

The big picture window in the living room was growing light enough to see by. I sat up.

"Where are Anastasia and Gemma? It's almost daylight."

"They're not back yet," Grant said.

Shit. "Should we go look for them? Have you gotten any word back from them?"

Now Tina was sitting up, frowning, worried. "Jeffrey—"

I scrambled up, no longer bone tired. An adrenaline-fueled second wind pushed me. "We have to go look for them."

Nodding at Conrad, Grant said, "Tina, can you look after him?"

"I want to go, I want to help find him—"

"Someone has to stay here," Grant said. "If we lose the lodge to the hunters, we've lost everything."

She nodded and sat, clasping her hands. Her hair was limp, in need of a wash, pushed behind her ears. Her shirt and jeans were streaked with dirt and blood—Conrad's blood was all over both of us. Dark circles shadowed her eyes. I wondered if I looked that wrung out.

"We'll find him," I said, trying to sound hopeful. Had to stay hopeful.

Grant and I went outside. At the edge of the porch, I tipped my nose up and tested the air. I smelled the forest, the outdoors, like I always did, but I wanted to smell people. Vampires. Their cold, undead blood should have stood out among all this life.

"Find anything?" Grant asked me.

"Not yet." I stepped forward, all my senses firing.

I heard running. Not caring about stealth, someone crashed through the trees toward us.

"Someone's coming. Jeffrey," I said as he broke out of the trees and joined us in the clearing.

"Thank God," he said, gasping to catch his breath. He was sweat soaked. No telling how long he'd been running. "They've trapped Gemma, we need you."

Jeffrey led us back the way he'd come, about a mile through the woods around the lodge, to the edge of the meadow. He explained on the way, as well as he could around the hard breathing. We were all running on adrenaline by this point.

"We found the blind, a camouflaged tent full of equipment and weapons. We broke up as much of it as we could, scattered the ammunition, hid the weapons in the underbrush. There were silver bullets, silver arrows, stakes, crosses, bottles of what we think were holy water. And a cage. No sign of Cabe or Provost.

"We were on our way back to the lodge when something—it was like an explosion. Too loud for a gun-shot. It—it was a harpoon. I can't think of how else to describe it. It was automated. Anastasia said there wasn't anybody around, she would have sensed them if they were. But it got Gemma. It was a harpoon on a line and it dragged her into this . . . this cage." He was half jogging, half limping now, holding his side. His face twisted in pain. He'd better not have a heart attack on us.

He said, "They could have just staked her, but they didn't. They waited, and they triggered this . . . this thing. This trap."

We arrived and saw what he meant. Gemma was trapped in a cage, just tall enough to stand up in, just wide enough to grip both sides with her hands. Sheltered out of sight by a tree, it was portable, maybe set here only in the last day or so the way the grass under it was recently crushed. Steel and heavy, it would hold lions. A winch welded to the back had reeled in Gemma, who struggled against a harpoon sticking out of her right shoulder. The whole thing could have been automated, set on a trigger, operated by remote—we'd seen that the hunters had cam-eras and monitors set up. They could have moved their base since Grant interrogated Valenti. But as Jeffrey had said, they could have staked her just as easily as trapping her with harmless—to her—steel. This trap had a differ-ent purpose.

The cage was at the edge of the open meadow, and sunrise had begun. A band of full sunlight crept toward us across the grass.

Anastasia was talking Gemma down. Gemma herself

gritted her teeth and threw herself against the barbed spike in her shoulder.

"Gemma, darling, stay calm. Don't struggle. Don't thrash."

The younger vampire closed her eyes and settled, nodding in agreement.

Anastasia reached through the cage and held the spike, where it protruded from her back. "We'll work it out of you. Carefully, now."

Gemma eased herself forward, leaning against the spike, rolling her shoulder a little, struggling against the barb. Anastasia braced it still. I heard the wet, meaty sound of ripping flesh.

Vampires felt pain. I'd seen them get hurt. But they didn't bleed much, and they didn't need to breathe unless they were speaking. Gemma slid herself off that hook and didn't make a sound. When she was free, she fell forward, and Anastasia dropped the spike, where it dangled off the winch.

Anastasia glared at Grant. "Every magician is also an escape artist, yes? You can pick the lock?" She pointed to the door of the cage.

Grant was already kneeling before the lock, working on it with a couple of thin metal tools, his lock picks.

Gemma leaned forward, pressing herself against the bars of the cage, leaning toward Anastasia, reaching. Anastasia held the younger woman's face.

"Ani, I don't want to die," she said, gasping now in instinctive panic. She was still more human than not, had spent more years as a human than as a vampire.

"Hush," Anastasia said. "Stay calm. When he opens the door, we must fly to safety, do you understand?"

Gemma nodded quickly. Her face puckered and she started crying.

I had never seen the sun rise so quickly.

"Anastasia, go back to the lodge," Grant said, never turning his concentration from the lock.

"No, not without Gemma, I'm not leaving."

"You're in danger," he said. "Go back."

"No!"

"I'll save her. I'll get her out. But I can't worry about you both."

"Gemma—"

The girl was sobbing.

I said to Anastasia, "Some of the stories say you guys can turn to mist. You can vanish, reappear at will—"

"We can't just walk through walls and iron bars!" the elder vampire said. "She's just a child!"

"Anastasia, please," Jeffrey said, putting his arm around her shoulder, urging her away.

"Jeffrey," I said. "Go back to the lodge, the hunters' blind, whatever's closer. Get a tarp or a blanket or something we can put over the cage to shade it," I said. I'd started crying, too. I'd have thought I'd be out of tears by now. "Both of you, go!"

Anastasia turned and ran, Jeffrey following, struggling to keep up. I moved around the cage, putting myself between Gemma and the sun, as if my small body could shelter her.

Grant worked on the locks. He clenched his jaw and seemed to be struggling.

"Grant?"

"This type of lock would be easy, but there's a film of silicone sealant on the mechanism. It's glued shut."

Gemma pressed her back against the bars, as far away from the oncoming sunlight as she could get. Watching, I could almost see it move toward her, a reaching hand. Grant continued jamming his pick in the lock, working it in an arcane fashion that might as well have been magic.

With a pop and a click, the lock sprang and the door swung open. Grant took hold of Gemma's arms and pulled.

And the sunlight reached her.

"No!" Grant screamed in fierce defiance and clung to Gemma all the more.

But the light touched her legs and she caught fire, and the flames raced up her as if she were made of dry cotton. Her clothing didn't burn so fast but stayed for a moment as a shell around an inferno. Her eyes held terror, her gaze locked with Grant's, her mouth open in a silent wail.

Then the fire was gone and all was ash, specks drifting above on heated air. Grant knelt before streaks of soot and ash on the ground, his hands rigid in front of him, his skin burned to blisters.

The smell in the air was . . . I breathed through my mouth and tried to shut it out.

I moved to Grant, put my hand on his shoulder. The expression on his face was lost, the eyes sad. He looked old.

"I *had* her," he murmured. "I'd opened the lock. I'd *won*."

I wasn't sure he'd even noticed his hands. He hadn't moved them. They still curled as if they held Gemma's arm.

"You're hurt," I said. "Let's get inside."

He slumped against me, and I almost panicked, thinking I'd have to drag him back, thinking he'd die, too, and then what would I do?

"I'm so tired," he said, leaning on my shoulder. Just resting a moment.

"I know," I whispered.

Turning at the sound of running, I saw Jeffrey, standing with a wool blanket that might have come from the hunters' blind. When he saw us, he dropped it. His shoulders slumped, and grief pulled at his face.

A pair of gold filigree rings had survived the blaze. Gemma's rings. I picked them up, squeezed them in my hand, and nudged Grant. "Come on, we have to go."

Propping him up, I pulled him to his feet, and whatever moment of despair had gripped him vanished. He straightened, the look of cold stone settling over him. He folded his hands protectively to his chest and walked.

I picked up the blanket Jeffrey had dropped, held it up, showing the light that played through the fibers. Not a tight weave. "It probably wouldn't have been enough," I said, like that was any comfort.

"It might have been," he said. "If I'd been faster."

I hooked my arm through his and urged him on. Side by side, Jeffrey and I followed Grant back to the lodge.

Anastasia was waiting in the living room, toward the back, in shadows and away from the sunlight now pouring in through the windows. She had to know it was too late, but when we came in through the door she demanded, "Where is she?"

Grant, streaked with sweat and soot, could only look at her, his burned hands clawed in front of him.

Tina covered her mouth, her eyes narrowing with tears. Anastasia didn't say a word. Not to reprimand him, not to weep. She nodded once, then went to the basement door and descended into her cave.

I followed.

"Anastasia?"

At the bottom of the stairs, I found her sitting on the bed, a noble statue, gazing into the corner.

"Anastasia, I'm sorry. He tried. He almost had her."

"She died in his arms," she said. "I could see that. Right now, I have nothing to say. I need to rest. I hope to see you come nightfall."

Hesitating, I approached, opening my hand to her. Gemma's rings lay on my palm. Anastasia stared at them a moment, then retrieved them with cold fingers, closing them in her own fist.

I left her, climbing back up the stairs with feet made of lead.

chapter **20**

Tina, Jeffrey, and Grant were in the kitchen, tending to the magician's hands with ointment and bandages. Someone must have found a first-aid kit. Grant's jaw was taut, and he bore what must have been terrible pain without flinching.

Leaning on the counter, I watched, wondering what to do now. I asked myself what Cormac would do, and I couldn't think of an answer anymore. No, that wasn't true. He'd hole up somewhere defensible with a case of ammunition and shoot anything that moved.

Not a bad idea, that.

Jeffrey said, "Kitty, you should get some sleep. You look like you're about to collapse."

My muscles ached; my brain hurt. And the walls were closing in. "So do you."

"Is there a plan?" Tina said.

I shook my head. "I'm all out of plans."

"Anastasia can't leave until nightfall," Grant said, forcing his voice to stay steady. "Getting sleep in the meantime isn't a bad idea. We can rest in shifts while the others keep watch."

"They're still out there," Tina said. "You think they're still after us?"

"Of course they are," Grant muttered, harsh with pain.

"But they have to sleep, too," Jeffrey said. "Maybe they'll leave us alone for a while."

Maybe they would. Maybe we'd have a few hours' respite. "I'll take the first watch," I said.

"No," Jeffrey said. "Tina's right, you're half asleep already."

"I'm fine."

He touched my shoulder and guided me to the second sofa, and I was too tired to shrug him off.

I woke up not knowing how I managed to fall asleep at all, but exhaustion had caught up with me. But I didn't exactly feel refreshed. I still felt hunted, all my muscles tied in knots, my hackles permanently taut. When I looked around the living room, it was with suspicion, searching for the thing that was wrong. Looking to see who was missing now.

Grant was asleep on a bed of blankets on the floor by the fireplace. His injured hands wrapped with gauze bandages lay on his chest. Tina was slumped in a chair, also asleep. Jeffrey sat in a chair near the window, out of sight from the outside, where another beautiful sunny day in the mountains shone through.

Conrad, sitting up, his injured leg stretched out on the

other sofa, was awake and looking at me. He actually seemed a little better—more relaxed, not so pale. His leg had been washed and bound with gauze and tape. Blood still seeped through the bandages. He really needed a hospital. That goal seemed a tiny bit out of our reach at the moment.

"Hi," I said, slowly drawing myself into the moment.

"Hi," he answered.

"What's been happening? What have I missed?"

"I don't know. I've been kind of out of it. The others have been taking turns keeping watch."

"How are you doing?" I asked.

He smiled wryly and shook his head. "It's gone numb."

That couldn't be a good sign. "We'll get out of this. Everything'll turn out."

That sounded lame, didn't it? I glanced away in apology.

His voice was soft but steady now. As long as he didn't move, the pain seemed manageable. "You're married, right?"

"Yeah." The reminder of Ben sent an ache through my heart. I couldn't think about him right now—just think about getting through the next few hours.

"You have kids?" he said.

"No."

"You want kids? Are you and your husband trying for them?"

My smile got tighter as the old wound twinged in my gut. "It's not a matter of what I want. Lycanthropes can't carry a baby to term. Shape-shifting causes a miscarriage."

"Oh. I'm sorry."

"Yeah. Life's a bitch."

"I didn't think I wanted them. My wife—Trish—talked me into it. I could never say no to her. But when Toby came along—God, I didn't think I'd feel that way. It's like the whole world shifted so everything centered on him. This amazing little *thing*. Toby, then Hannah . . ."

He wiped his nose on his shirt. That whole life-flashing-before-your-eyes thing? Maybe it happened sometimes, but I had a feeling that just three faces were flashing before Conrad's eyes.

"We're going to get out of this," I said weakly. "You'll see them again."

He gave a painful chuckle. "Yeah. Sure. Okay." Unconvinced.

"Get some rest," I said. "In case we have to go running again."

"I want to be awake. When the next thing happens, I don't want to be asleep."

Yeah. I got that.

"Jeffrey?" Conrad craned his neck, looking for the psychic, wincing as he jostled his leg.

Jeffrey came over. He didn't look any better than the rest of us. A beard had started growing, his hair was shaggy and uncombed, and his face was pale. Jeffrey was one of the most upbeat people I knew. I'd never seen him so grim. He didn't even speak, just waited for Conrad to continue.

"Jeffrey," he said, full of emotion. "I'm sorry. I'm sorry I didn't believe. I want—can I talk to Natalie? I want to talk to her. Can you help me?"

Jeffrey smiled, though sadly. "Just talk to her, Conrad. She'll hear. She's always heard you."

"And my kids. If anything happens to me, I'll still be able to see them, I can talk to them—will you help me talk to them? I just want them to know—"

"Don't think about it," Jeffrey said. "It's not worth thinking about." He went back to the window, staying at the edge, sneaking careful looks out. He was tense, arms crossed, jaw set. I wanted to hug him. Like that would help.

Conrad settled back on the sofa, staring miserably into space.

I went to find something to eat. Drank a cup of flat soda and a slice of bread and peanut butter that went down like sawdust.

"Tina, Grant, Kitty—" Jeffrey called. The others woke and sat up instantly; they may not have slept at all. "I saw something. They're out there—one of them is, at least. In the trees there."

"What do you see?" Grant said. He didn't act injured at all, except that he kept his hands cradled in front of him, sheltered.

"I think it's Provost."

I thought for a minute. "You think we can catch him?"

Grant said, "Where's the rifle?"

"We lost it with Lee," I said, thinking I probably should have picked it up. I consoled myself by believing it had been damaged in the explosion. "Who has the handgun?"

Looking around, I found it on the kitchen counter. I grabbed it, checked the ammunition. Still full.

"Can you use it?" Tina said.

"I'd have to get out in the open—he'd get me before I got him," I said.

Jeffrey said, "So that's it? We're talking about killing him?"

I said, "I think we're firmly in them-or-us territory. As nice as it would be to see them convicted of murder, they're not going to sit still for that."

Jeffrey looked at Grant. When the psychic spoke, he sounded unhappy. Maybe he dealt with enough death that he didn't want to go around causing it. "You have a spell for this? Maybe some of the hypnotism?"

"I'd need to use my hands," Grant said, moving to the window. "Where?"

Jeffrey told him, describing the place at the edge of the clearing, near Valenti's old spot.

"What is it you keep saying, Kitty?" the magician said. "Flush them out?"

"Who gets the short straw on that one?" I said.

"What if you went out the back? Then shifted to your wolf form and came at him from behind? He's looking for people coming out the front."

I had so many arguments against that plan. It was a horrible plan. As hyped up as I was at the moment, I couldn't be sure I wouldn't turn wolf and head for the hills, never to be seen again. I might try to join that pack of wild wolves we'd run into. Then again, I was pissed off enough that I might be all too happy to go after Provost and tear him to shreds. But if I didn't kill him, if he didn't die—I never wanted to be responsible for infecting another person with this disease. Even someone like Provost. *Especially* someone like him. Homicidal bastard as werewolf? Bad scene, there.

"You're not saying anything," Grant said.

"I think you're overestimating my ability to follow a plan once I shift."

"What if you didn't follow a plan? What if you just ran, got out of here, and went for help?" Jeffrey said. "Even if you didn't remember what you were doing as a wolf, you'd remember when you woke up, right?"

"Assuming I didn't run up against silver razor wire or get caught in another insane trap." The whole lodge had become a trap, of course.

"I keep expecting them to attack the lodge," Grant murmured. "We don't have anywhere else to go."

That, more than any other reason, was why we had to do something. If we didn't, they would.

"I don't have to be a wolf to flush him out," I said. "But are we scaring him, catching him, or killing him?"

Nobody answered until Conrad said from the sofa, "Do we have a choice?"

I had killed to protect me and mine before. I could do it again. I drew the handgun from my pocket, checked the chamber and safety one more time. Loaded with silver bullets, of course, which made me twitch. But Provost and his party hadn't brought along any other kind, apparently. I felt horribly ostentatious doing the checking—bad action-film girl, right here.

"Distract him," I said. "Keep him looking out front. Make him think he can get a shot off." Then I'd sneak up from behind. It was a Cormac-grade plan.

I left them and went to the back door. Quietly opened it. Didn't make a sound. Stepped out.

And fell back as the wall beside me exploded. Another

gunshot blasted as I slammed shut the door and hunched on the floor.

Grant, Tina, and Jeffrey came running.

"Cabe," I said, picking myself up, checking myself over. Some scratches from flying splinters marked my arm, but I could handle that. Just as long as nothing silver touched me, I'd be fine.

Tina huffed, turning away in a show of frustration. "So they're waiting us out."

"We have to think of something," Grant said. He started pacing, slow, moderate steps. He winced with pain.

Jeffrey was looking at the front door. "I want to try something. Kitty, can you stay out of sight?"

"What are you going to do?" I said.

"Just don't let Provost see you through the window."

He went to the front door and opened it.

Tina gasped and reached after him. "Jeffrey, don't!"

Jeffrey called out, so the man in the trees could hear, "Joey! We want to make a deal! Let's talk!"

Grant joined Tina by the front door to listen. Still holding the gun, I crouched nearby, under the window.

"What do you think you're doing?" Grant demanded.

Jeffrey kept calling. "You've made your point! Cabe just shot Kitty out back—"

I thought I saw where this was going. I ducked and listened.

"Except for the vampire in the basement, the monsters are all gone. The rest of us are human. We know this is all about the monsters. If you let us go, the four of us will walk away. We'll leave the vampire to you."

It just might work.

The thing was, Provost and Cabe couldn't let anybody

walk away. They'd already killed their witnesses, the show's assistants. But maybe he didn't know that we knew that. Jeffrey was good with people. Maybe he really could lure him into the open. All I needed was a clear shot . . .

"Conrad and Odysseus are hurt. We need to get to a hospital. We just want to talk to you, Joey. Stay there if you want, but talk to me."

A long moment passed. This wasn't going to work. Provost was in communication with Cabe, who might or might not have seen whether he actually shot me. I wanted to yell to Jeffrey to get back inside.

From the trees, Provost yelled, "The werewolf bitch is really dead?"

Jeffrey hesitated, but it didn't sound like a man about to lie. It sounded like fear, grief, helplessness. All things we were feeling anyway. "Death by silver bullet isn't pretty. But I'm sure you know that."

Provost's answer was filled with mirth, with victory. "You're a dead man, Jeffrey Miles. You're all dead."

Provost appeared, moving out from behind the shelter of a pine tree. Like Valenti, he had transformed himself from the slick Hollywood guy. He wore black fatigues, a belt holster—gun in place, I noted—a knife at his belt, combat boots.

In seconds I'd have a shot. I was lining him up. Jeffrey said over his shoulder, "Don't shoot him. He's not holding a weapon. I want to see where this goes."

He had better be right about this.

"Just tell me why," Jeffrey said. "I keep trying to understand this."

When Provost smiled, it was a slanted, wicked expression. "There's nothing to understand. None of you is human. You, the psychic bitch, the magician, the atheist. You're still monsters. The things you do? Makes you all witches. And you ought to be burned!"

Atheist? I had to assume he was talking about Conrad, who didn't have a magical cell in his body. I glanced at Conrad and muttered, "Since when does being an atheist make someone a monster?"

"It does to the kind of people who threaten to burn witches," he said. "Trust me, I've heard this line before."

Provost was still ranting. "We wanted to see if we could kill monsters. Turns out we can, and we're going to show the world how to do it," he said. He walked toward the lodge now, casually, step by step. Carelessly, almost. He had to know we had the weapons we'd taken from Valenti. Maybe he really thought Jeffrey didn't have it in him to shoot anyone. But Jeffrey didn't have to.

"Ron Valenti doesn't agree with you," Jeffrey said, and Provost stopped walking. "In fact, he's pretty upset."

Provost said, "You haven't really talked to him."

Jeffrey shrugged. "You might as well burn this place to the ground, because it's going to be very haunted when this is all over. Then again, all that negative energy doesn't need a place to anchor to. It's hanging over you, Joey."

Provost was frowning now. "This isn't about Valenti. It's about who gets out of here alive."

"You're right. I'm just telling you—free consultation— that this isn't going to end here. But you might get yourself a few points to balance that out if you let us go. I know you believe all that—some kind of balance, some kind of life after death—or Tina and I wouldn't be here. I'm making the offer: let us go. Because if you kill us, you're never getting rid of us."

It didn't work quite so simply. Jeffrey had said as much. But maybe Provost didn't know that, and maybe he was just keyed up enough to believe it. The men looked at each other across the clearing. Jeffrey faced Provost with all the courage in the universe. Arms at his sides, calm, non-threatening. Treating Provost like he was an approaching predator.

Provost shot him. A quick draw, he'd grabbed his gun from his holster, aimed and fired in a heartbeat, before any of us could react. Jeffrey fell back, boneless.

I stood, leveled my gun out the door, and fired at Provost.

I didn't practice much and wasn't very good at the gun thing, but I hit him. He staggered, his right arm flung back, the gun flying from his grip.

Which was good, because I lost it. I flung my own gun aside and ran at Provost.

From the stress of the last few days, the rage at losing friends and good people for no reason at all, I lost control. Wolf had been battering at me, at the mental bars of the cage that kept her calm, since all this started. I'd shot Provost, but she—we—wanted more. Wanted his blood in our mouth, his flesh in our teeth.

I was Changing without even feeling it.

The fury in me felt molten. Like I had turned into fire, liquid iron. The Change had never come so smoothly, so painlessly. I had always fought it, but this time, Wolf was simply there when I wished it. My limbs melted. I stretched my fingers and they were claws. I hunched my back, bared my teeth. My clothing tore away.

I run fast, with Wolf's speed and strength. He doesn't have time to reach for his fallen weapon. I shove into him,

and my claws are into him. I can't see through the anger,
I only feel. Hear his scream. He doesn't think I have it
in me to tear his throat out. No one ever thinks I have it
in me.

For a moment we look into each other's eyes. I can't
imagine what he sees in mine, what amber fire is blazing
in them. But I see that he is frightened—eyes ringed with
white, terrified. I *dig*—

*On the ground now, her weight has toppled him. Teeth
around his neck, not letting go, shaking her head to rip
the skin. Blood fills her mouth, a taste of ecstasy. Flesh
gives way. He shrieks in her ear, hits her with fists. Only
makes her more angry. Not dead yet, but he already
smells rotten. Snarling, clawing, ripping, she mauls.*

*A distant memory recognizes a voice that calls, "Kitty!
Get back, get inside!" One of the two-legged ones, but
familiar, and the voice within her, her other half, urges
her: listen. Go. Too dangerous in the open.*

*She raises her head to look, sees the male who called
her running toward her and sees another male in the
trees. Her nose flares, takes this one's scent, and the
wrongness of it shocks her. He is weapons, steel, fire. Her
other half knows this means terrible danger. Only one option: run to safety. But she has no den here, no pack, no
safety—except the house, which smells lived-in, denlike.
Closest safety she'll find.*

*She runs for the door she burst from only a moment
ago. Leaps past chaos, a male and female dragging two
others. An explosion, a hot streak ripping through air.*

Part of her expects to feel an impact, expects that this is her death. She doesn't stop running, even after she passes through the door.

She's felt nothing, no pain. The weapon of smoke and fire missed.

Another explosion sounds, very close—the female stands at the door, holding another weapon straight. It fires, bursts of heat and thunder, again and again, until the man slams shut the door and they both collapse, along with two bodies that smell richly of blood.

She licks her snout, which is covered with blood. She is standing by the far wall, tail rigid, hackles raised, a low warning growl breathing out each time she exhales. Waiting for the next attack.

"Oh God, oh God. Odysseus, Tina—what do we do about her?" Another man is sitting up, staring. He smells like old blood. Injured. Easy prey. He's staring right at her, and this makes her angry. She directs her growls at him, and he cringes.

"Conrad, don't look at her. Look away. Conrad! Look at me!"

The injured one looks away. She was almost ready to pounce to show him which of them was stronger.

"Tina, can you see outside? What's he doing?"

"He's staying there—he hasn't left the trees. Jeffrey, how's Jeffrey, oh, my God—"

The room has filled with blood. Makes her hungry. The two-legged ones are trembling like a frightened herd.

"Kitty—she wouldn't really," the female says. "She's in there somewhere, right? She wouldn't really attack us."

"Tina, stop looking at her." This is the strong male,

the one who called her inside. "Walk very calmly along the wall to the kitchen. Find the pantry—there should be some canned food left. Open a can of chicken or tuna."

Movement. The female is edging along the wall. She's strong—the only person here who doesn't smell injured. Let her go.

The male is speaking, his voice like soft fur. He's looking at the floor near her. "Shh, Kitty. It's all right. Danger's over for now. It's all right."

The calming voice helps. The fury ebbs. But she's still standing with her back to a wall and the smell of an enemy in the room. Where is her pack? Her mate? The growl turns into a whine.

The female puts something on the floor and quickly edges away—a new scent. Meat, but not fresh. Not fresh, but available, a few paces away. Hunger has become more important than the rest. She pads to the scent, finds several mouthfuls. She eats warily, keeping a watch on the group of two-legged people. Finishes the carrion quickly, but it settles her.

She does not mean to sleep, but weariness pulls her under.

I had blood and skin under my fingernails. I picked at it.

Either I didn't remember what had happened, or I didn't want to. I could guess. The last thing I remembered was Provost's face, white with fear. Yeah, I could guess what had happened. I hadn't even felt the Change come. I'd just snapped. That had never happened before.

If I stayed numb, I wouldn't have to think about the implications.

Someone had put a blanket over me. I lay against the far wall, nearest the kitchen. My muscles were stiff, as if I'd slept curled in a tight ball. Looking across the room, I was having trouble recognizing what I was seeing. My mind was still filled with wolfish vision and the taste of blood. I could smell death.

A body lay against the wall, covered with a sheet, dead. I made a wish, took a breath, and let out a moan, because I smelled Jeffrey. Provost had been so close, Jeffrey couldn't have survived the shot. Still, I couldn't believe it. Wouldn't. I just wouldn't deal with that right now.

There was another person lying on the floor, breathing fast, painfully, in the way of the seriously injured. I recognized his scent, too.

Joey Provost was alive.

chapter 21

I wrapped the blanket around my naked self and stood in the middle of the living room, assessing. I clamped my mouth shut because I was afraid I might throw up. If ever I had a right to spontaneously vomit, this was it.

I didn't want to have to take care of Provost. I'd rather shoot him.

Conrad was asleep on the sofa. Grant sat on a chair in the middle of the living room, like he could hold us together with his presence. He sat nearest the injured Provost but didn't seem to be looking at him. Tina sat on the floor, near the window but not looking out. At first I thought she was asleep, the way she held her head propped on her hand. Her other hand rested on a Ouija board sitting next to her. She looked at me. She'd been crying.

I couldn't talk. I couldn't open my mouth or I would scream. I wished I had stayed Wolf. The world was simpler when I was Wolf.

"Kitty?" Grant said.

Now I was looking at Provost. He lay on a blanket, covered by another blanket. His shirt had been stripped.

He panted, tossed in a delirium, his arms clenched, hands clawing.

I stepped to him, knelt beside him.

"There's something wrong with him," Grant said softly.

Besides being infected with lycanthropy? The words stalled in my throat. If I opened my mouth I'd throw up, so I kept my mouth shut.

I put my hand on Provost's forehead—he was burning with fever. Normal, for a recent victim of a werewolf bite. He'd thrash in a haze for a few days while his wounds healed and while his body transformed itself from the inside out. He smelled ill, injured. Under all that, though, I caught a new scent, musky, animal. Wolfish. Fur, just under the skin. I'd promised myself I would never do this to anyone, I never wanted to, he should be dead—

"Kitty," Grant said. I shook my head, bringing myself back. Rubbed sleep and tears from my eyes. I needed clothes. I pulled the blanket tighter around myself.

I saw what Grant was talking about, about there being something wrong. He had enough arcane lore, he must have had some idea what a bite from a werewolf did. Provost's wounds, shredded flesh across his neck and shoulder, were healing: scabs had formed, blood seeped from surface wounds. That was normal. However, where the bullet I fired had hit him, a chunk of flesh taken out of his bicep, wasn't healing. Here, the wound was black, oozing pus along with blood.

I swallowed and managed to scratch out, "Did the bullet go all the way through?"

"Yes," Grant said. "It's a flesh wound."

Then I laughed. I sounded ridiculous, hysterical. I

curled up, hugged my knees, and laughed. This was so fucked up, I ought to be taking notes.

Patiently, Grant waited for me.

I got myself back under control. "Silver allergy. The silver bullet went through him before he was infected. But there must be a trace of it that's reacting to the lycanthropy. Not enough to kill him. If the bullet had stayed in him, though, he'd have the full-blown allergy. He'd be dead. I wish he were dead." I laughed again, then covered my face to try to stop the tears. Copious, hysterical tears.

Tina had moved closer to us, studying Provost along with us. She reached out to me, but I leaned away from her. "Don't touch me," I whispered. I wanted to Change again. I wanted to get out of here, to bite someone.

"Kitty—" Grant said.

"Any sign of Cabe?"

"No. Maybe he'll cut his losses and leave us alone."

"Not likely," I said. Before he could respond, I stood, tightening the blanket yet again. "I need some clothes."

I went upstairs.

The face in the bedroom mirror was the face of a monster. I studied it, the crazy blond hair that hadn't been brushed in two days, the bloodshot eyes, the ragged frown. I wanted to see my friends, my pack, my mate. I wanted to go home.

"Tell me, Cormac. What am I supposed to do now?" I muttered.

You just keep going. He'd say, you just keep on keeping on until you're dead. But don't make it easy on the bastards by rolling over for them.

I wasn't dead yet. We still had a lodge full of people

who weren't dead yet, and the bad guys were down to one man standing.

When I came downstairs, I was dressed in fresh clothes, hair brushed and pinned up, face washed. Still on the edge of hysterical, but at least I was upright. Two legs for the rest of the day, I promised myself.

Tina was sitting at the dining room table now, a blank sheet of paper in front of her, holding a pen over it. This was an old mediumistic talent—automatic writing. Some people believed spirits could communicate by causing the hand of a psychic to write out messages. Most of it was fake, but it really worked for Tina. She expected to receive a message. It wasn't happening.

I sat next to her. Didn't have to say a word. Our hearts— our grief—showed all over our faces. She fell into my arms, sobbing. I hugged her as tight as I could. Didn't say a word, because there was nothing I could say. I held her until she pulled away, scrubbing her eyes, lips tight with a sad smile.

She glanced at the pad of paper. "I don't know why I think he'll talk to me. He has no reason to—"

"Maybe he needs time. Maybe you need time."

She nodded, almost frantically. "Yeah, maybe that's it."

Grant joined us, standing on the other side of the table, looking down on us. He also had a scruffy beard started. His gaze was as alert and stony as ever.

"Kitty. Provost is waking up," he said.

I didn't want that to have anything to do with me, but

I went over to where the hunter lay. We had words to exchange, him and me.

Provost was rubbing his face, trying to sit up, and falling back, weakened. He groaned and seemed uncertain, looking around in confusion. When he saw me, he let out a scream and tried to scramble away. A chair and his own weakness stopped him.

"Hi there," I said, frowning.

His face showed blank terror. He knew what was happening to him. He groaned, and his words came out slurred. "Why—why did you do this to me?"

"Not my fault. You were supposed to die."

His wounds were looking better, the scabs more established, ringed with healing pink flesh. Even the silver-tainted one looked better. It had stopped oozing. It would heal, but it might leave a scar. Moaning in denial, Provost writhed, like he could burrow through the floor to get away from me. "Damn you, damn you, damn you . . ."

"Now let me ask you a question," I said. "Why did you think you could get away with this?"

"Fuck you," he said.

"Aw, isn't that sweet? The thing is, Joey, you're one of us now. You're one of *me*. A bloodthirsty monster. And that wasn't part of the plan at all, was it? Did you really think you were going to get out of this in one piece?" I was feeling vicious. All of my sympathy was for myself, having to deal with this guy.

Provost shook his head. He squeezed his eyes shut, like he could block out the world. "You were a bunch of dumb celebrities. Suckered in. It'd be like fish in a barrel."

"Well," I said flatly. "That's nice."

"Monsters like you—you're not that tough. We'll get you in the end."

Us and them. It always came down to us and them. But it wasn't so black and white. Us and them broke down into interlacing Venn diagrams; sometimes someone in an "us" column became "them," depending on how you changed the categories and definitions. You could always find something in common. Provost regarded me with so much hate and contempt, I couldn't fathom it. Nonetheless, I was probably turning at least that much hate and contempt back on him. I liked to think there was a difference between us: he'd earned my contempt through his actions. He'd killed my friends.

"Here's what's going to happen," I said. "You're going to be sick for a few more days, but your wounds will heal, and you'll come out of this good as new. Better than new. The next full moon, you'll Change. And I'll tell you right now, it's fucking hell. You'll either learn to live with it, or you won't. Either way, you're going to learn to live with it or not in a silver-lined prison cell. Got it?"

"Cabe's still out there. He'll finish you. He'll still finish you!"

"Then he'll finish you," I said. "Because like I said, you're one of us now."

I walked away, and he threw curses at my back, eventually breaking down into sobs, and the sobs faded into a hysterical prayer, "Kill me, please God, kill me, kill me . . ."

Arms crossed, shoulders hunched, I paced along the wall like a caged animal. Part of me was all ready to oblige him. Bullet in his head, my hands around his throat, that'd be the end of it. Shouldn't be too hard—I was a monster, after all.

After his frenzied outburst, he passed out in short order.

We had to get out of here. I could do it, I could run—with only one of them out there now, it should be easier. Cabe couldn't watch both doors. I'd go, I'd get help. All Cabe had to do was burn the house down and he'd win. Couldn't let that happen. Had to run, soon—

"Kitty."

I stopped and looked, startled, wanting to growl at the interruption.

His face a mask, Grant regarded me. He and Tina had moved to the living room to watch my exchange with Provost. She sat on the sofa next to Conrad, head bowed, hands over her ears, like she was trying to shut out the world. Conrad switched between staring at Provost, Grant, and me. Like he didn't know whom to be more frightened of.

"Kitty," Grant said. "We need you to stay human. Please."

I couldn't guess what the others saw in me. A monster, probably, just like Provost saw in me. They were all human. Us and them.

Hands over my face, I slumped against the wall and slid to the floor. Keep it together. Just a little while longer, keep it together. We'd get out of this. We could use Provost to get out of this. We could stop Cabe. We were almost there.

I scrubbed my face, which was wet. The tears just started, quietly leaking. I tried to smile. Tried to make it an apology. But Provost's smell, the evidence of what I'd done, filled the room, oppressive.

"I always said I'd never do this. I'd never infect someone else with this. I never wanted to be responsible for someone like that." I wiped my nose on my sleeve, turned away.

Grant said, "It'll be dark soon. We'll wait for Anastasia."

That was as good a plan as any for the moment.

Tina and Conrad slept fitfully. Grant and I kept watch, sneaking looks out the front window, checking the fronts and the backs of the house, looking for any changes. Waiting for tear gas canisters to come flying through the windows. The situation remained quiet. Provost remained unconscious. Twilight fell, and we lit the candles and found the flashlights.

I listened for footsteps on the basement stairs, for the sound of the door opening. Didn't hear them. She moved quietly and didn't allow any sound to escape, so that she seemed to just appear at the edge of the living room, dressed elegantly as always, flowing black slacks and a silk top, her hair knotted and pinned at the back of her head. It was as if nothing had happened, she stood so calmly.

What she saw in the living room must have seemed like a war zone. Jeffrey's body under a blanket. Provost feverish and sweating, drifting in and out. The rest of us huddled in on ourselves, wearing the haunted gazes of refugees.

After a long moment she said, "You've been busy."

I stifled a laugh.

"What's the situation?" she said.

Grant answered: "Cabe is still out there, watching the house. He's probably trapped one of the doors and is keeping an eye on the other."

"Have you thought about using this one as a bargaining chip?" She nodded at Provost.

"We were waiting for you," Grant said.

"Ah. I can tell you what I'd prefer to do with him. I need to keep up my strength, after all."

"What happened to using him as a bargaining chip?" Tina said.

"We'll still have him for that," she said, her voice too sweet. Sugarcoated poison.

None of us stopped her from kneeling beside Provost, raising his wrist to her mouth, and drinking. The injured man groaned, started to thrash, but she rested a hand on his forehead. He continued to moan in delirium, but his body calmed. After a few moments, she let him go.

"I've drunk from two of them," she said, licking her lips dramatically. "I'd love to taste the third."

Tina made a sound and looked away, while Conrad huddled even farther back on the sofa.

Anastasia stood and smoothed her clothing. "I'm sorry I missed the events that led to this. Kitty, you must have been spectacular. I confess, I wouldn't have expected it from you. Did you intend to turn him?"

"I intended to kill him," I said.

"Ah." A frown turned her mouth. "He won't make it. His kind rarely do. Give him access to a gun and he'll kill himself."

"Save me from having to do it," I muttered, and everyone looked at me. I glared back, daring them to argue with me. I wasn't much interested in being nice and moral anymore. We all had our breaking points.

Anastasia went to the window and studied the falling night outside. "This is a war of attrition. Messy. But if the numbers hold, we're winning."

"Small comfort," I said.

"Kitty, please stop feeling sorry for yourself. I haven't survived for eight hundred years to give up now."

"I'm not feeling sorry for myself. I'm just tired. And that's an understatement." I was even too tired to pounce on that scrap of information. Eight hundred years. I didn't care. Scratching my hair, I got up and tried to get my brain working. "I could try running for help again. Cabe can't watch all of us. If we can set up some kind of distraction—"

The explosion of a shot fired, and the picture window in the living room shattered. Candles flickered, Tina screamed, all of us ducked—except for Anastasia, who leaned over to peer through the now-empty space.

"Well," she said. "The move's been made. The endgame begins."

chapter 22

We still had the handgun, but not much else in the way of weapons. Maybe he'd stand still long enough for us to throw tear gas at him. Nothing else would work at range, which left us with trying to lure him out. Because that had worked so well the last time. With a breeze coming in from outside now, I could smell danger, more guns, gunpowder. Cabe, the only unfamiliar scent on the air.

"He's right outside," I said. "He's moving in."

Something arced through the open window and cracked on the floor. A rock or something. Something metallic. Tina spotted it first, lunged for it, grabbed it—a grenade. She threw herself on that grenade, literally. I yelled at her—I couldn't lose anyone else—

She cocked back and threw it back through the window. It exploded on the dirt clearing outside, a sound of thunder and a roiling orange fireball, debris scattering in all directions. Rock and gravel struck the house like bullets. We all ducked away from the destruction.

Another shot rang out—Cabe taking advantage of the confusion. Tina was standing right in front of the window, only seconds after she'd gotten rid of the grenade. As if Cabe had expected something like this, like the grenade had been just a distraction. The shot hit her torso. She fell. I screamed.

Grant was at her side before I could think to move. "She's alive!" he called. Tina herself backed up his statement a moment later.

"Shit!" she groaned.

At that moment, I could have been easily persuaded to believe in the power of prayer. *Please, God and whatever other powers are watching, get us through this.*

"I need a distraction out front," I said. I found the handgun on the kitchen counter. It had only four shots left; it would have to be enough.

Anastasia pulled Provost off the floor. "Get up, you. Time to be useful." She slapped his face a couple of times, and he slowly came out of his daze. When he saw the vampire holding him up by his arm, her nails digging into his skin, he panicked. Jerking away from her, he thrashed, pounded with his fists, screamed. Anastasia's grip never weakened.

She grabbed his chin and forced him to look at her. "I could finish you without even thinking of it. Just like I finished your friend Valenti. I guarantee you it won't be an easy death." She caught him in her gaze, and he calmed, hanging limply in her hands. His face went taut, despairing, but he stopped fighting her. He was trapped, hypnotized.

Part of me wanted to leap to his defense, and the feeling horrified me. That was my Wolf, sensing another, weaker wolf in danger—*our* wolf. There was an instinct to protect him. But this man was evil. I wouldn't claim him. Couldn't. *Not this one,* I told my whining Wolf and turned away.

Anastasia hauled Provost through the front door, shoving him in front of her as a shield.

Grant and I looked at each other. This was it.

"Go," he said. "I'll keep an eye on the front."

I didn't go out through the back door, in case it was trapped. But there was a window on the side of the house. I opened it and popped out the screen. Moved very, very carefully. Listening hard, smelling all around the edges for gunpowder, wooden stakes, silver arrows, anything that might be a weapon. The ground under the window looked fine. Here goes, then.

Quietly, I lowered myself out the window to the ground. When I didn't blow up, I ran to the corner and edged along the porch until I could see Cabe.

He could have given Rambo a run for his money. He was down to a T-shirt, black pants, and combat boots, but he was outfitted for war: rifle in his hand, gun in a shoulder holster, crossbow slung over his shoulder, a pouch on one hip holding arrows, a pouch on the other hip holding a bundle of gardening stakes. Several more grenades on a bandolier.

He could have blown us all up, but he wanted to do this face-to-face. He wanted to go down to the wire. I could see it in his eyes. Fucking maniac.

Anastasia was speaking. "We killed Valenti; this one here's as good as dead. You can't win, Mr. Cabe."

Cabe fired the rifle. I flinched, simultaneously trying to see what had happened. Bullets couldn't hurt Anastasia, I wasn't worried about her, so what had he shot?

Provost slid out of Anastasia's arms and fell dead. I choked on a shout.

Cabe dropped the rifle and threw something at the vampire, a fast and haphazard pitch. Water splashed from a bottle, like the small bottle of liquid that Valenti had carried. Anastasia was lunging at Cabe when the spray hit her, and she lost her composure. She put up her hands in defense, cringed, slouched away, and didn't make a sound as the holy water burned like acid on her face and hands.

Next, Cabe swung up his crossbow—already loaded, ready to fire a wood bolt through Anastasia's heart, now that she was vulnerable.

I leveled my gun; I had him in my sights, squeezed the trigger.

Blood sprayed from Cabe's thigh. He cried out, staggered, dropped to his knees. The crossbow tumbled from his grip. But he was still alive and going for the stakes at his hip.

Okay, so I really needed to practice with this gun thing some more. Mental note.

Only partially recovered, Anastasia struck at him, more slowly than she should have moved, not at all like her elegant, brutal self, and he stopped her midstride, holding a stake up, gripped with both hands, ready to impale her. She stopped, teeth bared. The tableau paused; then Cabe climbed to his feet. His thigh was a bloody mess. He didn't seem to notice.

"You!" Cabe shouted, glancing at me. "You fire again and I'll kill her! I can do it!"

Did the man have no pain receptors? Maybe he didn't. I emerged from my shelter behind the porch. Lowered the gun, just a little.

"Not good enough!" he said. "Put it down! Drop it!"

Quick mental calculation: if I dropped it, how quickly could I pick it back up again? Could he really stake her before I shot him? Could he stake her before she reacted? The wooden point was a foot from her chest. Anything could happen. Grant stood on the porch, probably making the same calculations I was.

Frozen, I couldn't make a decision. But my hand opened and I let the gun go.

Cabe jumped toward Anastasia, stake raised, shouting in rage. She braced, preparing a defense, teeth bared, hissing. I dove for the gun, running forward in the same motion.

Grant leapt forward—putting himself in front of Anastasia, protecting her—and grappled with Cabe. It happened too fast; I didn't see what led to Odysseus Grant falling, holding his bandaged hands to his chest. But I could guess: he'd put himself in front of the stake meant for the vampire. He clutched the length of it sticking from his rib cage. Cabe stood over him, stunned, staring, panting like a wild beast.

I steadied myself, aimed the way I'd been taught, and fired the last of the gun's shots. Cabe jerked, fell back, and didn't move again.

The world fell silent, still, my hearing masked with cotton by the sound of those gunshots. I'd killed again— too late, this time.

Anastasia crouched by Grant's head, held his shoulders, and stared at the stake in his chest with a shocked gaze. Red rashes from the holy water streaked her beautiful face, which was creased with either pain or grief. She hadn't even looked so distraught when we lost Gemma.

Numb, I dropped to my knees beside them, gripped Grant's wrists, which were braced around the protruding stake, and searched him for life and movement. His eyes were open, looking back at me, and his lips smiled faintly. A time like this, and he smiled.

Tell me what to do, I pleaded silently, meeting his gaze. I had gone feral, Wolf in my eyes, in my senses, unable to form words.

"Kitty," he murmured, coughed, and I squeezed tighter, urging him to lie back, not to struggle. But he never listened to me. "It's a trance—tell them."

He coughed, and blood bubbled at the corner of his mouth. Air bubbled in the blood around the wound at his chest.

"Odysseus," Anastasia breathed.

"Slows heart rate. Blood pressure." Another cough, with more red foam sliding down his chin. "Not dead. Tell them."

He met my gaze, nodded once, then closed his eyes. Laid his head back, almost in Anastasia's lap. His breathing slowed, then slowed again. My hands were on his wrists, I felt his pulse, I heard his heart—it also slowed. Dimmed.

"No," I murmured, my voice finally unsticking. "No, Grant, no, no—"

Anastasia squeezed my shoulder, and I looked at her with round eyes, wolfish. My throat was tight, preparing to howl.

"Kitty," she said, her voice low. "He knows what he's doing. A trance, so he won't bleed out. He's saving himself."

If anyone could do such a thing, it would be Grant. I shook my head. "It won't do any good—we're still stuck here. He needs an ambulance *now,* Tina needs an ambulance—"

Anastasia went to Cabe's body and started searching it. "One of them has to have a satellite phone—they had to have a way of calling out."

I couldn't do anything else for Grant; I couldn't find a pulse and assumed he was unconscious. He didn't *smell* dead. So I went inside to check on Tina.

She'd managed to pull herself to the door. Curled up, hugging her middle, she looked out. Blood covered her hands. Her eyes were bright and, unbelievably, she was smiling.

"Tina." Kneeling by her, I took hold of her shoulder.

"It's okay. Kitty, it's going to be okay," she said, gasping. "Listen."

"What? What is it? Tina—"

She gripped my arm with bloody hands. "Listen!"

I held my breath and listened. At first, I thought it was thunder, a distant rumble. But it didn't fade. It was regular, steady, and getting louder.

The thump of a helicopter motor filled the valley. A helicopter. Oh my God.

I ran off the porch, calling, "Anastasia!"

"I hear it," she said, standing and looking toward the meadow and airstrip.

Still running, I headed down the path and looked up. A searchlight panned over me from above. I waved my arms, jumped up and down, shouted. The aircraft could have belonged to Provost and friends, it could have opened fire on me, and I was too tired to care.

But the helicopter was red, with the words "Search and Rescue" painted on the side.

chapter 23

In moments, the yard in front of the lodge turned to chaos. A pair of EMTs arrived with their kits and got to work. I tried to explain, but the words came out jumbled. I wasn't making any sense, but really, the scene before us was clear. Plenty of blood, plenty of bodies for them to work on.

"Jesus," one of the EMTs said, crouching by the inert magician. "Did somebody think he was a vampire or what?"

"I can't find a pulse," his partner said.

"He's not dead. He's in a trance," Anastasia said. The guy looked at her blankly for a moment, opened his mouth like he might argue, but she must have put the whammy on him, because after a moment he nodded, and they got to work on Grant. Bandages, neck brace, more bandages.

Another pair of EMTs huddled over Cabe and Provost, but without the urgency they'd shown with Grant. Anastasia and I watched it all like it was some kind of movie.

"Inside," I called to them, struggling for coherency. "There's two people injured inside. Please." They nodded and ran into the lodge. Tina, I hoped she was okay, I hoped she'd be okay—

Another man approached. He wore a jumpsuit and a jacket, headphones over his ears. He seemed to be talking into a headset—the pilot, maybe?

"Are you two all right?" he asked.

We were covered in blood. I swallowed, still feeling like I was choking, or howling, or something. "I don't know how to answer that."

He gave a wry smile. "Fair enough."

"How?" I said, my breaths coming in hiccups. "How did you get here? How did you know?"

"The police got a call from a guy named Ben O'Farrell. Is one of you Kitty Norville?"

Tears brimmed my eyes and spilled over. My knight in shining armor. Hell, yeah. "That's me."

"He said he couldn't get a call through and thought something fishy might be going on. We did some checking. Then a hiker from the Pine View Lodge up the trail reported finding a body that had been shot with arrows. We came out here assuming the worst."

"You have no idea," I said.

"The police are right behind us in another chopper. They'll want to talk to you about what happened here."

Softly, I said, "And we'll be happy to tell them."

"There are more bodies inside and out by the airstrip," Anastasia said.

The pilot turned an unhappy expression to the house and winced. Under his breath he said, "It's going to be a long night."

Not as long as the last couple.

* * *

We ended up at a Montana Highway Patrol station near Kalispell.

The detective in charge of the case didn't want to believe us, but the story we told was so crazy, we couldn't have made it up. Especially since the guy questioned us separately and we gave him exactly the same story, which matched the evidence. At the hospital, state troopers interviewed Conrad; he told them the same thing. We all backed each other up, and the police couldn't argue. Also, Anastasia might have done some of her own brand of persuasion; the detective was probably watching her eyes the entire time. By the time he let us go, he was smiling vaguely and murmuring about how we weren't under any suspicion at all, and if there was anything he could do to help, and so on. We asked him to drive us to the hospital where the others had been taken. Once there, he talked the staff into letting us into the ICU. Half the night had passed since the search-and-rescue helicopter took the others to the hospital. We hadn't heard anything since and were desperate for news.

Tina was still in surgery and not out of the woods yet. She'd been shot in the stomach, had suffered organ damage. The doctors were doing everything they could, we were told. Conrad had been in and out of surgery and was recovering. His wounds had been cleaned and stabilized, but the doctors were worried about infection and necrosis. If infection set in—a possibility given the depth and severity of the wounds—they'd have to amputate. But they were hopeful it wouldn't come to that.

Grant was in ICU. The surgeon on his case was on hand to explain that the stake had punctured Grant's left lung but not his heart. A few hours of surgery repaired the damage. He'd be in the hospital's ICU for at least another day, waiting for complications to strike. Even when he pulled out of danger, he'd be ill, weakened, for a long time. I was almost disappointed that he was mortal, after all, a standard substandard human being requiring doctors and all the rest. At the same time, it made me like him even more. He was vulnerable but still a fighter. Mere mortal humans made great fighters because they had so much to lose.

After we washed up and changed clothes—our old clothes were soaked with blood—the doctor let us stay with Grant for a little while. Anastasia and I waited at his bedside.

He was asleep and stable, his treated and newly bandaged hands resting over his middle. A machine beeped the steady rhythm of his heart. He had too many tubes hooked up to him—in his nose, in his arm, looping around and over him. He didn't smell healthy. This whole place smelled like illness, making my nose wrinkle. Instinctively, Wolf wanted to run from the illness, the sick combination of blood and antiseptic, but I felt so much better just sitting here, watching him sleep. The crags and furrows in his face smoothed out a bit, and he looked younger, settled against the flat white hospital pillow, a sheet pulled over his chest, penned in by the rails of the bed. He looked asleep now, instead of the stony quiet of the trance.

I sat within reach of his hand, so I could hold it when he woke up. Not that he'd appreciate it, but I'd try anyway. Anastasia stood at the foot of the bed, arms crossed, still managing to look elegant in the T-shirt and sweatpants the police had given her. Her wounds were healing, the rashes on her skin fading, but she looked tired. Her shoulders slouched a little, which was almost shocking to see. Her gaze was cryptic, like she didn't know what to make of this mere mortal who'd nearly given his life for her.

"That trance is an old escape-artist's trick," she said finally. "Those stunts when they stay buried for ten hours, or underwater for an impossible length of time—they're controlling their own metabolism. It isn't magic at all. Odysseus Grant is a very impressive man."

"Yeah," I said softly.

"If he were awake, I'd apologize. And thank him."

I shook my head. "I don't think he expects anything like that."

"No," she murmured. "He wouldn't." Then whatever maudlin mood she'd been in passed. She straightened, the old imperious—vampiric—stance returning. She would rebuild her life, her existence, starting now. As she'd no doubt done many times before. Eight hundred years, she'd said. "This isn't over, Kitty. This is only the start."

Not this again. "I thought we decided this wasn't a conspiracy. This was crazies out in the woods—"

"I'm not talking about Provost and his compatriots. Not directly. But this is a symptom. There's a war coming. And people like us can't hide from it if we're exposed, dragged into public. Even five years ago the police never would have considered entertaining the story we told them tonight. But now they must. This will continue. You've already attracted so much attention—"

"I'll hide," I said. "I can go back to hiding."

She smiled, a sly, haunting turn of lips. She could see into the future, not because she was psychic, like Tina or

Jeffrey, but because she had been watching the patterns for so long, she knew where they were leading.

"I've watched you for a week now. You won't hide. You'll *lead*."

I didn't want that responsibility. I didn't want that label, and I didn't want her cold, expectant gaze on me, *demanding*. But denying it didn't make her wrong. People listened to me—I based my whole career on that. I'd worked for that. Now I had to face up to the consequences of it: People *listened* to me. What was I going to do with that power?

"Yeah," I admitted. "If no one else will."

"There are alliances. Some—like Roman's—have spent a long time consolidating the wrong kind of power. Using it to tip people like Joey Provost and Eli Cabe into evil. It is far past time that people who would align against such powers form our own alliance."

Grant's monitor beeped steadily. I'd have expected a more portentous soundtrack to this kind of conversation. Something epic, to mark the shifting of my world.

"You make it sound so dramatic," I said, my voice flat.

"If you learn anything more about the Long Game, about Roman. About people like Cabe and his ilk, anything working to bring that kind of darkness into the world—call me." She drew a business card from an unseen pocket and held it to me until I took it. "If you need help, call me."

"And you'll do the same, I assume."

"That's what an alliance is. Tell Odysseus the same applies to him. Give him the number." She nodded at the man on the bed, then glanced at the window. "I need to go. It's nearly dawn." She turned to the door, like she planned on slipping out, just like that. Vanishing into shadow as vampires were wont to do.

"Wait!" I said, standing, preparing to chase after her. Fortunately, she stopped. "Where? Where will you go? Where is it safe for you?"

She smiled indulgently. In any other situation it would have been patronizing, but we were too tired for that. "Kitty, you don't get to be my age without having a few contingency plans. All I need is a dark place to spend the day. There are plenty of dark places around." Her lips thinned.

"Be careful," I said, which sounded stupid. Amid the million other things I could have said—thank you; was that even real; or help, because I can't do this alone—it was the only one I could articulate.

"Give Rick my regards when you get back to Denver," she said.

I watched her walk down the corridor, losing sight of her almost immediately even in the sparsely populated, early morning hospital. She blended in—she didn't want to be seen, so just like that she was gone. Also, my view was distracted by another figure coming toward me down the same hallway. A scruffy-haired guy in khaki pants and an untucked shirt, a worried frown pulling at his features and a desperate, wolfish look in his eyes. And I knew that smell a mile away.

"Ben!" I called, not caring how the sound echoed.

He froze a moment when he spotted me leaving the doorway to Grant's room. Like he didn't believe it was me. Like he had to take a breath, just to be sure. Then we ran.

We slammed into each other, wrapped each other up,

pressed our faces against the other's bare necks, breathing in skin. I couldn't hold him tightly enough; my fingers kneaded his shirt.

"It's okay," he said, close to my ear, and didn't let up his embrace enough for me to draw air and reply. I just cried, leaking tears onto his skin. He murmured, stroked my hair, and that was the first time I thought maybe everything really would be all right.

We sat outside Grant's room. I pulled Ben's arm over my shoulders and leaned into him. I didn't want to stop touching him. Never again.

I explained, in as few words as possible. "It was a trap, the whole thing was a trap. Three guys just like Cormac but psychotic. They almost got us all."

"I talked to the cops before I got here. I had to give them a statement before they'd tell me where you were. I don't know what to tell you, Kitty. Nobody's ever seen anything like this."

"But I bet it's happened before," I said. "Maybe not like this. But mass hunting of supernaturals?" I shook my head. Witch hunts, without the publicity. Without history taking note. Yeah, I could see it.

"I *know* hunters—I know people like that. I can't understand why they'd go after such high-profile targets. All of you'd be missed. Jerome Macy, Jeffrey Miles—" He stopped, shook his head.

I didn't want to think about Jeffrey. Or Jerome, Gemma, Ariel—

So I stopped. Just for now.

"I think maybe that was the point," I said, voice a whisper, because I was officially out of energy. I could let Ben take care of me for a little while. "We're all out in the open, and they didn't like it. They wanted to make an example, take us down. They might not even have cared if they got caught."

"They did it on principle? Is that what you're saying?"

There's a war coming, Anastasia had said. And maybe *she* was crazy, fanatical, paranoid—

Or maybe she wasn't.

"I think that's what I'm saying," I said, smiling thinly.

He squeezed me again and didn't seem any more likely to let go of me than I was to let go of him. Good.

"Cormac's going to be proud of you," he said. "When he hears about all this."

"Yeah? Have you talked to him? Does he know about this?" I wanted to get his opinion. Could we have done something differently? Something that would have saved a few more of us—

Stop. Think about it later.

"You can tell him all about it when we go pick him up from Cañon City."

I sat up to look Ben in the eye. Leaned on his chest, clutching his shirt. He was smiling. Grinning, even. I said, "He's getting out? He got parole?"

"He got parole."

Epilogue

A couple of weeks passed.

I sat in the studio, resting my head on my hand, staring at the mike, trying to concentrate. This had been going on for a couple of minutes now.

". . . then I tried leaving milk in a saucer, because one of the books I read said that works to calm brownies. But every morning the milk is gone and the house is a mess again. So then I wondered, what kind of milk? I used two percent, but maybe I should be using whole milk? Or half-and-half? But that's closer to cream, and the book specifically said milk. And it's pasteurized—is that going to make a difference? None of the books say anything about whether pasteurized milk works. My sister thinks I should have a priest in to exorcise the place, but that seems a little, oh, I don't know, *violent,* and if I could make the brownies feel more at home they might actually help out a little, like in the stories, even though I'm not a shoemaker or anything like that . . ."

I tapped my finger on the arm of my chair as I swiveled back and forth in a quarter-circle, like a kid in detention.

I'd been staring at my microphone so long it was blurring. My headphones itched. And this woman just kept talking. It was hypnotic.

My caller had a very serious problem, surely. It just didn't seem like it to me at the moment. Especially not after the last couple of weeks.

Finally I interrupted, like I should have done a long time ago. "Margaret, are you sure it's brownies that are wrecking your house every night? Maybe the saucers of milk aren't working because it's not brownies."

"Well, what else could it be? I swear, I go to sleep at night, don't hear a thing, and when I wake up there are dishes knocked down and broken, my Beanie Baby collection is scattered everywhere, the pillows are shredded, and what else could it be?"

Lightbulb moment. "Do you have cats?"

"Yes. Six."

It wasn't brownies. It was crazy-cat-lady syndrome. I needed a separate hotline for callers like this. "Margaret, have you considered that maybe your cats are a bit rambunctious and may be the ones wrecking your house?"

"Well, of course I have," she said, sounding indignant. Not that I could blame her. "But if it were the cats, wouldn't I hear something?"

"I don't know. Are you a sound sleeper?"

"Can anyone possibly be *that* sound a sleeper? Even medicated?"

"Wait a minute," I said, losing patience. "You have six cats and you take sleeping pills at night?"

"Well . . . yes . . ."

"Okay. That's just *asking* for it. I think you need to call a different show."

"But—"

I hung up on her, sorry I had only a button to slam and not a whole handset, which would have been more satisfying. Not that I wanted to lose my temper. Not that I was feeling violent.

I couldn't take another call right now. I couldn't stand another call. I couldn't deal with another not-problem. It was all I could do not to lean into the mike and yell, "Get a life."

But I'd get over it.

"Sorry, people. My tolerance for bull seems to have gone way down lately. I hope you'll understand and forgive me, but I think for tonight I've just about had it for calls. I'd like each and every one of you out there to consider your problems for a moment and consider that maybe they're not as epic as you think they are. The solution may be staring you in the face. Or it may be you've let a mere annoyance take over your life until it's become a problem. And while you're considering your problems and grasping for solutions, you should also take a moment to find that one good thing that makes getting through the tough times worthwhile. Those of us who spend our nights awake and watchful need those reminders, that sunrises are beautiful and worth waiting for."

God, I was going to start crying again if I kept this up. No crying. I was just having a bad night. Fortunately, Matt in the sound booth tapped his watch, telling me time was up. I took a breath, reset my mental state, and managed to sound cheerful when I gave my usual wrap-up.

"This is Kitty Norville, voice of the night. Stay safe out there, people." The on-air sign dimmed, and I sat back, exhausted.

The mass murder I'd managed to escape had been all over the news. I'd spent the last show talking about it, fielding questions, condemning the kinds of people who perpetrated these crimes, but mostly talking about my friends who'd died. Begging the world, or whatever part of it listened to the show, not to let anything like this happen again. Be kind to each other.

The same message I tried to deliver every week: be kind. Not that it was helping.

"Kitty?" Matt said.

"I'm fine," I said flatly, before he could ask the question.

He hesitated, then said, "Okay." But he didn't sound convinced.

And I wanted people to stop fussing over me.

The police, working with the FBI, had pieced together most of the story, and it wasn't pretty.

Joey Provost really was a TV producer and really had been working for SuperByte Entertainment for several years. But he also had ties to a couple of whacked-out right-wing "clubs" that promoted various shades of fascism and gun mania, and the members all had impressive weapons collections stashed at home. Through those leads, he'd met Cabe and Valenti. Cabe was the hunter among them, with a fascination for the supernatural. He'd probably done most of the nitty-gritty planning and designed most of the traps. The three men had met, hit it off, and decided they didn't like the way entertainment and popular culture were going. They didn't like that monsters and the occult were being legitimized and glamorized. They wanted to strike back, so they cooked up a plan: trap the worst offenders of this movement, wipe them out, and distribute a film of the accomplishment. They were declaring their own little war. Provost pitched the front show to SuperByte, who then inadvertently funded the enterprise. The company itself was absolved of wrongdoing, except maybe for the mistake of trusting Provost in the first place. The producer hired Valenti and Cabe. During filming, they chose their moment, shut down production, and slaughtered the witnesses. Then they launched their own show. The clips they'd filmed of us talking about each other and how much we missed our families were meant to be our own obituaries.

None of the three had prior criminal records, but their activities, known associates, and known obsessions were indicative. None of it raised flags until you put the three of them together and added lighter fluid. Individually, they never would have acted. Together as their own little army, they egged each other on to destruction. Their egos, their sense of superiority, had never let them think for a moment that they could fail. I remembered Valenti, in Anastasia's arms, as the full realization of what was happening to him dawned. And maybe Anastasia was right, and they'd been encouraged by someone like Roman.

They'd planned so well. They'd known so much about what they were facing. But in the end they hadn't had a fucking clue.

I'd called the families of Jerome, Lee, Ariel, and Jeffrey. Not that there was anything I could say. But I was one of the last people to see their loved ones alive and wanted to bear witness. My chattiness failed me, of course. All I could say was I'm sorry, which was so inadequate.

As far as I could tell, Gemma and Dorian didn't have

families. I couldn't track them, except through Anastasia, and she already knew how I felt.

Like he often did, Ben picked me up after the show. I climbed in the passenger seat, and he didn't say a word, for which I was grateful. He just leaned over, touched my face, and kissed my cheek, resting his lips there for a long time. I leaned into the touch.

It was going to be okay.

Tina survived. She got better. The first time I saw her back on her own show, I cheered. Her cohosts were babying her, I could tell. They wouldn't let her carry any equipment and helped her out of their van. That she didn't argue with them said a lot about how hurt she really was. But she was back in action, and it felt like a big middle finger to Provost and company. We talked often, but not about Jeffrey. When she was ready, she'd bring him up. Me—I had no doubt he was still around, looking out for her.

Conrad also lived, and so did his leg. I got e-mails from him all the time. Updates, pictures of his kids— at the pool, on the beach, playing ball. Conrad was still processing. For him, the only way to believe that it had all happened was to keep in touch with our insane little survivor group. Whatever worked. He was also planning his next book—about his moment of epiphany, and about reconciling skepticism with the supernatural. I promised him an interview for it. I was happy for him, and grateful we'd been able to save him. No, not grateful—relieved.

Relieved that I hadn't had to call his wife and kids to tell them I was sorry.

Grant came to see me at my office a couple of weeks after. He'd spent time in Montana recuperating and was on his way to Vegas to return to his magic show. Another middle finger to the bad guys. When he sat down in the chair across from my desk, he moved slowly. He still looked ill, which was disconcerting. He was one of the strongest people I knew, but his face sagged, shadows marking his eyes. He sat unevenly, favoring his left, injured side.

We studied each other for a long moment. Hunting for the nonvisible scars.

"Well," I said. "We made it."

Ducking his gaze, he hid a smile. "I admit, I had some doubts for a while."

"Naw, I never did," I said, grinning and lying.

"How are you holding up?" he said, when I should have been the one asking.

I sighed. "I'm very, very angry. And I think Anastasia's right. There's a war brewing."

"But Roman wasn't involved with this."

"Maybe not directly. Maybe not literally. But I think they're both symptoms of the same thing," I said.

"Good versus evil?" he said, brow raised.

I shrugged. "Let's say order versus chaos. Kindness versus fear. No, never mind. False dichotomies, all of them."

His smile quirked. "You're learning."

"Anastasia wanted you to have her card." I handed him the copy I'd made of it.

He didn't look at it but folded the page with scarred

hands and tucked it in a pocket. "So Roman is recruiting his alliance, and Anastasia is recruiting hers. Do you wonder where this is all going to end?"

I shook my head. "I don't think it will. I think this same damn thing's been going on for thousands of years. It's just our turn to play the game now."

"Well, then. Until next time." He stood to leave, I stood to see him out. With anyone else, I'd have stepped forward for a hug, but that wry smile was all I was going to get from him. After he left, I sat at my desk, staring at his empty chair for a long time, ignoring the nervous knot in my stomach.

Cañon City was a small town in the foothills between the prairie and the Rocky Mountains. It was also, at least to people living in Colorado, synonymous with the several prison complexes that occupied a good chunk of land here, marked by miles of tall chain-link fence topped with razor wire and clusters of concrete institutional buildings. The Colorado Territorial Correctional Facility was in town, right off the highway. That was where we stopped. The late-summer sun baked off the blacktop and concrete, and I squinted against the glare of it. The whole prison area shone like its own little nightmare.

I was pacing by the car. Ben leaned against the hood, trying not to pace, but he had his arms tightly crossed and was tapping his foot. We were both fidgeting.

"Is it time yet?" I said.

"There's still ten minutes." He didn't even have to look at his watch, which led me to think he'd been all but watching it since we arrived ten minutes ago. We'd gotten here early because we didn't want to be late. The last thing we wanted was to have Cormac get out and not have anyone here waiting. We owed it to him not to fail on that little thing.

I paced because I kept thinking about how I almost wasn't here at all.

Finally, Ben uncrossed his arms and straightened from the car.

"It's time?" I said.

He just smiled and started walking toward the first of the chain-link fences. I rushed to join him, grabbing his hand. We squeezed tightly and walked on together.

Ben knew where to go, and I realized he'd probably done this before with clients. I'd come here dozens of times to visit Cormac over the last couple of years, but this was a different gate, a different part of the complex. It felt like a new start. Maybe that was the idea.

Just inside the gate in the fence here was a white plankboard guardhouse. Beyond that looked like three more stages of chain-link fence, forming a series of cages that led to the first of the cinderblock buildings. The idea of cages made my hair stand on end. I wanted to start pacing again.

A guy in a uniform stepped out of the guardhouse and started unlocking one of the interior gates. Another guard emerged from the building and did the same.

"The suspense is killing me," I hissed. Ben didn't say anything but just kept watching.

Then a tall, lanky man in a pair of faded jeans and a gray T-shirt stepped out of the building. He had brown hair and a trimmed mustache and carried a canvas duffel bag over his shoulder. He shook hands with the guard by the building, who locked the gate behind him as he walked on.

God, that was a really long walk.

It probably wasn't more than thirty yards, but when you were waiting on the other side, it took forever. Especially when Cormac couldn't seem to be bothered to speed up his usual calm saunter. But I recognized Cormac by that walk.

At the gatehouse, he stopped and signed something on a clipboard offered to him by the guard there. Then *they* shook hands.

"Time off for good behavior," Ben said to me. "You can always tell because the guards actually look happy for him."

I had started bouncing a little.

Then the last gate opened, and Cormac was standing outside.

He paused for a long time. Tipped his head back, looking into the sky, just breathing. The gate wheeled shut behind him, and he didn't move. I resisted an urge to run forward and instead gave him time.

He seemed to shake himself free of the introspective moment. Then he looked like Cormac again, calm and watchful. *Then* we went forward to meet him.

Ben reached him first, hand outstretched. "Welcome back to the land of the living."

"Jesus Christ, you have no idea," Cormac said, his relief plain.

They shook hands and fell into a guy hug, one-armed, thumping each other's backs. My eyes started tearing up. I quickly wiped them clear before anyone could see.

Ben was rambling. "Are you okay? Is everything okay? They didn't hassle you, did they? Here, let me take that." They argued over his bag for a minute. Rolling his eyes, Cormac finally let Ben slide the duffel bag off his shoulder.

"I'm fine, everything's fine, don't coddle me, I just want to get out of here."

Then Cormac and I faced each other.

He was taller than me, so I had to look up at him. He'd spent much of the last two years indoors, and it showed. He was paler than I remembered; before prison, he'd always had the burnished tan of a real outdoorsman.

But he was *here,* finally, and he looked good. Still strong, his eyes still clear and focused. He regarded me wryly.

"Well?" he said. The word carried weight, because the last time I'd faced him like this I'd been single, and we'd had something. But that was a long time ago, and right now I felt only relief. For his sake, for Ben's, for me. Now it finally felt like we could all move forward.

I fell into his arms, and he clung to me like I was an anchor. He was solid in my embrace, real, which was good, because maybe part of me hadn't believed he was back until now. I turned my face to his neck and took a deep breath.

I had always associated Cormac with leather, gun oil, toughness. The smells of a hard-bitten attitude and a guy who meant business. That scent had faded from him, replaced by other smells: concrete dormitory, institutional soap, faint sweat raised by the heat of the day. A new Cormac. Or maybe this was a purer Cormac, with the weapons and harshness stripped away. This was going to take some getting used to.

We pulled away, and I felt myself grinning like a maniac.

"What is it?" he said.

I shook my head. "It's just really good to see you on the outside."

"Let's get the hell out of here," Ben said, glancing over his shoulder. "I keep thinking they're going to change their minds and come running back here for you."

That was enough to make me want to grab both of them and rush, but we walked toward the parking lot. Cormac kept looking around, a thin smile on his face. I was still grinning.

"I need to thank you for saving my life," I said.

Cormac glanced at me. "Not again—"

"No. This is a couple weeks ago."

Now he looked confused. "What are you talking about?"

"Never mind."

He smirked. "All right. What almost killed you this time?"

I laughed. I couldn't help it.

"You know," Ben said. "Things might have been a little calmer for you on the inside."

"Don't count on that," Cormac said flatly.

"Okay, what aren't you telling us?"

"Long story." Well, he hadn't lost that inscrutable smile, had he? "You know what? I want a steak," he said. "A real steak. Thick. Rare."

My mouth watered at the thought.

"There's a place just up the road," Ben said. "I think it caters to ex-cons craving real food."

"Good," Cormac said.

I ended up walking between them, so I wrapped my arms around both their middles and pulled them close. Cormac draped an arm over my shoulder; Ben hugged me, and we matched strides. And it felt right.

Our pack of three was whole again.